THE HARROWING OF DOOM

The tread of armored boots echoed up the vaults of St Peter. The stained glass windows seemed to tremble at the monarch's step. Zargo had never seen Doom this close. Doom was tall, but his presence turned him into a colossus. He filled Zargo's vision and consciousness until it seemed he should burst through the tiny walls and roof of the church. A faint hum and metallic clicks came from Doom's armor, and Zargo suddenly knew what the machinery of fate sounded like.

He looked up at the mask and quailed before its titanium grimace. Even worse were the eyes, looking out from behind rectangular slits, eyes that had seen so much, eyes that *knew,* where Zargo had only the weak fabric of belief. Doom's hooded cape, somehow untouched by rain, draped the metal of the armor, its dark green suggesting the sorcerous power of the natural framing the wizardry of technology.

CW00956210

LEGEND OF THE FIVE RINGS
Curse of Honor

WARHAMMER 40,000:
SPACE MARINE BATTLES
The Death of Antagonis
Overfiend

WARHAMMER 40,000: YARRICK
Chains of Golgotha
Imperial Creed
The Pyres of Armageddon

THE HORUS HERESY
The Damnation of Pythos
The Unburdened
Ruinstorm

WARHAMMER 40,000:
PRIMARCHS
Vulkan: Lord of Drakes
Roboute Guilliman: Lord of
Ultramar
Spear of Ultramar

WARHAMMER 40,000:
THE BEAST ARISES
The Last Wall
The Hunt for Vulcan
Watchers in Death

WARHAMMER 40,000:
SPACE WOLF
Curse of the Wulfen

WARHAMMER 40,000:
GREY KNIGHTS
Sons of Titan
Warden of the Blade
Castellan

WARHAMMER 40,000:
SPACE MARINE LEGENDS
Lemartes

WARHAMMER 40,000:
LORDS OF THE SPACE MARINES
Mephiston: Lord of Death

WARHAMMER 40,000: WARLORD
Fury of the God-Machine

WARHAMMER 40,000:
SANCTUS REACH
Maledictus

WARHAMMER: AGE OF SIGMAR
Mortarch of Blood
The Dominion of Bones

WARHAMMER HORROR
The House of Night and Chain

JEN BLAYLOCK THRILLERS
Crown Fire
Kornukopia
The Valedictorians

Gethsemane Hall
The Thunder of Madness

MARVEL UNTOLD

THE HARROWING OF DOOM

DAVID ANNANDALE

ACONYTE®

FOR MARVEL PUBLISHING

VP Production & Special Projects: Jeff Youngquist
Assistant Editor, Special Projects: Caitlin O'Connell
Manager, Licensed Publishing: Jeremy West
VP, Licensed Publishing: Sven Larsen
SVP Print, Sales & Marketing: David Gabriel
Editor in Chief: C B Cebulski

Doctor Doom created by Stan Lee & Jack Kirby

First published by Aconyte Books in 2020
ISBN 978-1-83908-052-4
Ebook ISBN 978-1-83908-053-1

Cover art by Fabio Listrani

Distributed in North America by Simon & Schuster Inc, New York, USA
Printed in the United States of America
9 8 7 6 5 4 3 2 1

ACONYTE BOOKS

An imprint of Asmodee Entertainment Ltd
Mercury House, Shipstones Business Centre
North Gate, Nottingham NG7 7FN, UK
aconytebooks.com // twitter.com/aconytebooks

For Margaux, and the dreams we celebrate.

PROLOGUE

"I know thee for a man of many thoughts,
And deeds of good and ill, extreme in both,
Fated and fatal in thy sufferings."

BYRON, *MANFRED*, II.ii.34-6

April 30.

The bonfires of Latveria burned high on Walpurgis Night. They burned in the market squares of Doomstadt, the roar of the flames echoing down the narrow streets, the glow catching the steep gables of the houses and turning their shadows into claws that stretched across the cobblestones, wavering and hungry. They burned before the churches of St Peter and St Blaise, and the gargoyles on the façades seemed to shift back and forth, eager to take flight and revel in the night's dark work. One burned on the rooftop of the Werner Academy, the blaze high and isolated against the night like an eye both fearful and knowing. They burned too in the countryside outside of the city of Doomstadt. They burned with special purpose there, where the night lay heaviest, unbroken by the doubtful refuge of streetlamps.

The people danced around the bonfires. Arms linked, faces turned upward to see the flames strike at the night, they danced and they chanted. Their chants were pleas for protection.

In Latveria, the people did not plead for protection from witches. They pled for the protection *of* witches.

In Doomstadt, the city named for the witch revered above all others, costumed children ran in groups down the streets. Some of the children in each group were disguised as demons. The others were gargoyles. To anyone not born in Latveria, it would have been difficult to tell the two apart, based on appearance. All the children bore horns and fangs. There were wings of cardboard and crêpe paper, even made of leather stretched over a wire framework. It was the actions that distinguished the demons from the gargoyles.

The demons ran ahead of the gargoyles. They yowled outside the doors of houses where the windows were lit by brass lanterns in the shape of gaping skulls. When the doors opened, the gargoyles descended on the demons with snarls and chased them away, before the group reformed and the performers were rewarded with pyro-wands to throw on the bonfires and smear the night with eruptions of blue and green and violet.

On Walpurgis Night, Latveria embraced its paradoxes. Evil against evil, monsters against monsters, in the land where angels had vanished from its myths. On Walpurgis Night, the darkness danced, and the people danced with it. The people feared the shadows and they loved them. The bonfires threw light, but at their edges, the darkness, imperious, was stronger than ever.

Shadows ruled over Latveria. And one shadow was supreme, its dominion absolute.

On Walpurgis Night, he who cast it walked abroad in his kingdom.

His was the shadow that was feared above all others. His was the shadow that defined Latveria. Without it, there was no Latveria. His shadow threw itself over every square inch of the land, and, midnight or noon, it was always there. The truth of Walpurgis Night in Latveria was that his was the shadow in whose honor the bonfires burned and the people chanted. The dancers and the demons and the gargoyles might not fully understand this truth. The celebration and its rituals were ancient, but all the centuries of observance and the slow accretion of variations had been tending to their present form, their present purpose. The people might only sense the truth. Victor von Doom grasped it, because his being had shaped it.

The nature of Walpurgis Night in Latveria was one of his works, and he walked far beyond the walls of Castle Doom that he might look upon this work and see that it was good.

On other nights, on other days, Doom would march through the arteries of his city with the majesty of a god, his passage preceded and followed by the heavy boots of his honor guard. Walpurgis Night was different. On the night of shadows, he chose to be one. He walked alone, the deepest darkness passing next to the revels, allowing himself to appear only as a glimpse, a glint of armor, the vanishing swirl of a cape. In this way, his presence spread to become all of the night. Wherever the people looked, they sensed him. He was everywhere. They felt his gaze, though they could not see him, and knew they must do all they could to propitiate him.

There were other reasons why Doom walked abroad and observed the celebrations. The rite of Walpurgis was an old one. It was powerful. Things stirred on this date. Deep currents flowed, and they demanded his attention. When he journeyed into the hills beyond the city, and the bonfires became little more than fireflies dotting the darkness, he could sense the warp and weft of the night more clearly. He could feel forces at work, and how thin the barrier between the world and the ones that came after it had become.

Doom climbed higher in the hills. Above the tree line, the wind was strong. He spread his arms, and his cape billowed. Like the tip of an iceberg, the wind was the trace of the greater current on the other side of the barrier. Walpurgis Night seethed with potential. The awareness of what it could become had haunted the unconscious of lesser minds for millennia. It haunted Doom too, because it felt like an answer he could not yet use.

Doom stopped at the top of the hill. He turned around to look back at Doomstadt, at the glowering lights of Castle Doom rising from its central peak, and at the bonfires flickering across the landscape. This was his domain. It was not his only one. And on this night, there were others that felt so close he could almost reach out a titanium-clad hand and seize them.

Walpurgis Night offered so much.

So different from Midsummer.

The thought made him grimace. The solstice was less than two months away. The year was swinging around, bringing with it the duel, and the burden of shame, and guilt, and rage, and frustration that marked the event. Hell must already be laughing at him, laughing in anticipation of his appointed fight with its champion, and the defeat that would come, as it had year after year after year. The defeat that would mean Hell would keep the soul of Cynthia von Doom for another twelve months.

Your son can command that a city bear your name, Mother, but he cannot free you.

He had fought the duel more than fifteen times. So many times that he knew how the coming one would end, no matter what champion Hell sent. His defeat was as certain as the need to fight. He would never turn away from the duel. And because he could not, he would go into battle with the sickening, treacherous sliver of hope that this time, *this time*, things would be different. On Walpurgis Night, with the duel still far enough away that he could think about it with a degree of calm, he felt immune to that hope. But it would come, like a cancer triumphing over remission, to torment him before the battle, and deepen the agony afterward.

This time. This time.

The words were poison. They tasted of death and futility.

Doom knew he would always be defeated. Hell never made a contract that it could lose. The Midsummer Night duel would always be on Hell's terms, never his. He was trapped in a bargain as foul as the one that had trapped his mother's soul.

She had been desperate to save her fellow Romani people from the persecutions of Baron (soon to be King) Vladimir Fortunov. She had given her soul to Mephisto in exchange for the powers to defeat Vladimir. Mephisto had cheated her.

He had given her power, too much power to control. She had failed to bring down Vladimir, and had inadvertently killed a village-full of the innocent.

Mephisto had used Cynthia von Doom's need to save her people, her urge to do good, to damn her. And he was using her son's need to save her in turn, to hold him in a cycle of endless defeat and humiliation.

The wind gusted. It moaned with the echo of spirits. Midnight was long past. The witching hour was close, and the barrier was gossamer-thin. Doom breathed deeply, tasting, though his mask's filter, the air growing colder with the touch of unquiet tombs.

If only there was a way to change the terms of the duel. If only there was a way to make Midsummer more like Walpurgis Night. This was the night most holy to his mother. This was the night that honored her most of all.

If only…

The great bells in the high tower of the castle struck three. The witching hour began. With the last reverberation of the toll, revelation came to Victor von Doom.

I have been a fool. I have been wrong to see the duel as the failed means to an end. It is what it can lead to that is important.

Walpurgis Night was not the respite before Midsummer. He must force Midsummer to be the stepping stone to Walpurgis.

He would have his terms.

I will take Hell by the throat, and I will squeeze.

Doom laughed. Amplified by projection units in his helmet, the laughter echoed across the hills. It rolled over the villages, and through the streets of Doomstadt. The shadows rose high at its thunder, and the bonfires quavered. The people faltered in the chants, and they shivered.

The darkness had spoken, and they feared what it would command.

PART I

MIDSUMMER'S NOOSE

"Patience – and patience! Hence – that word was made
For brutes of burthen, not for birds of prey!
Preach it to mortals of a dust like thine, –
I am not of thine order."

BYRON, MANFRED, II.i.35-8

CHAPTER 1

Mount Sivàr raised its barren crown east of Doomstadt, Latveria's border with Romania. It was isolated from the rest of the chain, as if it had marched west, the vanguard of granite invasion. Trees clustered thickly around the lower half of Sivàr's upheaval, then halted abruptly. Above the trees, the slope was not steep at first, but it was a brutal vista of rockslide debris and deep gorges. Then the peak thrust up, its sides nearly vertical, its faces bleak and savage. When the rising sun cast its shadow over the land, it was like the second coming of night.

Doom's flight to Sivàr brought him to the mountain as the heat of the day faded, and gloom deepened on the western flank. He used his waist-mounted jetpacks to bring him to a point a few hundred yards below the line where the rubble-strewn slopes gave way to the naked face of the mountain. His goal was near the peak. He could have flown directly there. But that would not have been a strategic approach. There were ways of winning a struggle where the opponent never even knew there had been one, just as there were errors that would create a battle for which there was no need.

There was a power in the high reaches of Mount Sivàr. Doom had never tested himself against it. It was not his intention to do so now. Such a struggle would not be useful to him. He had other things in mind for the dweller in the peak.

He began the long climb. It was still possible to walk at this altitude. His titanium boots rang loudly against stone as he strode effortlessly between the leaning piles of granite. He was pleased with the sound of his march. Let his arrival be known. Let the mountain be aware of who had come.

His path through the wounds of stone became long and tortuous. Massive rockfalls blocked his way in one direction, and then a jagged crevasse stopped the way forward in another. Every time his route was barred, he resisted the temptation simply to fly over the obstacle. Instead, he surveyed the landscape carefully, every boulder and crack and patch of scree turned into an individual datum, the mountain slope nothing more than an object of analysis to be anatomized and understood. She who lived on the mountain had set terms to control what she believed was her corner of the Earth. Doom would follow the terms so rigorously, he would make them his own.

She had her path up and down the mountain. It was one that she traveled safely, and that she believed guarded her. He would walk it, and she would wonder if it was truly a work of her will after all.

The grey of evening had come when Doom reached the end of the rubble and reached the mountain face, a sheer black monolith in the failing light. Climbing Mount Sivàr, even with equipment, would be suicidal for even the most expert alpinist. Doom smiled tightly behind his mask. The pleasure came less from the challenge than from the ease with which he would best it.

He spoke the incantation softly, the syllables weaving together to form a command, whispered yet iron. What was hidden shed its veil. A narrow ledge appeared before him. It was less than three feet wide, its edge crumbling and treacherous. It zigzagged its way up the mountain face, a barely visible thread. This was the path she walked. This was how she descended from her home and returned.

Doom started up the path. He marched swiftly, though he knew the consequence of each step before he took it. The fall of dusk did not hinder him. His helm lenses would soon switch automatically to night-vision, and as he walked, he kept up a steady, rhythmic litany of sorcery. The spells were minor, so slight that they required no effort, and barely any movement. His fingers subtly traced delicate glyphs in the air. He murmured so only he could hear his words, though the world obeyed all the same.

He came upon the first of the wards at the start of the second switchback. Revealed by his will, its cat's cradle of intersecting lines glowed a soft violet. It was a simple ward of warning, created to be unfelt by the one who triggered it, but its caster would know in that instant that someone was ascending her path. Doom could have dispelled it with a gesture. Instead, he stepped onto it. He saw the flash of its signal shoot to the mountain peak. He stayed where he was, arms crossed.

Look down. The night will not trouble your eyes any more than it will mine. Look. Know who is here. Know that you have time to prepare. Know that I do not come in stealth, or as the lightning.

He stayed there a full minute, then moved on.

The wards became more numerous the higher he climbed. Many of them were traps. They made gaps in the path look like solid stone, or they called upon falls of rock. These he disarmed, though the warnings he continued to trigger.

Heed your sentinels. I draw near.

The climb was a long one. It was full night before he was halfway up. There was time to contemplate the encounter to come. More than a mountain separated Doom from the power in the heights. Decades had passed since they had last seen each other. Decades heavy with history, freighted with pain. Their paths had been set by the same tragedy. It haunted them both. They were caught in its grip. Doom saw an escape for himself, and so he needed her help. She would, he was sure, respond to the same need. But she would have to be convinced that the escape was there. She had lived so long under this shadow, she would find it difficult to believe there was a chance of liberation.

At the witching hour, Doom reached the top of the mountain. He had timed his arrival for this moment, exactly one day after his Walpurgis Night illumination. This hour belonged to him, but also to the power on the mountain. It had belonged to his mother once too.

The concealed ledge came to an end at the mouth of a cave just below the frowning, heavy brow of the peak. A black standing stone of polished granite stood beside the entrance. Its network of runes glowed crimson at his approach. He stopped a few feet from the stone, just outside the cave. This was the most powerful of the wards. Another step forward, and he would trigger its response. The latent spells hummed with a sub-aural but psychically resonant pulse. Unleashed, their attack would be massive. Disarming the wards would itself be a challenge. He refused it. Instead, facing the torchlit glow of the cave, he opened the next phase of the campaign he had begun thousands of feet below.

My terms, though you do not know it.

"Maria von Helm," he called. "Doom has come, and will speak with you."

He waited. The wind blew his cape, but he was as still as the stone. He waited, knowing she had heard him. He was immovable as the mountain, and more patient. She would answer him before he spoke again.

The cave entrance extended less than ten feet into the mountainside before it turned sharply, hiding the rest of the dwelling from the outside. After several minutes, a shadow appeared around the wall, preceding the emergence of the witch of Sivar.

She walked slowly toward Doom, stopping just before the threshold. The few feet that separated them might as well have been a gulf of leagues. The sorceress stood straight, though she showed the erosion of her haunted years. She would have been in her seventies, but she had the lines of someone who had experienced thirty years more. Her eyes were dark, barely visible beneath her lids, and glinted with power. Her grey hair was cut short, as if roughly hacked with a knife. She wore a simple black robe whose edges blurred with the shadows of the floor. Her expression was wary, defiant.

"Why are you here?" Helm asked.

"There is something we must do together."

She grunted. "I don't think so. We have never had anything to do with each other. It is better that way."

"Only that isn't really, true, is it?" said Doom. "The past has a common hold on us."

"That past is long dead." Helm shifted, as if preparing to leave.

Doom remained motionless. He was not going anywhere. "It is the past that brings me here," he said. "It is the past that means you will agree that we must work together. I do not think you will turn your back on Cynthia von Doom a second time."

Helm jerked as if struck. "I never turned my back on her," she murmured.

Doom said nothing, waiting.

"I failed her," Helm said, the truth as hard to contain now as grief had been all those years ago. Her voice was heavy with more than forty years of guilt.

Cynthia von Doom had been Helm's friend, and her mentor. Helm had learned from her, studied with her. "You fought at her side against Baron Vladimir Fortunov," Doom said. "You tried to stop his atrocities against our Romani clan. You were not at her side the night she died, though."

She did not deny it. "I tried to stop her from summoning Mephisto. I knew the cost would be too high."

"You knew the power he gave her would kill the innocents she wanted to protect?"

"I didn't know what the cost would be. Just that it would be terrible. I *tried*."

"'I tried,'" Doom repeated. "How often do we use those words to excuse our failure?"

Helm was silent.

"All the time," Doom said, answering his own question. "We use them all the time. Oh, I have tried too, sorceress. I *have tried.*" He bit the words off and spat them out. "I have fought for my mother's soul, year after year after year, and I have failed her, *failed* her, every single time. I did not stop fighting for her, though. Why did you?"

Again, no answer.

"I finished the work that you and she began. You did not defeat Baron Vladimir. Quite the reverse. He became *King* Vladimir, and then his persecutions truly knew no limits. I stopped them. I slew the king."

"Our grief took us in different directions," Helm said.

It certainly did. Helm had withdrawn from the world after Cynthia's death. She had delved deeper and deeper into the occult sciences, growing in wisdom and power. Yet that power had been idle, doing little more than warning off any who would wish Helm harm, or seek to conscript her to their cause. Helm's single focus had been to prepare for her own inevitable encounter with the powers of Hell. She had been present when Cynthia had summoned Mephisto, and Hell never forgot anyone who drew its attention.

Her obsession meant that she and Doom had lived by an unspoken contract. She did not seek to interfere with his governance of Latveria, or in any of his projects. In return, he ignored her and let her be. They had never spoken. He had been an infant the last time she had tried, *tried,* to alter the course of events in Latveria for the better.

"And this is where your grief took you," said Doom. "Your grief, and your fear. This is where you have been hiding for all these years. Perhaps you do not like to think of this as a hiding place. Retreat, a sanctuary, a strong point. Are these the words you would prefer? Are they the lies you wish would give you peace?"

"I have no peace."

"I believe you. Neither do I."

"I believe you, too," said Helm. "But even though the past imprisons us, that is not enough to make me work with you."

"Yet you will."

"Oh? Do you think you can force me? Are you going to match your sorcery against mine?"

"We might both prefer that I do not," Doom said calmly. "Nor do I have to, because you will not refuse me."

"I already have," said Helm. "There is nothing you can say that would interest me."

There were few who had dared speak like that to him who were still alive. He felt no anger today, no ruffled pride. Her defiance amused him, because he knew how this encounter would end. "And if I said you could liberate yourself from the past?" said Doom. "If I showed you the chance of redemption?"

That held her. She breathed in heavily, then exhaled, her sigh becoming a plea. "How?"

"By freeing the soul of my mother."

Her eyes had widened with hope. Now they narrowed again. "Do not try to fool me with a false dream," she said. "Of course I would wish to free her. That means more to me than you know."

I know exactly what it means to you. It would mean not just that you had made amends to the past, but that there was hope for your own escape from Hell's clutches.

"But I know what happens on Midsummer Night," Helm continued. "The tremors from your battles reach even to here. I cannot join you in them. There is no hope there. There is only futility."

"Of course there is," said Doom. "That is why I do not ask you to join me in the Midsummer rite. I know I cannot change the outcome of those duels. I am no longer interested in making Hell agree to release her. I will no longer play its game to its preordained conclusion."

"What do you plan to do?"

He had her interest again.

"I am going to storm the gates. I am going to harrow Hell."

The sorceress stared at Doom. Disbelief and hope and excitement chased each other over her face. He had spoken to her fears and her regrets, and he had her now. *This is your moment of capitulation. You'll realize that, perhaps, in times to come.*

"You can do this?" Helm croaked.

"With your help. Our mastery of sorcery is different, because our disciplines of focus are different. United, imagine our power. Remember what you and my mother could do together. Imagine that a thousand-fold. You and I will lay siege to Hell, and it will not withstand us."

Helm gazed at him. Doom sensed her trying to take his measure, and weighing the risk of destruction against the end of fear. At last, she said, "Yes."

That was all. A single word, barely loud enough to hear

over the wind. With it, Helm committed herself to the full scope of the great work that lay ahead of them. With it, she made herself his more than she could possibly imagine.

Helm took a step back and to the side. The runes on the standing stone faded away. Victorious, Doom entered.

"Let us speak of the triumph to come," he said.

CHAPTER 2

It was two days after the Walpurgis Night celebrations. The remains of the bonfire in the square before St Peter Church had still not been entirely cleared away. The blackened logs marred the central paving stones. It was raining, and ashy water ran in streaks from the dead fire. The blot nagged at Father Grigori Zargo as he stood in the shelter of the church porch after vespers, seeing off his parishioners as they filed out. He avoided looking at it, resolutely concentrating on the faces of the people as they stopped to speak with him, but it was there in the corner of his eye, the flaw that could not be ignored.

Zargo mouthed blessings and pleasantries. They came too easily, too automatically, and his mind kept turning to the bonfire. He wondered, as he did every year, if the delay in the clearing of the square was the result of a deliberate policy. He wondered if it amused Doom for the remnants of the pagan rite to linger outside the church, as if a point were being made about their equal standing in Latveria. Because that was how Zargo saw the Walpurgis Night celebrations. They were utterly removed from any Christian sense of the date. Older beliefs had taken over. The fact that a saint had given her name to the night was forgotten. In Latveria, the night roiled with the occult, the magical, the superstitious. Evil was fought with other evil. If Doom *was* making a point, it wasn't necessary. Zargo hardly needed reminding. After all, almost every person he now greeted he had seen dancing before the bonfire. He was painfully aware of the retreating tide of faith.

One of the faces drew his full attention. "Hello," he said to Ilona Sandor. "It's good to see you."

"You too, Father." Sandor took his hand and smiled.

They had known each other a long time. They had been friends since childhood, and that, as Zargo measured the years, was two lifetimes ago. For a time, they had followed the same calling as adults. Over ten years ago, his had changed. More grey in his beard now. More grey in Sandor's red hair, too.

Thunder rumbled, and the rain came down more heavily, white sheets of water hammering pavement. People hurried out of the square, but Sandor lingered.

"Nasty evening," she commented.

"You were lucky to be spared this on Walpurgis Night," said Zargo, unable to keep all the bitterness from his tone.

"We were," Sandor agreed.

"Did you enjoy yourself?" he asked.

She gave him a knowing look. "Yes. Yes, I did. You saw me?"

"I saw everyone in the square."

"You spent the night in the church again." In prayer. Or at

least, as much as he could, when he wasn't driven to punish himself by watching the revels.

"Yes."

She sighed. "Why do you put yourself through that every year?"

"Because I have to. Does anyone remember that Walpurgis is the name of a saint?"

"Oh, I'm sure they do," Sandor said, avoiding his gaze.

"Did you?"

She grimaced apologetically.

"You see? The pagan rite is so strong, it's taking the name away from the saint. It's turning *Walpurgis* into a word that means witchcraft. Especially here."

"And you're going to turn that around by yourself, through prayer?"

"Probably not. But I still have to try."

Sandor put a hand on his arm. "You're too hard on yourself. And on us. St Peter was not empty this evening. It won't be tomorrow, either, or the next day."

"What does that mean?" This was not a question he would have asked anyone else. It would be wrong for him to show distress to his flock, especially distress that could be interpreted as doubt. His and Sandor's paths had diverged, and they had grown apart, but they were still close. She knew him better than anyone else. "What is the nature of the faith being practiced here?"

Sandor laughed uneasily. She glanced at the sheeting rain, then said, "That sounds like the opening to a conversation better suited to a quiet booth in a tavern."

"Please don't make light of this," said Zargo.

"I wasn't trying to."

"Then please tell me, what does it mean for you, Ilona, to take part in opposed communions?"

"That isn't something I've ever given thought to."

Zargo pressed harder. "Are your prayers in here any different from the chants on Walpurgis Night? Are they just another form of incantation?"

Sandor wasn't laughing now. "How far are you going to take these questions, Grigori?" she asked softly. She looked around again, nervously this time, and when she faced him, her expression was stern. "Remember where we are."

This is Latveria. "Sorry," said Zargo. If he had gone much further, he might have said something that might reach the wrong ears. He had verged on condemning witchcraft. "I must be tired." Now *there* was an incantation. It was the formulated phrase that washed away all seriousness from the words that came before it. *Just overtired. I didn't mean anything. Don't listen to me.*

"That must be it," Sandor said. "Get some rest. You'll feel better."

Zargo nodded, sad that this, like so many other conversations in his life, had to end before it had truly begun, and cancel itself out. He and Sandor would utter pleasantries now, and then part. *Nothing has happened. There is nothing to see. There is nothing to question us about.* "Blessings upon you," he said.

"Thank you, Father. And with you."

There. The standard phrases, void of real meaning, serving only to ease the social mechanics of departure.

Sandor left the shelter of the porch and jogged off across

the square. Zargo watched her until she vanished, and with her the conversation they might have had. He stared at the rain, and at the vague, dark blot of the bonfire remains. Then he stepped out into the downpour and walked slowly towards the site of the burn. He was drenched in seconds. Water slicked his hair and poured down his neck. It ran into his eyes, and he had to keep wiping his face just to be able to see where he was going. He sloshed through puddles, his cassock taking on extra pounds of sodden weight.

He stopped in front of the blackened bones of the bonfire and let the storm beat down on him.

So. What was the point of all that? What did he really think he could accomplish? Was he trying to browbeat Sandor into some kind of repentance?

I wouldn't do that to her. I wouldn't be that unfair.

Only he had come very close to doing precisely that.

Let him who is without sin cast the first stone.

He winced and took his penance under the rain. He had no right to chastise Sandor or any other member of his congregation, not with his history. No one who knew anything about Latveria had the right to condemn its people for hypocrisy. Not when their absolute monarch was a sorcerer. Not given the things that every Latverian knew to be true about the supernatural, things that did not require faith because dark miracles were witnessed so often, they might seem mundane if they were not so terrifying.

What chance did mere faith have against the omnipresent reality of witchcraft?

This is the way things are.

He stared at the soaked, charred logs, and tried not to turn them into a metaphor for his struggle. He could not change anything in Latveria. Yet he had to try. And yet he could not fight as hard as he might without incurring the wrath of its ruler. This was his paradox. He wanted to be a rock and a refuge for his flock, but he did not want to be noticed by Doom. All that was left was to struggle on in the most unobtrusive and foredoomed ways.

Coward. You pointless coward.

Pointless cowardice or pointless martyrdom. At least the former didn't seem as stupid, he supposed.

There was no let-up of the rain. It was trying to smash him down into the paving stones. He could not get any wetter, but he was tired of punishment, so he turned around and made his way back to the church. His cassock clung to his body like a soaked curtain, impeding his gait. His shoes squelched.

He paused when he crossed the threshold, standing at the end of the nave, dripping onto the marble floor. He gave the hem of his cassock a desultory wring, then walked on towards the altar. The servers had cleaned up and left, leaving him alone. He was very conscious of the space, of the emptiness in the air. He looked up at the height of the gothic vault, and the cold distance between himself and the ceiling. Instead of inspired awe, he felt alone. It was as if Walpurgis Night had stained the church, the bonfire and the revels draining it of its strength.

That isn't true. Nothing has changed here. I'm the one who has weakened.

He knelt at the altar. He began to pray for strength, had just lowered his head to his clasped hands, when the church door slammed shut with a reverberating boom.

Zargo jumped to his feet and whirled around.

Doom was striding up the nave toward him.

I have been noticed.

Zargo's knees shook. His throat was suddenly so dry he could not swallow.

The tread of armored boots echoed up the vaults of St Peter. The stained glass windows seemed to tremble at the monarch's step. Zargo felt as if he were sinking down through the floor of the church. He had never seen Doom this close. Doom was tall, but his presence turned him into a colossus. He filled Zargo's vision and consciousness until it seemed he should burst through the tiny walls and roof of the church. A faint hum and metallic clicks came from Doom's armor, and Zargo suddenly knew what the machinery of fate sounded like. Doom stopped a few paces away, and that was too close for what remained of Zargo's courage. He looked up at the mask and quailed before its titanium grimace. Even worse were the eyes, looking out from behind rectangular slits, eyes that had seen so much, eyes that *knew*, where Zargo had only the weak fabric of belief. Doom's hooded cape, somehow untouched by rain, draped the metal of the armor, its dark green suggesting the sorcerous power of the natural framing the wizardry of technology.

"Your Excellency," Zargo stammered. Fear thickened his tongue. *What did I say, Ilona? What did he hear? Was I seditious?* He stopped short of launching into a babbled mix of apologies and pleading. That would only make him look guiltier, and would do no good. All he could do was meet his end with dignity. He prayed for the strength to accomplish even that.

Surrounded by the ocean of his terror was a tiny island of surprise that Doom would trouble himself to squash someone so insignificant.

"Your Excellency," Zargo said again. "Is there something I can…"

Doom cut him off. "I require your assistance, Grigori Zargo."

That voice. Rasping through the filter of the mask, yet deep in timbre, profound as the heavy posaune of a pipe organ, commanding as a hurricane.

Zargo blinked, astonished. The first words Doom had ever spoken to him were the last he had ever expected to hear from the monarch. "My assistance," he managed. "Of course. Of course. Forgive me, but I am surprised, Excellency."

"I imagine so," said Doom, with what sounded like the flint of amusement. "It is not a priest, though, that I have come to speak with."

"I don't understand," said Zargo, his heart sinking. "I can't see how else I would be of any use to you."

"As a priest, you are of no use to me at all. This was not always your calling, however."

"No, it wasn't," Zargo whispered. He dreaded what was coming.

"Before you entered the church," said Doom, "your education was at the Werner Academy. So was your profession."

"Yes." Zargo's voice became even smaller. He cursed the past that was reaching out for him.

Relentless, Doom hauled the past into the present. "You were trained to be an occult historian."

"I was, Excellency. But this was years ago."

Doom made an impatient gesture. "That is irrelevant. Time does not erase your debt to Latveria, and thus to me."

"I was not meant to lecture on the occult." He surprised himself with his defiance. He would not lie to Doom, or to himself.

"Perhaps not," Doom allowed. He looked back at the pews for a moment. "Perhaps you are better suited to this form of audience, at least when it comes to the choice between lectern and pulpit. You were granted permission to change profession when you decided you had a calling."

"And I am grateful–"

"Being granted that permission did not erase the obligation to the state conferred by your academic education," Doom interrupted. "If anything, that debt has increased. Beginning today, you must repay it."

My obligation to the state. And the state is you. "As an occult historian?" said Zargo. "I mean no offense, Excellency, but am I really the best choice? Surely you have a better choice of historians in those working at the Werner Academy right now. Ilona Sandor, for instance. Her erudition was much greater than mine ten years ago. That must be even more true now."

"It is. And if I have need of Professor Sandor, I will make use of her. None of the current academics, or students for that matter, match my requirements. None of them have the precise skills I know you to have."

Zargo shook his head. "I am not exceptional."

"You are. Will you dispute my judgment?"

"No," Zargo said hastily. "No, of course not, your Excellency." He surrendered. "What would you have me do?"

"Your specialization was ley lines, their history and their detection."

"That's right." In spite of himself, he became curious. Deep inside, long-smothered embers flared to life.

He had always been religious. He had always found it hard to reconcile the orthodoxies of his faith with the practice of the occult. But when, in the early years of Doom's rule, he had taken the compulsory Academic Aptitude Exam, and found himself directed to geomancy at the recently founded Werner Academy, he had found it hard to dispute the results of the Exam. He *did* have a gift for the field. The research excited him. The insights excited him even more.

But all of it was wrong, too. He was good at the study of geomancy. He was very good. That meant he was good at witchcraft, and he could not face so great a sin. His faith warred with his assigned field, and his faith won. While he was still a researcher, before he became a practitioner, he turned away from the thrill of geomancy for the certainties of God.

He *was* grateful that his change in calling had been accepted. He had left Latveria. Its seminaries, such as still existed, were too influenced by the occultism he was fleeing. He had found his training in Nigeria instead, at a seminary in Ibadan. The years there had been the most peaceful of this life. He had found the fellowship, the belonging, and the certainties that he had been longing for.

It had been hard to return to Latveria. But that *was* where he had been born. If he could bring a more disciplined faith to the country, if he could save even one soul, then he was duty-bound to try.

He had tried. He was still trying. And those precious certainties were proving hard to hold on to.

Such thoughts flashed across his mind. Now Doom had come to find him, specifically. And though he was frightened, he was also flattered. And he wanted to know what it was that had brought the lord of Latveria to him.

"You also worked on their cataloguing, I believe," said Doom.

"On the impossibility of doing so comprehensively," Zargo corrected automatically.

"Quite," said Doom, and Zargo sensed he was pleased. "There is a confluence that I need, and that you will find."

"I will try, Excellency, but after all these years, I'm not sure about my skills."

"I am, so your doubts don't matter. You will present yourself at the castle gates tomorrow morning at six."

"Yes, Excellency."

Doom walked away without another word. His presence filled the church so completely, he might have been holding it in his hand, up until the moment that the door clanged shut behind him. Even then, his shadow lingered. Zargo could still feel his gaze. Now that it had been turned on him, he would never be free of it.

Zargo staggered over to the front row of pews and collapsed on them. His breath came in long, ragged gasps. His hands shook. The cold of his soaked cassock was nothing compared to the ice running through his blood. When he thought he could walk without falling, he pushed himself up from the pew and stumbled to the rear of the church, out the exit and into the small rectory nestled like a barnacle against the east wall of St Peter. In his chambers he changed out of his wet clothes, then grabbed a bottle of scotch and poured himself a double shot. Liquid smoke went down his throat. Warmth blossomed in his chest. He sank down on the bed, fighting the shivers, and stared blankly at the ceiling.

Tomorrow morning he would return to a past that disgusted him. He dreaded the road Doom would force him to walk.

He dreaded it all the more because of the treacherous excitement stirring in his heart.

CHAPTER 3

Zargo jolted awake, unable to breathe. A heavy hand covered his mouth. Another pressed down on his chest, pinning him to the bed. He flailed, striking arms as rigid and thick as wooden posts. The hand over his mouth kept his panicked scream inside, turning it into a whining moan. He thrashed harder, but the man who held him down didn't seem to notice.

"Settle down, Father," said a voice he didn't recognize. It came from somewhere near the foot of the bed. "Don't struggle, and things will go much more comfortably for you."

Though his assailant had not covered his nose, he felt that he couldn't breathe. His body was convinced it had to fight or die. He shuddered with the effort to fight down the panic. He forced his arms down. He held them at his side, hands splayed. He reminded himself that he could breathe.

When he was still, the voice said, "That's better. Are you going to be sensible? If Emil releases you, there will be no screaming or stupid attempts to get away?"

Zargo grunted what he hoped was an affirmative. He held himself immobile.

"I think he's going to behave, Emil. Sit him up."

The huge hands released Zargo, then grabbed him under the shoulders and heaved him up until his back was resting against the wooden headboard.

Sitting on the battered dresser opposite the bed, a storm lantern turned low cast a dim light in the room. Prince Rudolfo Fortunov, son and heir of the deposed and slain King Vladimir, reclined in the chair next to the dresser, rocking it on its back legs. The other man took a step back from Zargo after lifting the priest into position, his face shadowed but still recognizable. Zargo had seen Emil Seefeld at the vespers service. He had shaken his bone-crusher hand afterwards. Seefeld had been a regular member of Zargo's congregation for years. He was big, his shoulders rounded from the labor of fields, but broad as a wall. He had always been quiet in the church, expressionless. The smirk he bore now revealed a thuggishness Zargo had never seen before.

Be very careful. He's enjoying this. Don't give him an excuse to enjoy it more.

Rudolfo Fortunov was smaller than Seefeld. Most people were. But he looked harder. His features, weathered by years of battle and living in the rough, still had the chiseled pride of his family. Even matted with dirt, the way his short brown hair swept back conjured thoughts of royal portraits in oil. His eyes had the aura of command that reminded Zargo a bit of Doom's, but there were years of frustration there too. The world was supposed to belong to the prince, and he did not forgive it for failing in its duty.

Zargo rubbed his shoulder where Seefeld had gripped him. If Seefeld had pulled a bit faster or harder, he would have dislocated the joint.

"What do you–" Zargo began.

Seefeld slapped him, jerking his head hard. "You don't have permission to speak."

"Easy, Emil," Fortunov said, his face unmoved and cold. "I think Father Grigori was just trying to be agreeable." He smiled, friendly as winter. "You'll have to forgive Emil," he said to Zargo. "He's been coming to your services for a long time. I'm afraid your sermons bored him sick." Fortunov shrugged. "Given that, we have to expect he's going to want to get a little of his own back."

Zargo held a hand against his numb cheek. "He's been watching me all the time?"

Fortunov's smile became genuine. He was pleased. "I have eyes everywhere," he said. "Sometimes they have to watch for a long time before they see something useful. This evening they did. They saw Doom pay you a visit."

Zargo said nothing.

Fortunov leaned forward. The front legs of the chair came down on the floor with a bang. "What did Doom want?" he said, very softly. The threat behind the words was huge.

"What will my life be worth if I tell you?" Zargo asked.

Seefeld slapped him again.

Fortunov cocked his head. "What do you think it will be if you don't? Think carefully about what you say next, because I'm not going to repeat my question, and this is your last chance to answer it."

The wire of Zargo's balancing act stretched out before him.

For most of his life, he had been pulled and pushed in one direction or another. By faith and by profession, by fear and duty, by calling and by commands. He was used to trying to find a balance. He was also used to dealing with the fact that there were times when no balance was to be found. He had to find one this, time, though. Doom to the left, Fortunov to the right, and if he fell, one or other would have him killed.

Zargo took his first step on the wire. It was the only one available to him in the moment. "Doom wants me to research ley lines," he said. *If I lie, he will have me killed*, he wanted to say to any device that might be listening.

"He wants a priest for that," Fortunov said, dripping disbelief.

Seefeld's right hand, the one that had been slapping Zargo, made a fist.

"I wasn't always a priest," Zargo said quickly.

Fortunov held up a finger, forestalling Seefeld. "And why does he want you to do this? What does he expect you to discover?"

"I don't know." That was true. He had no idea what the confluence was that Doom sought, or what it might mean.

"I'm not sure I believe you," said Fortunov.

Seefeld grabbed Zargo by the front of his buttoned pajama top and yanked him out of the bed.

"It's the truth!" Zargo pleaded. Seefeld was holding him high, forcing him to stand on tiptoes.

"You're making Emil cranky," Fortunov warned.

"I'm not trying to!"

Fortunov steepled his fingers. "Do I have this right? Doom himself comes to see you, a priest, and not a member of the Werner Academy, and asks you to head up an occult investigation project for reasons that are unclear to you."

"Is it so strange that that seems strange?" Zargo asked.

"Now you're being witty," said Fortunov. "Don't be witty. That makes *me* cranky. Emil."

Seefeld punched Zargo in the stomach. Zargo had known the blow would have to come. He had tried to brace himself for it. He failed. There was no preparing for the violence of the impact and the pain. He doubled over, tearing free of Seefeld's grip, mouth gaping for air that would not come. He stumbled backwards, away from Seefeld, past Fortunov, stumbled as he had known he would have to, stumbled so he could remain balanced on the wire, stumbled all the way back to the outside wall where he fell with such force that his elbow smashed the pane of the bedroom window. Glass fell to the street, breaking the quiet of the night. Zargo drew air and his cry was unfeigned, instinctive and loud.

Seefeld was on him the next instant, and grabbed him by the throat. "Don't you call for help," he snarled. "Don't you dare."

Zargo didn't shout. He didn't have to. He heard the whistle of the night watch, and the sound of running feet in the distance. The alarm had been raised.

Fortunov was on his feet. "*Idiot*," he hissed at Seefeld.

"It was *him*," the big man whined, giving Zargo a shake.

"And who gave him the chance?" He grabbed Zargo's arm and punched Seefeld's shoulder. "Go! Now! We have to go!"

Seefeld scrambled out of the second story window, reached up for the overhang and pulled himself onto the roof.

Fortunov squeezed Zargo's arm. His grip was iron. Zargo

felt how small and brittle the bones of his arm were.

"Our conversation is not over," Fortunov told him. "It is only just beginning. Do you understand me? You are going to tell me what Doom is up to. Be certain of that." He shoved Zargo to the floor and went out the window.

Zargo struggled to his feet and lurched to the windowsill. The street behind St Peter Church was narrow. The gabled eaves of the rectory and the houses opposite were barely six feet apart. Fortunov and Seefeld leapt across the gap and fled across the rooftops, heading to the right as the whistles and running bootsteps approached from the left. He lost sight of them before the night watch arrived, but he pointed from the window when he saw the officers, then fell back on his bed as the pursuit began. He wished the nightmare was over. He knew it was only beginning.

Kariana Verlak, captain of the Castle Guard, nudged a piece of broken glass with the toe of her boot. She looked up at the window from which it had come, then back to Sergeant Kurt Genschow of the night watch. *Fortunov*, she thought, with a mixture of anger and determination. *You were lucky you escaped before I arrived.* "Where did you lose track of them?" she asked.

"Two streets over, captain," said Genschow.

"Show me."

Genschow led the way up the stairs of the house facing the rectory. They emerged on the steep roof, in a moonlit landscape of grey slate, punctuated by smoking chimneys. They crossed to the roof of the next house and climbed to its peak.

Genschow pointed south. "They were spotted from the street, but pursuit there was impossible."

"And when you gave chase on the roof, they had too much of a lead," said Verlak.

"Exactly."

They clambered down the other side of the roof and kept going on a diagonal path across the gables, leaping twice over a street, until they reached a cluster of roofs which was being combed by a squad of the night watch. More officers on the roof peaks on the other side of this street fruitlessly scanned the night for signs of the fugitives.

"They dropped out of sight when they went down this side of the roofs," said Genschow. "There was no sign of them after that."

Where did you go, traitor? "Did you have anyone at street level here?" The night watch on the ground would be able to converge quickly at target intersections to act as spotters of the men jumping across the gaps above.

"We did. They never saw anyone cross this street. They might have missed Fortunov in the dark."

"Or he never crossed at all."

Genschow nodded. "We're conducting room by room searches of the houses on this block." His shrug conveyed how much luck the night watch had had, and how he expected things to go.

Verlak grunted. She climbed back up to survey the roofs nearby. Everything was angles and deep shadows. It was unlikely anything useful could be found before daylight, if then.

Still, if this was the last roof Fortunov had been seen on,

his means of disappearance might be somewhere close.

The shadows next to a chimney caught her eye. There was a patch at its base, where the walls of two houses met, that seemed deeper than the rest. She approached and found a narrow gap, a couple of feet long and less than a foot wide, between the houses.

"A man could fit down this," she said.

"Barely," said Genschow. "And if he didn't fall to his death or get stuck partway down, he'd be trapped at the bottom."

"Where does this lead?"

"Nowhere. There's no alley below. It's just a space. The two houses aren't perfectly adjoined."

"You've checked?"

"We sent lights down. There's nothing."

Verlak thought for a moment. "No," she decided. "There's something. If it doesn't look like something Fortunov could use, then what it looks like is misleading. Let's go."

Back at street level, she rounded up officers with flashlights and had them open up the nearest sewer access, half a block down from where the two houses joined.

"Oh no," said Genschow.

"Oh yes," Verlak told him.

"How did he do it?"

"Let's find out."

They climbed down into the sewer. Beneath low, curved ceilings of damp brickwork, there was a narrow walkway next to the canal of foul water. Verlak took one of the flashlights and led the way, breathing through her mouth. After a short distance, she turned down a narrow tunnel. The walkway was slippery, barely more than a ledge, and she had to walk carefully. She aimed the light up at the ceiling. Now that she knew she was looking for a shaft, she found the access point almost immediately.

"Do you see?" she asked Genschow. "You can just make out where they cut." Faint lines ran across the brickwork, easy to miss but telltale in their regularity. They formed a rectangle the same size and shape as the gap at the chimney base. "Get someone up there," Verlak said. "There will be some kind of trap door mechanism. They had that shaft prepared for their escape. They probably had a rope to get down, though that will be gone now."

"This won't be the only hatch like this, will it?" Genschow asked, sounding dismayed.

"No, it won't be, and that means a search." She knew what she was demanding. Hundreds of miles of sewer and abandoned mining tunnels honeycombed the foundations of Doomstadt. Even with drones, it would be a massive, perhaps impossible, task to find every escape route Fortunov and his rebels had created. But each one that was blocked would reduce his freedom of movement by that much, and bring her closer to putting a bullet between his traitor eyes. She lived for the moment she would perform that service for her king.

They left the sewers, and Genschow relayed Verlak's commands, setting the tunnel search in motion. Verlak and the sergeant made their way back to the rectory. Two guards were posted by the outside door, the block was cordoned off.

"Has the priest been questioned?" Verlak asked.

"No, captain. We waited for you, given that Fortunov was involved."

"Good. Maintain the same practice here. Anything that has anything to do with Father Grigori Zargo is to be reported directly to me."

She looked up at the broken window.

"Sloppy work," said Genschow. "Fortunov wouldn't have had to run if he'd been a bit more careful."

"Indeed," Verlak said dryly. "Unlike him to be so clumsy, isn't it?"

"What do you mean?"

"So unlike him as to be improbable."

"You think the broken window wasn't an accident?"

"I'm sure it wasn't."

"Why would Fortunov want to alert us?" Genschow asked, confused.

"It wasn't Fortunov or his man who broke the window." She crunched broken glass beneath her heel. "This was a cry for help."

The guards had let Zargo get dressed, though they had not allowed him to leave the bedroom. His cassock made him feel a bit more like himself, even a little bit less helpless, and he could use every comforting illusion he could find. He sat on the edge of the bed, waiting for the interrogation to come, thinking about how he would keep his balance on the tightrope.

Nothing to do except try. I can't dismount. They won't let me.

His wait ended when Kariana Verlak entered the room and shut the door behind her. Zargo had never spoken to the captain of the Castle Guard. He had seen her from a distance, and that was how any sane person preferred to keep Verlak.

Having to speak to her was never a sign that things were going well for you. *Things aren't going well for me, are they?*

He wasn't sure who unnerved him more, Verlak or Fortunov.

She stood before Zargo, eyeing him closely before speaking. She had a patrician bearing in her uniform's dark greatcoat with her hawk-like features and ramrod posture. Her parents had been peasants, though. There was no trace of the old aristocratic families of Latveria in her bloodline, and her ferocity in the defense of Doom's order was the stuff of fearful awe.

She will know everything about me. She will know things about me that even I don't know.

The only way to take another step on the tightrope was to be utterly honest.

"So you had a visit from Rudolfo Fortunov," Verlak said.

Zargo nodded. "Aided by Emil Seefeld."

"I see."

Her tone was expressionless, and Zargo couldn't tell if it was news to her or not that Seefeld was a rebel.

"They came to ask why our lord visited me last evening," Zargo continued.

"What did you tell them?"

"The same as I am telling you: everything I know." *Which, I hope, is so little that it won't matter.*

"A risky strategy, Father," said Verlak.

"What else is there for me to do? If I had lied to Fortunov, he would have had Seefeld kill me. If I lie to you, my prospects won't be any better."

"On that last point, we agree."

"You should know something else. Fortunov expects me to keep talking."

"The solution to this situation, then, would be for you not to learn anything that would be of interest to him," said Verlak. "Is that right?"

"The thought had occurred to me," Zargo said, wondering if he could dare allow himself to hope she and Doom would think the same.

Verlak's thin smile dispelled the hope. "The lord of Latveria has chosen you," she said. "Your only course of action is to carry out the work he has commanded of you. It's really that simple."

The news that he was not about to be shot was not as comforting as he might have thought.

"And when Fortunov comes again?" Zargo asked.

"You're that confident he will?"

"I mean no offense, captain, but aren't you?" He broke out in a sweat as he asked the question. He was giving offense even if he didn't mean it. He was implying that Verlak would not catch Fortunov. He was gambling on the idea that she was as honest with herself as he was being with her.

Verlak said nothing for a long moment. Then she turned to the door. "Get up," she snapped. "You're coming with me."

The tightrope had trembled. But Zargo hadn't fallen. He could take another step.

CHAPTER 4

The tower rising from the center of Castle Doom was so broad it appeared squat to the eye, even though it was one of the tallest of the castle's structures. It had the ribbed metal dome of an observatory, though its peak was a wide, level platform. The roof and walls were a black deeper than interstellar. They absorbed light and reflected none. The tower brooded over its secrets and waited to unleash its power.

Inside, the upper third was a single, cavernous laboratory. The curved walls were built up in inverted terraces, each level of stonework looming out a bit further over the one below. Multi-jointed and multi-tooled servo-arms extended from rails fixed to each terrace. They could reach any part of the lab at the command of their master. Ringed by walls of layered obsidian and titanium, a circular pool, shimmering silver, dominated the central floor space. Doom walked around the pool, and the servo-arms adjusted their positions in reaction to the movements of his fingers. He created a column of empty space above the pool, reaching all the way up to the center of the dome. Around the base of the tower's vault, another massive set of retracted servo-arms held the great mirror and lens of the observatory's telescope next to the walls.

Doom finished his inspection. The lab was ready. Its potential was unlimited and purified of all traces of previous work. The empty space above the ring seemed to hum with latent creation. It was a void that would be filled. It was where the Harrower would come to be.

The single door to the lab was heavy with an inner layer of lead shielding. Its bronze surface was engraved with a pentagram enclosed by a magic circle. Symbols of both protection and invocation ran between the circle's double lines. The moment Doom was satisfied with the positions of the servo-arms, the door opened. An old man entered. His hair and beard were white, though his posture was unbowed by age. He was Doom's advisor, the man who had raised him from his orphaned childhood, and the only human being on Earth that Doom trusted implicitly.

"Boris," said Doom. "If I have not praised your timing recently, then I have been remiss."

"It is simply my duty to you, your Excellency," Boris said, sounding pleased.

"Is she here?" Doom asked.

"Yes. Maria von Helm waits in the great hall."

"Good."

"Shall I have her shown to her quarters?"

"No. Bring her here. Our work must begin at once."

"As you wish." He hesitated.

"What is it, Boris?"

"She has asked about the archives."

"Then she is not wasting time," Doom said, satisfied. "I will take her there myself."

"How much liberty is she to be allowed there?" Boris asked.

"She is to have complete freedom there and elsewhere in the castle. She is not to be hampered in any way, and she is to have full cooperation. If she needs something, then she is to have it. Am I clear?"

"You are, your Excellency."

Behind his mask, Doom's lips pulled back in a tight grin. "You look concerned, old friend."

"Vassily Dubrov will take it hard if she has a free hand in the archives."

"That is none of my concern."

Boris tried again. "Dubrov is a proud man."

"Then that is a flaw to be corrected, as it should have been by now. I do not understand how he has not learned humility after so many years, but if he must be educated now, then so be it. The archives are not his fiefdom."

"Of course not," said Boris.

"And that is not an illusion he will be permitted to have," Doom added.

"Understood." Boris looked as if he might say more, but knew better. Instead, he changed the subject. "What of the priest?" he asked. "Captain Verlak has him under guard."

"Did she take him to a cell?"

"No, to one of the Chambers of Contemplation."

For Doom, the spare, unadorned rooms high in the towers were places of quiet, where he could be free of distraction as he looked out over the vistas of Doomstadt and the landscape beyond. For others, placed there with the doors locked, they were places where waiting turned contemplation into terror and anticipation into dread.

"Leave him to his thoughts for now," Doom said. "That will make him more pliable. Let us go and greet Helm."

Is this what you want?

Maria von Helm had begun asking herself the question even before she had agreed to work with Doom. It came to her partway through their conversation on Mount Sivàr, insistent and disturbing as a haunting. Some part of her had already known she would say *yes*, and that part writhed with uncertainty. The question had swirled through her dreams and her waking hours ever since. It was more strident, almost desperate, now that she was in Castle Doom.

The scale of the palace was enormous. She was in the center of a hall hundreds of feet long and thirty feet high. Stained glass windows mounted just below the arched ceiling let in daylight filtered through shades of red and green. Suits of armor lined the walls at regular intervals, guarding the shelves of leather-clad volumes on recessed bookcases. Above the shelves were paintings of Latverian landscapes. The hall was firm in what it valued, and what it valued was Latveria, knowledge and power.

She could not remember when she had last been in so huge an interior. On Mount Sivàr, she had either been outside, uncontained by walls, or inside her cave. She could touch its ceiling by reaching up. Its chambers were cramped, but they had felt less like a prison than the castle. Here, she was painfully conscious of being inside the embodiment of Doom's will.

The spider had invited her into his web. She had come voluntarily.

Is this what you want?

Yes. I think so. I wouldn't be here if it wasn't.

Will the spider ever let us go?

If what I do with him succeeds, it won't matter if he lets us go or not. She would be free of her greater prison, the one whose cell door had slammed closed on her the night Cynthia had died. Her true jailer was on the other side of death's veil. If she could be free of that terror, then what happened to her on this side of the veil was irrelevant.

Yes, this was what she wanted. If she could free Cynthia, she could free herself.

The question refused to be satisfied.

Very well. She would have to live with it.

Doom appeared at the far end of the hall and strode toward her. She walked to meet him halfway. If they were to be partners in the endeavor, she would act like one. *This is your web, but I am no fly.*

"I am glad you have come," Doom said. He gestured for her to walk with him, and they headed back down the hall. "The work ahead of us will be long. We should begin at once."

He led her down other long, majestic corridors, through an iron door, and then up a long, stone, spiral staircase.

"Have you thought about where we should begin?" Helm asked as they climbed the steps.

"On separate paths," said Doom.

"What do you mean by that?"

"I will show you."

They reached the top of the stairs, and another massive

door admitted them to the laboratory. *The center of the web*, Helm thought. The network of servo-arms poised above her looked ready to seize anything the spider wanted. Banks of computers and tanks of chemicals lined the periphery of the chamber, but Helm was surprised by how much empty space there was.

"The raw material for the Harrower has yet to be gathered," Doom said, guessing her thoughts. "This, though, is where it will be constructed, and where it will do its work."

They stopped at the edge of the silver pool. At first Helm thought she was looking at mercury, then she wasn't sure. "What is that liquid?" she asked.

"Nanobots," said Doom. "The configurations possible here are infinite, and the response immediate." The moment he finished speaking, the surface formed into an interlocked pattern of occult symbols, and became solid. What had resembled mercury now looked like steel.

"How many times have you used this material like this?" Helm asked, concerned.

"Many times."

"Then the charge it carries is…"

"Enormous. Yes. And it is under my control."

"I don't see how you can be so sure."

"Yet I am, because it is mine. So is this." He pointed up.

The dome of the ceiling hummed, and ribbed sections pulled back, opening up a space wide enough for the 300-inch lens and mirror. The servo-arms moved them into alignment with each other. Initially they were a foot apart, both at the threshold of the aperture. More nanobots streamed out of the walls and formed the body of the telescope. It extended quickly, the lens carried further and further out of the dome of the observatory. Some of the body came down into the lab, but not so far that it intruded on the central column of empty space going from the pool to the level center of the dome.

When the telescope was complete, the silver pool shifted again. It turned into a picture of the clouds and sky above Doomstadt. The resolution was so complete, the picture reproduced in such depth, that vertigo assailed Helm. She almost toppled into the sky beneath her.

She gasped. "You project the forces of the stars onto this material," Helm said, awed.

"As above, so below," said Doom. "Before we are done, as below, so above. This is merely our starting point, though." He waved a hand, and the telescope disassembled itself, the roof closed, and the pool became silver again. "The saying has become a commonplace that any sufficiently advanced technology is indistinguishable from magic. But that is merely an expression of perspective. What we will do operates at the true point of indiscernibility, where the most advanced technology and the most advanced magic become one."

"Technology is not something I know anything about," Helm said.

"No, your studies have been purely hermetic. I *do* know a lot about the intersection that we will use, but not everything. These are the two paths we will begin on, then. I have shown you this laboratory so you are aware of where our goals will converge. Do not concern yourself about it otherwise. I will focus my research here. You will follow the dictates of your own expertise and go as far as you can toward our objective.

When we encounter the walls to our progress, and we will, that is when we shall pool our resources. We will go further, faster, if your explorations are not hampered by mine. Is that agreeable?"

"It is, if you mean what you say. I will not have you looking over my shoulder, then?"

Doom shook his head. "Your views are not mine. That is crucial. That is why you're here."

Helm looked at the pool of silver nanobots. She thought again about the scale of what they were setting out to do. What Doom had shown her here made her uneasy, and they would be tampering with energies far greater and more terrible before long. This was simply the doorway to a mad dream.

Is this what you want?

Yes. Oh yes, it is.

The exhilaration of the possible was already overcoming her reservations.

"Good," she said. "Good." She took a deep breath. "I think it's time I saw your archives."

"I think it is," said Doom.

The archives' reading hall was deep in the foundations of Castle Doom, directly beneath the laboratory tower. Helm's initial impression was that this was an architectural inversion of the lab, an enormous amphitheater whose sides she could not see. She could tell she and Doom had entered a bowl from the way the walls curved away from the door, vanishing into the gloom. She guessed they were midway down the slope of the bowl, though she could not see how far the terraces of monolithic bookcases went up behind her. Stone walkways cut down the slope, connecting the terraces, and leading to the bottom of the amphitheater, where sat a huge reading table and a single, equally huge chair. Lighting everywhere except at the table was low, just enough for nearest shelves and the materials on them to be visible.

The reading hall was a sea of shadows. Helm thought about the knowledge contained in this space. That, she thought, was where the real shadows came from.

A man in dark robes climbed the walkway to meet them as they descended towards the floor of the hall. His back and shoulders were rounded from a life of hunching over documents. Thin lank gray hair framed a sallow face that might not have seen the sun in years. His wrinkled flesh had the yellowed texture of decaying parchment, and hung from his skull like melting wax. There was something familiar about him, though, and the sense that she should know who this was startled Helm.

"Your Excellency," the man said, his tone even more obsequious than his low bow. "You honor me with your presence."

Doom acknowledged him with a grunt. "Maria von Helm," he said, "this is Vassily Dubrov. He is the chief archivist. He will provide you with whatever you need."

"Dubrov?" Helm asked, startled. "Are you a relation of Ivor Dubrov?"

"I am. He was my uncle. Did you know him?"

"Not well. And that was a long time ago." Faded memories stirred, none of them welcome. She remembered Ivor's nephew now, as he had been then. The archivist had been in his early teens when she had last seen him.

Dubrov scuttled down ahead of them to the reading hall floor. The table was easily fifteen feet long, large enough to be a banquet table, but it was clear no plate had ever touched its polished oak surface. Helm would have room to lay out a vast array of documents. The chair was massive too, a throne of mahogany and brass. She would disappear in it. But the light here was good, and she was sure that if anywhere in the world held the knowledge that she needed to find and interpret, it was this hall.

"Tell me what you require, and I will bring it to you," Dubrov told Helm.

"Thank you. I will start with the *Lemegeton*, the *Cyprianus*, the *Zekerboni* and the *Grand Grimoire*. It would be helpful, too, for you to show me how the materials are organized, so I can find my way around."

"I'm sure that won't be necessary," said Dubrov. "It will be much more efficient if you just give me your requests."

"It's not a question of efficiency. It's a question of serendipity, and of not artificially narrowing the paths of my research. There will be books and papers here that I don't know about and don't know that I need, and I won't know without the happenstance of stumbling upon them. I will need to explore."

Dubrov's pallor became even more pronounced. "*Explore?*" he said, as if she had suggested setting the hall on fire. "Oh, I don't think that can be done. I don't think so at all."

"It can and it will," said Doom.

"Your pardon, your Excellency, your pardon." Dubrov spoke quickly, bowing and shrinking away before the most powerful shadow.

"You will have the run of the archives," Doom said to Helm. "Go wherever you like. Find whatever you need."

"Thank you," said Helm.

"Is that understood?" Doom asked Dubrov.

"Absolutely, your Excellency. As you wish, as you wish." The archivist was bent so low he was almost crawling.

"There will be no obstruction of any kind to Maria von Helm."

"Or course, of course, of course, I didn't mean…"

"Why aren't you already retrieving the grimoires she requested?"

"Your pardon, your pardon, your pardon."

Helm watched him scuttle away, feeling the same distaste she had felt for his uncle more than fifteen years ago.

When he was gone, Doom said, "When you want, Boris will show you to your quarters."

Helm nodded. "I think I should begin my research first." She was surrounded by a storehouse of occult knowledge that had few equals anywhere in the world. The excitement for the work was growing. There was no question in her mind now.

This was what she wanted.

Dubrov loaded another grimoire onto a book cart. The cart was wheelless, its antigrav drivers holding it a few inches off the ground. It required very little strength to push. Even so, Dubrov leaned into it as if it were a burden. He needed something to strain against, to work off some of his anger.

As he emerged from the aisle onto a ramp, he saw Helm one level up, moving along the shelves with a rapt expression.

She had a hand out, her fingers just brushing the spines of the books as she gazed at them. The sight enraged Dubrov. Helm hadn't been here an hour, and she was touching the books, *touching* them, *touching everything* as if the archives were hers.

Dubrov forced himself to look away. He maneuvered the cart onto the ramp and headed slowly down to the reading table. His chest was tight with anger. It was hard to breathe with the decades' worth of fury suddenly squeezing him in a fist.

Had she known Ivor Dubrov? Had she known the heir to the title of *Count* Ivor Dubrov?

Not well. And that was a long time ago.

Long by whose memory? Not long as far as Dubrov was concerned. Nor should for Helm. *She destroyed two families.* That wasn't the sort of thing it should be easy to forget.

We have a shared destiny, witch. It could have been a golden one. You made sure it wasn't.

There was nothing wrong with his memory. He had only been fourteen, but he remembered what it had been like, when the Helm and Dubrov families had arranged the union of Maria and Ivor. The Dubrovs had had the advantage of an older name, and of a distant familial connection to Baron Vladimir Fortunov. Their fortune, though, had been diminishing the past few generations, and Ivor's father, Sergei, had lost the rest of it. The Helms had money, and they wanted prestige. The marriage would have strengthened both families. Dubrov remembered the optimism that had reigned in the mildewing family manor house in those days. He remembered the excitement, the belief that everything was going to be better soon. His uncle entranced him with stories of the glory days to come. The marriage banns were read. The date was set.

And then Maria von Helm ruined everything.

She had refused the commands of her parents. She had rejected Ivor Dubrov.

That was bad enough. But then she joined Cynthia von Doom in her fight against Baron Vladimir. When that struggle failed, Maria fled, and the Helms fell. Vladimir burned their home and wiped them out to the last servant. And for the Dubrovs, it didn't matter that Ivor had been rejected. The fact that a union had been attempted was enough to taint the family by association. Only the kinship with the Fortunovs saved them from extermination.

Financial ruin came within months.

As a teenager, Vassily had resented Maria for the loss of personal comforts. He had blamed her for the poverty that had overwhelmed the Dubrovs, and for the humiliation of being forced from their ancestral home.

As an adult, he blamed her for the ultimate fall of the Dubrovs, too. In the last days of King Vladimir's reign, as the threat of Doom plunged the monarch into desperation and paranoia, Latveria had not been spared the convulsions that came with the collapse of a regime. Vladimir had imprisoned anyone he suspected of disloyalty, and his suspicions had turned on his distant cousins.

Vassily Dubrov had been the only one to survive Vladimir's prisons.

Dishonor, destitution, incarceration and torture. *Helm did this, and she doesn't even remember.*

Dubrov had, under Doom, found a measure of pride again.

Doom had freed him from the prisons, and with an unnerving eye for others' skills, made him the castle librarian. The archives were his domain. He was important here. He served only one master, and he had value. This was not the life he had been promised. At least it mattered. He was grateful to Doom for the meaningful life he had now.

And now Helm was here, in all her arrogance, to take it all away again.

Why did Doom bring her here?

Dubrov began unloading the grimoires onto the table. Each tome he set down felt like placing a brick in a wall. The question was the purpose of the wall. If Helm won, Dubrov was immuring his pride.

He would not let her win.

Dubrov feared Doom too much to hate him.

He did not fear Helm.

CHAPTER 5

Doom met with Verlak in his command chamber that connected to the Castle Guard operations center. Banks of screens covered the windowless walls, surrounding the swivel throne where he sat. The chair's arms held controls for the castle's surveillance and defense systems. The door to Operations was closed and sealed. The screens received all the feeds from the larger room beyond, but nothing that was said in the chamber could be monitored without. Verlak stood before Doom, the image of the frustrated hunter. She was burning with the need to be out in the field, chasing Fortunov to ground, yet stymied by the fact that there was no chase to be had for the moment.

Doom understood her anger and her frustration. He approved of both. They sprang from a loyalty that bordered on fury.

"Despite Fortunov's mistakes," Verlak said, "there isn't enough for us to know whether he is planning something or reacting to you. Determining that would help shape our strategy against him."

"It would not," said Doom. "With Fortunov, acting and reacting are one. He lays plans, many plans, I'm convinced of that, based on his coup attempts of the past. The plans lie dormant until opportunity arises. The nature of the opportunity determines the nature of the plan. Sometimes, he is more prepared than others."

None of that pleased Verlak. Her right hand twitched, as if she could strangle Fortunov here and now. "I believe he is an active danger," she said.

"Of course he's dangerous. The fact that he has avoided capture and execution is proof enough of that. Do you believe he is an *imminent* danger?"

"He may well be." Verlak turned to the screens. She tapped one, calling up an image of Fortunov's escape hatch in the sewer. "This shows a lot of preparation."

"How is the search proceeding?"

Verlak tapped a few more screens. "We've deployed squadrons of drones." Active scans of the tunnels appeared, the updating images shimmering grey and amber. "From their telemetry, we've already identified and sealed seven other camouflaged hatches. I will not pretend we will find them all quickly."

"I would not believe you if you did," said Doom. "What about at the rectory? Any useful evidence there?"

"Not much. Some soil from the soles of their boots. We've analyzed it, hoping to identify some geographical particularities." She called up the results. "Most of it is from the sewers and the streets of Doomstadt."

"Most," Doom repeated. "But not all."

Electron-microscope photos appeared, showing grains the

size of asteroids. "The sample of interest is very small," Verlak said. "Hardly conclusive."

"But it is of interest."

"Organic content and particle size distributions suggest the viniculture regions to the east of the city. That still gives him a massive area to hide in."

Doom thought for a moment, the geography appearing before his mind's eye faster than Verlak could summon the digital maps. "We might narrow things down a bit," he said. "Fortunov will favor the cliffside vintners over those on the plains."

"For the commanding heights?"

"Such as they are. Though we should not underestimate his ability to put limited resources to good use." He was contemptuous of Fortunov as an individual, and even more so of what passed for the deposed prince's ideals. The prince was wedded to a vision of feudal aristocracy that would never return. Fortunov had skills, though, and contempt for them would be a mistake. For almost a decade, since he had come of age, Fortunov had been fighting to reclaim the throne. He was an irritant, sometimes a dangerous one. "We should consider the Kavan family."

"Why them?"

"They have never appeared on your counterintelligence radar, have they?"

"No, they haven't."

"Such a low profile would be useful for someone like Fortunov, don't you think? They have prospered, and their service to me has been unblemished, but they do have old ties. Aristocracies never forget their fall. There are families in France whose anger over 1789 remains fresh."

"I'll have them placed under surveillance," said Verlak.

"Discreetly. There must be no possibility of their being aware of it."

"If Fortunov is there, we'll know, and we'll hit with such force he will have no chance of escape."

"No," said Doom. "Observe, from maximal distance, and do not act unless I give the command. We must not move against Fortunov until we know what he has set in motion. Attacking too soon can cause as much damage as acting too late."

"Unless we kill him."

"Assuming you succeed and that he doesn't disappear again. Even then, the risk is too high. Tell me, captain, do you believe Prince Rudolfo's love for Latveria exceeds his regard for himself?"

"Not for a second," she hissed, every syllable drenched in the venom of her hatred for the traitor.

"Precisely. Am I confident that he has not prepared contingencies that will trigger indiscriminate attacks in the event of his capture or death? I am not. Watch for him. Watch for what he might be planning. When we know what we must, we will act. When Fortunov is ready, he will break surface. And there are ways of encouraging him to do so. They have already borne fruit."

"I don't understand, your Excellency."

"There was a reason why I paid a personal visit to Grigori Zargo instead of simply having him summoned to the castle."

"Your visit was bait," Verlak realized.

"Yes. That is also why I did not have any guards posted on the church or rectory. And Fortunov took the bait."

"He told the priest they would meet again."

Doom nodded, pleased to see that Verlak was seeing the strategy now. "The hook is in his jaw."

"So Zargo is to be released?"

"He will be free to go as he pleases. Or at least, where he pleases in the furtherance of the task I will set him."

"How close a watch shall we set on him?"

"You will use two kinds. The first should be subtle, and not too close. Far enough back that Zargo does not detect his minders. Fortunov will spot them, though. He will be suspicious if he sees nothing at all. The other observers will be further back. They must not be seen at all."

"Will Fortunov be brazen enough to return to the rectory?"

"Highly doubtful. We must be prepared for the possibility that he will get at Zargo some other way, a way we won't see. But the priest will see. He will be our eyes and ears. He will help us find Fortunov, willingly or not. Knowingly or not."

It was afternoon before the door to the Chamber of Contemplation opened. If not for the chiming from the clock towers of Doomstadt, far below the rock of the castle, Zargo would have lost all sense of time. He had been alone with his thoughts and his fears long enough. He almost felt relief when Doom entered the chamber. At least the waiting to know the worst was over.

The great metal mask looked down at him for a long moment, and Zargo wondered if he was about to be thrown from the tower. His head swam with anticipatory vertigo.

Doom moved to the stone balcony instead of hurling Zargo from it. "You did well last night," he said.

"Did I?" *Did I really keep my balance on the wire?*

"Breaking the window. A clear signal of your intentions. That was quick thinking."

"Thank you, your Excellency. But Prince Rudolfo is going to come to me again."

"Of course he will, one way or another."

"What do I do?"

"You will tell him your truth."

Zargo saw a number of ways to interpret Doom's words. In every one of them, he saw himself as the object of satire. He was too frightened to take offense, and he was too tired to guess which meaning was the one Doom intended. "I don't understand," he said.

"No, you won't," said Doom. "Not everything. That will ensure your continued survival."

"I thank you for that," Zargo said without irony.

"Your survival is useful to me," said Doom. There was no irony in his words either.

"You said you want me to find an intersection of ley lines."

"Yes. The resources of the Werner Academy are open to you again. I presume you still know your way around its halls."

"I'll manage," Zargo said, dreading his return and the temptations that would come with it.

"As needed, you have the use of the castle's archives as well. Here you will work in conjunction with Maria von Helm."

The Witch of the Mountains. So, Doom had brought her down from her lair and out of the rumors and nighttime whispers of Latveria. If sorcery was an ocean, then Zargo was going to drown in it. He said nothing, waiting to hear the rest, and know the anchor that would drag him down.

"Correlate the geographical locations of the lines with historical events. Find the points most associated with Latveria's history of conjuration."

"There will be many," said Zargo. The chronicles of Latveria were more like a grimoire than a historical record. *The magic circle has greater resonance in our past than the cross.*

"Find the most powerful nexus," said Doom.

"That is not something anyone could identify with certainty," Zargo protested.

Doom turned away from the balcony. The implacable mask faced Zargo, and the priest shrank away. "You can, Father Zargo. You will. I have faith in you."

Zargo left the castle less than an hour later. He had a driver now, a taciturn man named Mirov, at the wheel of a car that Zargo thought of as a compact tank. The windows were thick, ostentatiously bulletproof. The body looked as if could fend off a rocket launcher.

Mirov said nothing as he drove, and Zargo had no desire to push the intercom button in the roof above him and attempt to engage the man in conversation. He spent the twenty minutes it took to reach the Werner Academy in silent prayer, seeking forgiveness for what he was about to do, and the strength to do it.

The driver *did* have music playing, though. The strains of Giazotto's "Adagio in G Minor" filled the passenger compartment, emerging from invisible speakers. The mournful majesty of the piece felt like more mockery, and for a while Zargo couldn't decide if it was Doom or Fate amusing themselves at his expense this time. The day was overcast again, and the rain began when the car was a few blocks away from the Academy. It ran down the windows in tears as the "Adagio" swelled, and then Zargo knew that Fate was to blame for the pathetic fallacy.

That's quite enough, isn't it? Isn't it?

The car pulled up before the wide, columned staircase leading to the main doors of the Werner Academy. Mirov got out and opened the door for Zargo. He remained silent when Zargo thanked him, and sat back in the driver's seat to wait.

The Werner Academy architecture was a mix of the neo-classical and the brutalist. It reigned over six blocks of Doomstadt, a monolith marked by cold grace. In honor of the man for whom it was named, it devoted its west wing to clinical research. Its east wing, where Zargo had studied and worked in the life he had tried to leave behind, was the country's center for occult sciences.

Ilona Sandor was waiting for him at the entrance. "I was told to expect you," she said.

"And you were instructed to welcome me back?"

"Not in so many words. If I can make this easier for you, Grigori, I will. I know coming back here is hard for you."

"Yet after all we talked about yesterday, here I am," he said with a twisted smile.

They started down the main hall. The lighting gave the stone walls and marble floor an amber glow. The air was filled with the memories of old things, of secret things, of the nomenclature of things that should not be named. Doors on either side opened into lecture theaters. Zargo made a conscious effort to look straight ahead, but he felt the memories of sitting on benches and speaking behind lecterns come for him, bringing with them the guilt for his share of the things he had helped name in his time here.

And now I'm back to do it again.

"I don't have to ask if it was your idea to come here," said Sandor.

"No, you don't."

"I also know you don't want to hear this, but the decision was a good one. This is where you belong, Grigori."

"You're right that I don't want to hear that. What I need, though–"

Sandor held up a hand, interrupting him. "I'm sorry," she said, "but that is something *I* don't want to hear. I think that's for the best, don't you? You know your way around."

"It's been years..." Zargo began.

"If you tell me you've forgotten how to find what you're looking for, I won't believe you."

He wished she was mistaken. He wished he had shed his years here. But the old instincts were coming back. He was *home*, and that horrified him. The corridors felt as familiar as the nave of St Peter.

"I'd rather you didn't tell me anything about why you're here unless absolutely necessary," Sandor continued.

"All right," said Zargo.

"If you want to talk about anything else, I'm ready to listen."

"Thank you." *What shall we talk about? That I think you're wrong that I belong here, but I'm terrified that you might be right?* Too many memories were rushing in, most of all the emotional memory of the bad excitement that had accompanied his work here, the feeling of sinking in greater and greater sin, and the thrill that had come with the horror. He had been lucky. The horror had outweighed the thrill, and he had escaped. The years of repentance seemed shallow now. The thrill was waiting just beyond his fear to return, stronger than ever.

Sandor left him at the doors to the Department of Geomancy. He walked as quickly as he could to its library, conscious of the looks he received from the students and faculty he passed. He kept his eye straight ahead and on the floor. He would not acknowledge their curiosity, or, worse, their satisfaction.

The library was as he remembered it, a long, wide hall, made airy by the skylight that ran the entire length of the ceiling. Galleries of bookshelves three floors high lined the walls, and large work tables took up most of the floor. It took Zargo only a few minutes to get the charts and chronicles he needed. It took him a bit longer to force himself to go to the doctoral theses cabinet and take out his own. He had burned his private copies, but that didn't matter. His work could not be undone, and there it was, confronting him with past sins, ready to help him engage in new ones.

He spread out the charts, and for the next few hours he pored over them, tracing lines and intersections, crossreferencing them with the notable eruptions of occult activity in the chronicles. For the first while, his search was like trying to find the wettest part of the ocean. Latveria's history seethed with the supernatural. But he became increasingly focused on his task, and the more he was absorbed, the more he began to see patterns. He was picking up where he had left off with his research. His thesis had argued that the charting of ley lines was not only incomplete, it was a task that never could be completed. There were always more currents of power than human investigation could detect at any one time. The currents were affected by each other, and by sorcerous activity. Like physical rivers, events could change their course. The most ancient and the most powerful were constant, but there were tides that seemed to sweep through them, too.

The theories in his dissertation had been put to the test and proven correct. It was the work that had led to his faculty position at the Werner Academy. It was also the cornerstone of his shame. He had done so much, *too* much, to help develop the practice of witchcraft.

But there had been pride, too, at the time, and passion for work well done. And the more he revisited knowledge he had tried to forget, and the more he found new patterns, and new connections, the more he felt the old eagerness returning. By late afternoon, he was too caught up in the chase to lie to himself that he was only making such progress because of obeying Doom's command.

He was back in the library again the next day, and every day that followed for a week and a half. He barely had the energy to drag himself through his services, and he found himself thinking about the problems of the lines and their confluence when he should have been praying.

The light from the skylight was turning grey on his tenth day when he sat back in his chair, rubbed his eyes, and looked again at the spot he had identified. Doom sought a confluence. The history of the location suggested such a confluence was there, though the charts indicated ley lines going near, but not through, the coordinates.

Zargo took a sheet of paper, placed it over the chart, and traced the lines. Then he added the uncharted lines he suspected were there, minor ones suggested by the rhythms of history.

The location was in the middle of nowhere. It was also in the center of a pentagon formed by the crossing of the lines. And it was precisely midway between Castle Doom and Mount Sivàr.

Zargo consulted another map. A road ran less than a mile past the target area.

You don't need to go there in person.

He resisted the idea for all of ten seconds.

Three hours later, as evening fell, Mirov turned the car off the road and the vehicle jounced over the barren land. The terrain was flat and stony. A shallow lake had been here, but had dried up after the construction of the Kanof Valley Dam to the north. In the center of the plain was a low hill. It had once been an island, and on its crown were the ruins of a small keep, built in the twelfth century, now only a tumbled foundation, stonework scattered like broken teeth.

Mirov brought the car to a stop at the base of the hill. Zargo got out and hurried to the top in the fading light. He scrambled over the waist-high remains of a wall. In the middle of the ruins, at the barely detectable peak of the hill, he stopped. He felt it at once. His body vibrated, as if it were a dowsing rod jerked suddenly down. He was at the center of centers. Energy writhed beneath the surface. The land hummed with potential.

"Found it," he said. "*Found it!*" he shouted. He gave in to the exhilaration of discovery. When the elation passed, the guilt that hit was the worst he'd felt since the day he had realized he must leave the Werner Academy.

In the gathering dusk, it was already harder to make his way down the hill without tripping than it had been coming up. When he got to the car, he collapsed on the back seat with a sigh. "Let's return to the castle," he said.

There was no answer.

"Mirov?" Zargo tapped on the plexiglass partition.

The driver turned around. It wasn't Mirov.

"So," said Rudolfo Fortunov. "What is it that you've found?"

CHAPTER 6

Two weeks before Midsummer, Doom brought Helm to the construction site. The work was progressing well. The excavations were complete, and the framework of the structure was taking shape. The hill Zargo had identified was coated entirely in iron. Immense flying forges had poured the molten metal over the ground, sparing only the ruins and the center of the peak. Silver had gone there, pure silver, forming a disk twenty feet in diameter inside the broken walls.

Five staircases radiated from the disk, proving access to the keep. Doom and Helm climbed the northern one. He watched Helm looking at the runes inscribed into the metal slope.

"Fine work," she said.

"The artisans know that only perfection is acceptable."

"I hope even that will be enough."

"It will be," said Doom. He had Fate in a stranglehold. He would not let go until he had his victory.

They reached the top of the hill and took in the panorama of the construction.

"It makes me think more of an arena than I thought it would," said Helm.

"Yes," said Doom. "The form unveils its function."

From the base of the hill, twenty-foot wide cylinders of silver-lined concrete stretched out for a quarter of a mile, rising as sharply curved pylons a hundred feet high, tapering to jagged points. More runes covered the complete surfaces. Though there were hundreds of yards of space separating the pylons, the sense of enclosure was strong. The hill, less than half the height of the pylons, did feel like it was at the center of an arena.

Or of a hand, with five clawed fingers frozen in the act of closing into a fist.

Generators surrounded the hill, and huge cables ran from them into the interior of the concrete. They were quiet for now. When they powered up, they would both tap into and feed the ley lines.

Doom contemplated the forces he would be unleashing then. There was some satisfaction in that. He was even allowing himself to feel eager for the duel on Midsummer Night. He could afford to.

This year, things will be different.

As soon as the words sprang to his mind, he banished them, wincing. They were cursed. He had told himself that same lie year after year. He could not afford to fall into old patterns this time.

Things are different.

Yes, that was better. The most important change had already

taken place. He knew he was not going to win. Victory wasn't even the goal.

That fact was tasting more and more bitter, though, as the duel with Hell drew closer. The power he was going to marshal this time, and the preparations he was making to shape the battle, were, thanks to Helm's aid, of an order he had never deployed before. It was tempting to imagine an outright victory. It was frustrating to think he was throwing all this effort into a certain defeat.

Not defeat. This will be a stepping stone. Remember that.

Another stepping stone. Zargo's identification of this site had been the first one. The next had been Helm's breakthrough. Doom had known what needed to be done. When Hell came for him, he would steal a portion of its essence. Helm had discovered how to do it.

The answer, when she had found it, turned out to be simple, in the way the principle of a fulcrum is simple. In the center of the silver disc was an engraving inlaid in iron. It was the Sator Square, one of the oldest charms in the magical lexicon.

SATOR
AREPO
TENET
OPERA
ROTAS

It had such a long history of widespread use as a basic invocation of protection that for Doom it was a banality, useless for his purposes, of mild interest for the puzzle of the translation of *AREPO*. Treating the word as a proper noun produced the mundanity of *the sower Arepo holds the wheel with care*. Helm, revisiting first principles and looking at them anew, had come to Doom in the lab four nights ago. She had been pale, but also excited, as she had pointed to the square in the grimoire she had been carrying.

"*Arepo*," she said. "The truth has been hidden before us all along. When I think of how often this has been used to heal, to protect, to save…" She shook her head. "The harm that has been lurking within…"

"You've found a new translation?" Doom asked.

"No. The illumination of an old, discarded one. *Arepo* is *arrepo*. 'I creep towards.'"

"Except it isn't," said Doom. "Not with that spelling. And the sentence is nonsensical with that translation."

"And that is why we have not seen the truth," Helm said. She shuddered. "The letter is missing, hiding, and so the meaning is concealed. *I creep towards* is hidden inside the meaningless letters. It lurks within the innocuous sentence, and the innocuous is the camouflage for the danger."

"An invocation disguised as protection," said Doom. The potential was exciting. *Well done, Helm.* She had seen what he had not, and new levers of power appeared before him.

"It's worse than an invocation," Helm said. "The hidden meaning is an expression of the will of the thing that is creeping. Using the square is not an act of power. It is an act of surrender to the hidden."

"But the sequence is a palindrome," Doom mused. "We can use that. Reversal does not change meaning, but consistent meaning does not erase the fact of reversal. We apply the square in the full knowledge of what it is. We use its truth against it, and to our purposes." *If Hell hides in the square, we will hide our intent even more deeply, and so complete our theft.*

Now, on the hill, Helm crouched and ran her hand over the inscription.

"What do you think?" Doom asked her.

"This is linked to the pylons?"

"It is. Through direct connections contained inside them, amplified by the paraneural web embedded in the iron covering the slopes, and by these means to the ley lines that mark out this region for what it is."

Helm straightened. She whistled.

"You're impressed," said Doom.

"And frightened. The risk is enormous."

"It is also the path forward."

"But if we should fail…"

"If *I* should fail, you mean. The duel is for me alone."

"I will bear my share of the responsibility for the disaster if the worst happens," said Helm.

"There will be no disaster," said Doom. He made the declaration an edict. "The champion of Hell and I will meet in combat. The struggle will meet its predestined end." He had never expressed the certainty of his defeat out loud. It galled him to do so. It galled him that so much time and effort was being put into construction that would not get him to victory. *Not victory here,* he reminded himself. *But the victory will come.* "And what we need to happen in the struggle will come to pass," he said.

Helm nodded slowly. "I believe you," she said. She closed her eyes for a moment. "The energy of this site is tremendous."

"Amplified, it will be unstoppable."

"I can believe that too." She turned to look down the eastern slope. "You were certainly right about Father Grigori."

The priest was midway down the hill, observing the installation of a line of spiked iron poles being sunk into the ground between the pylons. They were of varying heights. When their line was complete they would create a wave form on lines that marked the pentagon drawn by the ley lines. There was a theodolite on a tripod beside him. Once in a while, Zargo looked through it.

"Does he need that?" Helm asked.

"He only thinks he does," said Doom. "It's time he learned otherwise. The tool is only slowing him down."

They walked down to join Zargo. He spoke into a radio as they drew near. "No," he was saying. "Another yard to the right." The crane bringing down the current pole shifted its position slightly.

"You see," Doom said to Helm. "There will be no errors."

Zargo turned to face them. He looked exhausted, frightened, and in emotional pain. He was also excited.

You are being true to your real calling, Father. You may not understand that, but I do. For that, you should be grateful.

"Your work here is impressive, Father," said Helm.

"But wouldn't it be better yet if someone who knew what they were doing was overseeing this installation?" Zargo asked.

"You do know what you're doing," said Doom.

"I'm not a surveyor. I'm not a builder. All I ever was at the Academy was a researcher. I've had little experience in the field."

"Your lack of experience doesn't matter," Doom told him. "What is crucial is your talent."

"My talent?"

"You found this site because of your talent. Your research played only a small part. In fact, you are skilled at research *because* of your talent."

"I still don't understand," Zargo said, but he looked shaken.

"You feel the lines," Helm said gently. "You are a geomancer, Father Grigori. That is your talent."

Zargo shook his head. His lips formed a denial, but he could not speak it. Instead he turned away. He reached for the theodolite, but Doom took it from him and crushed the tripod in his grip.

"Your work will have greater precision without this prop," said Doom.

Zargo's outstretched hand dropped to his side. He stared at the crane. He was silent, and then, very, very quietly, he said, "Oh." The word was small, yet it held a world of despair and wonder.

He sees the truth of what he is. Good.

The truth might break Zargo. That was up to him. His work, though, would achieve a higher perfection, unsullied now by illusion.

The work was what mattered. Zargo's soul was not Doom's concern.

Verlak's apartment occupied to the top floor of a large house in Old Town in the ring road that followed the outermost circle of Castle Doom's fort, the wall that surrounded the canyondeep moat. She climbed the steep stairs, weary from the day, and unlocked the door. "Home," she called as she let herself in.

Elsa Orloff came out of the living room to meet her at

the entrance. She carried two glasses of scotch, and handed one to Verlak. "If your day was like mine, and I'm guessing it was…" she said.

"Oh, a good guess," Verlak said, kissing her wife and taking the glass. She sipped. Smoke and comfort flowed down her throat and into her chest.

They sat together on the sofa facing the gabled windows. The apartment looked south, at a view of Doomstadt's sea of roofs descending the rise to the castle's seat. With the coming of twilight, the angles of slate looked even more like waves frozen in anger.

"Rough day?" Verlak asked.

"Long," said the neurosurgeon. "Started with an aneurysm to clip. That went smoothly enough. We had complications set in during a partial corpus callosotomy."

"Bad ones."

"Complicated ones," Orloff deadpanned. "Saved the patient, but I think I might sleep for a week." She stretched and yawned. "At least I have something to show for the day. I take it there's still no sign of Fortunov?"

Verlak shook her head. Weeks of searching had produced nothing. Frustration and anger were robbing her of sleep. "He's not even bothering Zargo any more."

"Lucky Zargo."

Verlak grunted. Zargo's relief did her no good. She took another sip of the scotch. "I'll lay odds he's not far from the construction site, but he's covering his tracks well."

"He might not be there at all."

That did not make Verlak feel any better. She wasn't sure which was worse – Fortunov observing the construction of the Midsummer arena while she failed to find him, or that he was somewhere else entirely, beyond her remit to pursue. She was not able to take part in the active investigation, beyond receiving reports. Her first duty, subject to Doom's commands, was to the castle. Doom had added the arena to her responsibilities. She was having to delegate the hunt for Fortunov.

She kept thinking he had to be watching the construction site. It was where his interest had last been focused. For the hundredth time, Verlak pictured the site from the air, flipping mentally through drone footage. Her mind's eye tried to find the telltale bump in the terrain, the line that was too regular, the mistake that would reveal the hiding place.

Where are you? Where are you? Show me where you are, you coward, and I will free Latveria from your taint once and for all.

"Kariana?"

She realized Orloff had been speaking to her. "Sorry," she said. "What did you say?"

"I asked if you were staying home tonight."

"No. I have to head out again. There are some informers I need to speak to."

"You have officers who can do that."

"I need to be there," Verlak insisted. "This is Fortunov I'm trying to stop."

"Tell me honestly," said Orloff. "How dangerous is he?"

"It's what he represents that's so dangerous. You don't remember the regime of King Vladimir."

"Not clearly, no, thankfully." Fearing for her life under the violent tyranny of Vladimir, her parents had fled with her when she had come out to them as trans. They had not returned for many years, not until after Vladimir was dead and Doom was on the throne, the murderous Laws of the Person revoked, their enforcers imprisoned.

"All of my youth," Verlak said, "and all of my teenage years, were spent in *that* Latveria. I remember it in ways I wish I didn't. I will *never* let that family come within a dream of power again. Fortunov has to be stopped."

"And no one else can do it?" Orloff asked, gently now.

"I don't trust anyone else to do it."

The cave was in the hills above the northern end of the old lakebed, a third of the way between the construction site and the Kanof Valley Dam. Access to it was from a narrow cleft in the rock, barely large enough to crawl through. Fortunov was used to having to squirm like a worm for twenty feet to get in and out of the main chamber. Seefeld was bigger than he was, and blanched every time he had to make the effort. Some of the other soldiers under Fortunov's command couldn't get through at all.

The cave where Fortunov had gathered his council of war was part of a large network. There were other, larger, easier entrances to the complex, but they were miles away to the east, even further away from Doom's new project, and easier to spot. They were not to be used without Fortunov's express permission. He had given his permission for tonight. Many of his troops were already in the complex, along with the provisions they needed for weeks. The activity around concealed holes in the ground, dozens of miles from anywhere, would have been minimal. The prince felt safe as he and his lieutenants gathered around the table.

Makeshift shelves of scavenged wooden planks lined the walls, holding oil lanterns and maps. The table was more planks with two-by-fours for legs. It wobbled. The seats were empty oil drums. Unworthy, Fortunov thought, of the loyal sons and daughters of Latveria. The representatives of the old families had to crawl through stone and hide like rats in a country they should be ruling.

He knew what injustice and humiliation tasted like. They tasted of stale rations. They smelled of stagnant air.

There were ten of his loyalists around the table. Ten lieutenants to Fortunov, ten strong souls faithful to the dream of a restored Latveria. They were all Fortunov's age or older. They remembered what had been lost, and hated the man who had taken what was theirs.

"The latest reports from our observers," Fortunov said, "confirm what Zargo told us. Doom's project is looking more and more like an arena. So we should expect it to be complete in time for Midsummer."

There was a ripple of unease around the table at the mention of the date. No one knew the exact nature of Doom's battles on that night in June, but all of Latveria shook with their force.

"He's never constructed something like this for Midsummer before, has he?" said Leonid Kutuzov. He had once been a senior officer in King Vladimir's palace guard. The years had added lines to his face and pounds to his frame, but his bearing was as ramrod as ever. His small eyes looked out at the world with a viper's intensity. "That seems significant."

"It is," Fortunov confirmed. "And it's good news for us."

"How is that?" Natalya Rumyanova asked. She had once reigned over the ballrooms and social functions of Vladimir's court, a tyrant who wielded etiquette and slights with the lethal force of a barbed wire whip. She had taken to guerrilla warfare with a fervor and brutality that surprised only those who had not known her well.

"This is good news," said Fortunov, "because a project of this size will hold his attention, and draw his focus away from other places. He will be distracted. That is an opportunity for us."

"The castle will be no less well defended," said Kutuzov. "I don't see our chances of taking it being any better than they are right now, and they're miserable."

"The castle isn't our target," Rumyanova said quietly.

"Thank you, Natalya," said Fortunov. "You're seeing the possibilities. The castle is an ultimate target, but the opportunity needs to be there, both to seize it and to hold it. Even if we could get past its defenses, there's no point in the attempt if Doom will just take it back from us. The conditions have to be right. He has to be weakened."

"Distracted is halfway to weakened," said Vadim Shkurat, his shock of white hair nodding in pleased assent to his own words. The oldest of Fortunov's lieutenants, as old as Fortunov's father would have been now, if not for Doom, he enjoyed playing the part of the sage, and leaned toward the Delphic with his aphorisms. Fortunov would have lost patience with him years ago if he hadn't proved so resourceful in the field.

And in any case, in this instance, Shkurat was right.

"Exactly," said Fortunov. He leaned over the map. He put

his finger on the airport, then one location and then another in the city.

"Doomsport," Rumyanova said, murmuring the targets like an incantation. "The Werner Academy. Monument Park. The rail station…"

"Simultaneous attacks," Fortunov said. "Maximum chaos to be unleashed precisely when the terror of Doom's Midsummer Night battle is to be at its peak. In chaos there is opportunity."

"That doesn't mean we'll have a chance at the castle," said Kutuzov.

"No, but we will be ready if we do. And the destruction will be linked, in the minds of the people, to Doom's activities."

There was a brief, uncomfortable silence in the room, and Fortunov knew that his lieutenants were wrestling with the same frustrated thoughts as he. The hope of a popular uprising against Doom was something they all clung to. It was a dream as necessary as oxygen. What was as maddening as it was confusing was that nothing Fortunov and his loyalists had done to date had managed to stir the sleeping populace to action. The people couldn't be content to be such sheep. They couldn't be.

Maybe this time they would finally rise in anger.

Fortunov assigned the targets and the timeline for the assault. He ended the meeting when he was sure the plan was understood, and would be carried out exactly as he commanded. The men and women with him were loyal, and they were capable. He trusted them.

Up to a point.

When they had left, he turned to Seefeld, who had been

sitting silently in a corner. "I can see there is a question you're dying to ask, Emil," he said.

"I didn't hear you mention what our team's target is, your Highness. Don't we have one?"

"Oh, we do. We most certainly do. It's the most important one." And the one he would keep secret until the last possible moment. "When we attack it, the earth will shake, and Doom will fall."

CHAPTER 7

Sunset on Midsummer, and the sky was gorged with fire and blood. Streamers of clouds had rolled in toward the end of the afternoon, and they caught the rays of the descending sun, turning the firmament into war. The silver in the arena picked up the red, and it ran like blinding veins along the lengths of the pylons. The structure looked even more like a massive hand to Helm as she and Verlak walked with Doom to the top of the hill. The concrete and metal claws seemed to close when she saw them at the corners of her eyes.

I helped make this happen. And this is only the prologue.

The realization weighed more heavily on her as the crimson of the sky deepened, and the war on the ground drew closer. The implications of what she and Doom were attempting grew and grew. What they planned to do next was too immense to contemplate.

Doom walked around the top of the hill, looking out at the completed arena. He raised a hand, and a small panel slid aside in the wrist of his gauntlet, revealing a touch screen. He tapped it, and the arena powered up. Verlak jerked, startled by the sudden, seismic hum of energy through the hill and the pylons. Helm gasped, hit harder, and Verlak caught her as the older woman stumbled. The hair on her arms and the back of her neck stood straight. Her flesh crawled. The smell of ozone made her eyes water, and the air crackled as if it had turned brittle and was about to snap in two. What she felt most powerfully, though, was the thrum of sorcerous power underneath everything else. The physically generated energy was a wave towering higher and higher until Doom would unleash it, but the witchcraft was the tectonic disturbance beneath, the greater force that created the tsunami.

"Are you all right?" Verlak asked, shaken herself. Even those with no magical sensitivity would be affected by the activation of the arena. Its stirring to life would be felt for miles around, eldritch ripples spreading through the earth. And anyone close to the ley lines of the nexus would be assailed by premonitory shudders. Here in the center of the confluence of powers, even the dead would tremble.

"I will be," Helm said to Verlak. "Thank you." She took a heaving breath and adjusted to the violent tug of the currents.

Doom showed no ill effect. He tilted his head back slightly, and he stopped walking. In his stance, Helm saw satisfaction, and a reveling in what he had called into being. The power was not a threat to him, because it was his. The claw formed by the arena was the servant of Doom's titanium fist.

Helm had aided him, but this was Doom's work, and he saw that it was good.

How can defeat be coming tonight? Helm wondered. *How can we go further than what we have done here?*

Doom looked down at the silver platform and the engraved

Sator Square. A wind had sprung up with the activation of the arena, and Doom's cape stirred, his movements slow and majestic, like a bank of fog revealing and concealing the unforgiving strength of a mountain face.

"This is well done," said Doom. "All is ready." To Verlak he said, "Doomstadt is in your care, and yours alone, for the hours to come. You are its guardian."

Verlak went down on one knee. "I will not fail you, my lord. Though I'm ashamed that I haven't yet brought Fortunov in chains before you."

"He will strike tonight," said Doom. "We know he has been watching this site. We know that he knows it was constructed for tonight."

"Thanks to Zargo," Verlak said angrily, standing up again.

"That was part of his function," said Doom. "Thanks to him, exactly. We have his attention. Use that knowledge to your advantage tonight and protect the city from Fortunov."

"But if this is his focus, he might attack here."

There was the metallic rasp of Doom's short bark of laughter. "If he interferes here, then he will deserve what happens."

"I doubt he would be that foolish," said Helm. "Not if he has the slightest idea of what this site is for."

"I would be indebted to him if he were such a fool," Doom said. "I would be rid of him. But he is not a fool. Go now, Captain Verlak. You have your orders."

Verlak bowed and started back down the hill.

"You too," Doom said to Helm.

She hesitated. "I helped bring this about…" she began.

"You did, but this is not your fight. Go. At dawn, we will

meet again. That is when the construction of the Harrower will really begin. After all, this is nothing but a gathering of the materials."

The fact that he was absolutely right made Helm feel even more awed by the scale of their presumption.

"Go," Doom said again. "Leave me."

"I will not be far."

"As you will, but you *must* be beyond the perimeter of the arena. You know that."

"I do." Helm tried to find an appropriate farewell. *Good luck* and *fight well* sounded as grotesque as *see you later* and *have fun.* So she said nothing more and left.

Verlak was waiting at the base of the hill beside her vehicle. Helm waved her off and walked on, westward, over the dry lakebed. The sun was behind the further hills now, and the blood of the sky was turning darker, rotten. The clouds were heavier, their iron a mirror of the coating of the hill.

A storm is coming. We have brought the storm.

She looked back at the silhouette on the top of the hill, still except for the windblown cape. The lord of the storm waited alone for the lightning to strike.

The Friday evening service was over. St Peter Church was empty again, to Zargo's relief. He had been unable to concentrate. He knew he had spoken all the right words. He had led the prayers, said welcomes and goodbyes. He had even delivered a homily, though he could barely remember having written it, let alone its content. All he could think about was the night that was closing in, and that he had played a part in what was going to happen.

What is going to happen?

He didn't know. He couldn't know. He didn't want to guess, though his imagination leapt from horror to horror, assembling a catalogue of the apocalypse. It almost didn't matter what the precise nature of the catastrophe would be, because it *would* be a catastrophe. It could not be anything good. And he would have to bear his share of the burden of guilt.

Hypocrite. Hypocrite. Hypocrite.

The word had pulsed through his mind with every syllable he had spoken from the pulpit. It had blocked all comfort from prayer. He did not belong in these vestments, at this lectern. He did not belong in the church at all. He had shown his true nature.

Doom was right. He should be back at the Werner Academy, pursuing dark obsessions he would finally have to admit were his own.

"No," he murmured in the empty church. *No, no, no,* the echoes mocked.

Zargo knelt in front of the altar. He tried to pray. "Our Father," he began.

Hypocrite. Hypocrite. Hypocrite.

He sounded the words of the prayer, but he did not hear them. He did not feel them.

"Forgive me!" he shouted. The cry reverberated, then died. No one answered. "I should have said no," he whispered.

Said no to Doom? Who has done that and lived?

The truth was no excuse. "I should have tried harder."

Why didn't you?

"Because I was afraid."

Liar. Hypocrite.

Zargo buried his head in his hands. He *had* been frightened at the start. That was true. But what was also true was that the fear had fallen before the power of fascination, and of curiosity and of compulsion. By the end of construction, he had still been on the site because he had *needed* to see it completed.

I was proud.

When the last of the scaffolding was gone, and the cranes had driven away, and there was nothing but the long reach of those five pylons, curving up to grasp the hill, he had felt the rush, the pounding heart and the expanding chest of pride.

"Forgive me," he tried once more. Then he stopped. The words had no taste, no weight. They were dried pellets in his mouth.

Zargo sighed and pushed himself to his feet. There could be no forgiveness without a reckoning. If even then.

He left the nave and climbed the long spiral staircase in the north tower. He lost himself in the monotony of the exertion. After hundreds of steps, he emerged onto the roof of the tower, and moved to the north-east corner of the parapet. The gargoyle beside him leaned forward as if eager for the night's display.

The light was dying. The clouds were gathering. It would be dark soon.

Zargo wished it would stay dark until morning. He feared the light that would come soon, and what it would mean.

Verlak drove back into Doomstadt, struggling with shame and determination. She had a trust to fulfill, and she did not know how to do it. She had been chasing Fortunov down a series of dead ends. Human and drone surveillance, human and computer intelligence, all useless. Fortunov was a ghost, appearing only when he wanted to terrify Zargo.

He will strike tonight, Doom had said.

Where? How?

She wasn't even sure where she was driving. She could head back to the castle and monitor the surveillance feeds from there, but that would feel like she was physically isolating herself from the problem. If Fortunov attacked the castle, there were plenty of defenses that would deal with him, many of them automated. The castle would not stand or fall because of her presence or absence.

She needed to be on the streets of Doomstadt. Doom had commanded she protect the city, not the castle. But where in the city? And doing what?

She already given commands to the Watch for maximum vigilance. Drones were flying over the city like flocks of birds. Chatter on the radio as she drove was frustrating in its reassurance. All was normal. Nothing was going on.

She drove past the baroque dome of the Doomstadt Rathauz. A Kavan Vintners truck went by the other way, and she frowned with new frustration. The surveillance of the Kavans had produced no hint that the family was disloyal, or was anything other than an old aristocratic line that had survived by knowing when a regime's end had come. Even so, Verlak had not pulled the surveillance. Her tactics were patient even when she felt nothing of the kind. Doom had suggested she watch the Kavans, and as far as she was concerned, that was still the best intelligence she had, because it had come from Doom.

Verlak drove, watching the streets and sidewalks, scanning for something she did not know. The radio relayed endless reports of the status quo. Night was falling. Soon Doom would begin his battle. And then Fortunov would attack.

If Doom said that was what would happen, then it would. His predictions had the force of prophecy. She had seen proof of his foresight, again and again.

Where are you, traitor? Show your hand so I can cut it off.

She was waiting to turn onto a street running by Doomstadt Hospital when another Kavan Vintners truck crossed the intersection in front of her. She looked to the right, watching the truck rumble uphill.

Two Kavan trucks in the space of a few minutes. Not a coincidence she could believe in.

Deliveries? Just after sunset instead of the morning?

She didn't believe that either.

Verlak turned right and followed the truck north. Traffic was light, and she stayed a block back. She keyed her radio, transmitting to all her lieutenants. "Priority search for all Kavan Vintners trucks. I want to know where they are, and where they're going."

The truck she was following slowed down as it approached Doomstadt Hospital. It pulled over and stopped beside the loading bay.

Verlak's mouth dried. She thought of everyone in the hospital, knowing not one would be looking out and wondering about that truck. She thought about Elsa, and it was all she could do not to step on the accelerator and ram her car into the vehicle.

Don't. You might kill everyone.

Verlak stopped a block away and got out of her car. She crossed the street at the intersection.

A memorial park faced the hospital, dedicated to the victims of persecution under King Vladimir. Chestnut trees surrounded a wedge-shaped marble plinth. A row of five cast-iron hands emerged from the marble, fingers splayed in the last act of drowning. Only the tips of the fingers of the rearmost hand were visible, but the one at the point of the wedge was a fist of defiance. Verlak moved to the southern side of the plinth and looked around the point at the truck. The vehicle was almost directly opposite her. She could see the driver. He was sitting in the cab in a posture of relaxed boredom.

He *might* be waiting for his stock to be unloaded.

Wine? At the hospital? At ten o'clock at night?

He was definitely waiting for something. Verlak pulled her baton from her belt. She left her pistol holstered. Fortunov's people had never engaged in suicide attacks before. They were too interested in regaining their lives of privilege. Even so, she wasn't going to take the chance of shooting without knowing what she might trigger.

Do this right. In the name of everything you love, do this right.

Her radio earpiece began to feed her reports. The drones had spotted more Kavan trucks. A fleet was on the move. One was heading for the airport. One had arrived at the Werner Academy. Another at the Cynthia von Doom Memorial Park. Another at the Latverian Academy of the Sciences.

This is it. This is the attack.

For a moment she wondered what signal would launch the strike. The arrival of the truck at the airport? It was still a mile out from the terminal. They might have that much time.

Then she saw new meaning in the posture of the driver outside the hospital. He was leaning back, his head tilted up, turned slightly away from Verlak. He was looking at the sky. He was looking north-east.

In the direction of the arena.

When Doom's struggle began, the horizon to the zenith would burn.

Though he did not know it, it was Doom who would give the signal for the attacks.

"Move in!" Verlak radioed. "Neutralize all targets!"

She sprinted across the street.

And the sky flashed.

And the truck wailed a deafening siren.

CHAPTER 8

Doom watched the sunset's glow bleed away, and with it the last of the light. The clouds had gathered quickly and were pressing down hard. Full night was coming.

Hell was coming.

Doom closed his fists, and the nexus of ley lines responded. The deep powers of the earth, the powers that flowed in the pentagon marked by the furthest ends of the pylons, jerked at his will, and they lanced down the length of the pylons. The platform glowed like a silver moon, the letters of the Sator Square its runic craters. The silver veins leading from the pylons shone too. Doom's armor thrummed with the force of science and sorcery. They were entwining serpents, becoming a strength greater than either.

The power was immense. It was also not enough, not yet, because Hell was coming.

This time will be different.

The old hope, the old refrain, the old lie. *Don't let it take* hold. *Don't let it derail everything we've done. This time will be different, but only with discipline.* The closer the battle went as he and Helm planned, the better it went, the stronger the temptation would be to think he could win, once and for all, tonight. If he gave in to that temptation, that would be the moment of defeat.

Do not falter. Do not deviate from the true goal.

The light died. Night was here. It was time.

Doom steadied his breathing, bracing himself. He had changed the setting of the duel with the construction of the arena. He wondered what changes Hell would make. He was certain there would be changes. They had become Mephisto's delight over the years. For the first while, it had been Mephisto himself who had come annually to break Doom's hope and deliver the lesson of humiliation. Then, a bit more than five years ago, a different demon had appeared, a different champion drawn from Hell's nobility. Perhaps Mephisto had decided the annual ritual was beneath him. Perhaps it amused him to have Doom beaten by a different underling each time. For Doom, knowing the inevitable outcome did nothing to diminish his determination to win, and only magnified the fury and grief that came with each defeat.

This time, though. This time it was his turn to change the rules.

It does not matter who comes. The goal is the same for Mephisto. My goal is not. I will fight to win, but aim for the true goal, the one that will lead to the true victory.

His armor hummed. It and the arena were as charged as they could be. It was time to begin.

"Beneath is fire, above is darkness," Doom intoned, beginning the incantation of summoning that would begin the duel. The index finger of his right gauntlet burned with red light, and he drew sigils in the air. They appeared and lingered, floating in the dark, as he turned slowly and built them into a chain of smoldering meaning around him. "The north cannot hear. The south cannot see. The east cannot move. The west cannot dream. In the cold of the sun and the heat of the moon, I am here. Before time and behind death, I am here and await." He finished the circle and faced west. "Let the one who is summoned appear. Let what is appointed begin."

The night thickened. Darkness constricted. The clouds dropped lower, lower, funnels descending with a heavy stillness as if they were stalactites. The wind stilled, and the silence before the storm fell over the dry lakebed.

Then the trumpets sounded.

The blast, discordant yet magisterial, crashed over the landscape, carried by a wind so strong that, if not for the weight of Doom's armor, he would have been thrown from his perch on the hilltop. The wind would have taken him for its plaything, tossing him like a dead leaf while the blare of a thousand trumpets shook the earth. At the height of the shattering fanfare, light erupted from the ground at the base of the arena's hill. The light was diseased. It was unclean. It was a red the shade of hatred.

The light faded, revealing the demon. It was one of the kings of Hell. It had the body of a man clad in crimson armor streaked with black. It had the head of a lion. A viper coiled around its left arm, and its right hand held the reins of a monstrous bear. Though the beast had the shape of the animal it mimicked, it had black scales instead of fur. The red of the light that had brought the demon pulsed in the eyes and gaping maw of the bear.

This demon had never appeared at the duel before. It was another new foe, come to teach Doom humiliation. He would not give it easy satisfaction, and he knew who it was. He had long since learned all the names to have haunted the scribes of the demonology grimoires.

"Hail, Purson," Doom said acidly, turning the greeting into an insult, "seer of past and future, lord of secrets. You are welcome to this place."

Purson laughed. "I think you lie, worm." The voice was male, and deep, and with a liquid quality evoking rotten flesh sloughing off bones.

"Do I?" said Doom. "I would have thought you should know."

Purson cocked his head. "No lie, no lie," the demon said after a moment. "So, you welcome truly." He laughed again, and the sound was the child of a roar and cough. "You will rue the welcome, before dawn." He flicked the reins, and the bear began to pad up the iron slope. Its claws gouged the metal. The hill vibrated with its footsteps. "I know what is yours, Doom," Purson continued. "I know your future. I know your secrets."

No, you don't, Doom thought.

Purson looked around at the arena as the bear climbed toward Doom. "What do you think to keep from me here?" the demon chided. "What secret do you seek to conceal in these shapes?"

"None," said Doom. He spread his arms. "This arena is what you see. If you cannot divine its nature, then you are a poor lord of secrets."

Purson growled, and his viper hissed, darting its head forward.

Good. Good. Feel the insult. Grow angry. Doom understood wrath. It was wrath that had built the arena, but wrath turned cold and made into stone and iron and silver. He needed Purson's rage to be hot and instinctive, unthinking, and prone to error.

"You wear the arrogance of omniscience," Doom told the demon. "It is unearned. But come. I am happy to instruct you."

The lion's head bellowed in anger. Purson pointed forward and released the bear. The beast roared and charged.

"Did my barb strike home?" Doom snarled under his breath. He raised his arms, palms facing out towards the demon. He gathered the power of the arena in his hands. It strained to be set free. "Let me show you this secret," he said, and unleashed the blast.

A dual stream of electro-sorcerous beams shot out of his palms. They burned the night with quasar intensity, and they slammed into Purson's chest. The lenses of Doom's mask blacked out, shielding his eyes from the searing flash, rendering the battlefield for him in an instantly updating digital reconstruction. The explosion lit up the clouds, but not with day. It was a terrible silver night, a negative image of the dark, that filled the land. The impact knocked the demon off his mount. He hit the slope so hard that he carved a trench in it. Iron glowed and softened, but did not tear.

The bear did not slow. It hurled itself through the explosion. Fire ran over its scales, flowing like mercury. Its roar was louder than the explosion. It was the thunder of the future collapsing on Doom, and it immobilized him for a moment, for just long enough for the bear to reach the peak. It hit him like a battering ram. He flew back, but fired the jets at his waist at the same time, countering the force of his flight and keeping him upright. He arced back and up from the bear, and then shot back down again. He lanced the beast's eyes with the energy of the ley lines.

The bear screamed. It threw itself back and forth over the peak of the hill, paws slashing blindly. Doom dropped to the ground a few yards down and gathered the powers again for another strike at Purson.

Are you angry yet? Are you enraged?

The demon was gone. The hillside was empty.

Doom turned back to the bear, redirecting the power from attack to defense. He fired the jets again, pulling back from the hill, hoping he had time to get high enough to see the whole arena and spot Purson.

He was too late. The demon came around the hill to his left, running with the speed of anger, his armored boots leaving molten footprints in his wake. The viper whipped forward from his arm, growing in an instant to a hundred-foot length. Its jaws snapped shut around Doom's arm. His armor's force field was amplified by mystical energy. It was strong enough that he would not have noticed the point blank impact of an artillery shell. But the viper belonged to a king of Hell, and the force field cracked under the impact of its fangs. The invisible became visible, energy convulsing in violet flares.

The fangs went deeper, grazing the titanium of the armor.

Doom switched polarities again, overloading the force field and releasing the power at once. The viper released him, its body spasming as a redirected ley line hurtled through it.

He reactivated the force field in an eye blink. That was still far too long. Purson's attack with the viper had been a distraction. Before Doom could ready a counter, Purson was on him. Hellfire burst from the lion's maw. It enveloped Doom with the rage of a malevolent star. He could not see the night. He saw only the roil of the incandescent storm of flame. The shield overloaded and collapsed. The burn surrounded him. He flew up, trying to escape it, but there was no escape from the interior of Hell's sun. He fell, and when he hit the ground, it gave way.

He dropped into molten rock.

The streets were almost empty. When night fell on Midsummer, the people of Latveria took to their homes, where there was the illusion of safety, the bubble of comfort in which they could shelter and wait out the terror of Doom's storm. So there were few civilians around when the sirens began, and the sky flashed its terrible silver. But those few panicked and ran, and Verlak suddenly did not have a clear line of sight to the driver. In the seconds it took her to cross the boulevard, more people came pouring out of the hospital doors. They ran without purpose. The sirens triggered their instincts to flee. They reacted to the need to escape the place they were, but had no sense of where they must go.

The siren was too loud. It was too powerful. The strains of

fire engine and ambulance and watch vehicle were there, but so was the air raid warning, and so was something deeper, more atavistic. Verlak's pulse reacted to the shriek. Her hearing turned to breaking glass. Her eyes started to water. She had trouble keeping her gaze on the driver, who wore industrial earmuffs.

A cluster of the panicked saw her uniform and ran toward her, their terror overwhelming their natural fear of the Watch. The driver of the truck saw her, and he pulled out a gun. A man ran in front of her. He reached for her, eyes wide, mouth gabbling. Verlak knocked him out of the way at the same moment as the driver fired. The bullet punched into her chest plate. It felt like she had been punched in the bone. She ran harder and left the pain behind.

Stop him. Elsa is in that hospital.

Protect the city.

She threw her baton. The driver tried to duck. The baton clipped him in the side of the head and released its concussive charge, shattering the earmuffs. The man cried out and fell, releasing the gun. He clutched at his head and then scrabbled with clawed hands to open his jacket.

Verlak was on him. She took his pistol, yanked his hands away and tore his jacket open. He tried to stop her, but she was stronger and faster. There was a bulge in his inner pocket. She pulled the device out, expecting a detonator. She found a radio instead. It might as well have been a trigger. She pictured a signal sent and all the trucks detonating at once.

She had stopped that communication, and the truck's siren was still blaring. The siren, she realized, was a warning as well as being a psychological attack. *Fortunov doesn't seek a slaughter.* He was taking steps to avoid turning the populace against him.

But he risks a slaughter all the same.

She pictured the traitor shrugging over the deaths. *I warned them. They should have run.*

Verlak searched the driver, found the ignition key and nothing else. She retrieved her electro-baton, gave him another shock to incapacitate him until her reinforcements arrived, grabbed his earmuffs and ran to the back of the truck. The trailer was not just locked. It was welded shut. There would be no getting in to disable what was inside.

Her earpiece crackled. Other teams were discovering the same thing.

"We have until the sirens stop!" she radioed. She ran forward, jumped into the cab and started up the truck. "If you can destroy the trucks safely, do so. If not, get them away from civilians. Make for the river and the lake! Go!"

She stepped on the gas, and the truck lurched away from the curb. The engine strained with the weight in the trailer. Acceleration was painfully slow. She felt like she was driving a glacier. The siren swooped and wailed with skull-cracking intensity. Even with her ears protected, she kept seeing double. The earmuffs were only good enough to muffle the sound for the driver while he fled the scene. Verlak had to force herself to keep her hands on the wheel and not hold them against her ears. Warm trickles of blood ran past her lobes and down her neck.

Klyne River and Doom Lake. The only places a blast could go off with a chance of little damage and no loss of life. The river ran just south of the city. The lake was within the city, a north-south length that began just to the west of the castle mount. Verlak could not afford the distraction of trying to guess which body of water was closest to each of the other targets. She had to have faith in the officers of the Watch. She had to hold the hope that they would have time, just as she had to hope that she had.

The hospital was a couple of miles downhill from Old Town and less than a mile and a half to the east of Doom Lake. But there was a portion of Old Town, with its warren of narrow, twisting streets dipped south, between Verlak and the lake. She had no straight run to the waterfront. She had a choice between navigating the alleys of Old Town or making a long detour south to catch Victory Boulevard as it ran west.

She drove uphill, north, and took the first turn left. She knew Old Town. She had grown up there. She lived there still. She trusted in her knowledge of the streets to guide her to the lake. Even as she made the decision, her heart pounded harder. The fear rose of the siren suddenly stopping in the middle of the densely packed houses.

No choice. No choice. This is faster.

It had to be. She drove on instinct, the siren battering coherent thought from her head.

In two blocks, she was in Old Town. The siren cleared the streets ahead of her, but she yanked on the air horn too. The truck rode up on the sidewalks on both sides of the street. There was nowhere for Verlak to make hard left or right turns. The best she could do was choose the lesser of two evils when she came to a fork, and trust her memory that she did not choose a dead end.

With every ragged breath, she expected the siren to stop. How long a warning had Fortunov planned to give? Long enough for an evacuation, but not long enough for an intervention? But he hadn't counted on the trucks being spotted immediately.

Maybe. Maybe. *Maybe.*

A hope based on need, not facts.

She roared down a street so narrow that the eaves of the houses scraped against the trailer. Streetlights stripped off the rear view mirrors. The windows of the houses were so close that Verlak caught glimpses of the terrified people inside.

She was only a few blocks from the lakefront. There was shouting in her earpiece, but the siren was too loud, and she couldn't make anything out, did not know if she was hearing relief or panic in the scratching voices. She slapped at the earpiece and turned it off.

One more fork, one more tiny alley. It curved, and became even narrower. The eaves caught the truck again, pressed in closer, and the truck ground to a halt, stuck.

NO. No no no no no.

The siren wailed, and wailed, and her ears bled, and she felt the silence of death coming.

Verlak pressed hard on the accelerator, and the truck jerked forward, stopped, then jerked again, and it was free.

Wailing. Wailing.

Don't stop. Don't stop. Almost there.

Verlak barreled across Vista Boulevard. It snaked along the cliff edge above Doom Lake. A guardrail blocked the way to a fifty-foot drop.

The siren wailed. Verlak floored the accelerator. She fumbled for the handle to the driver's door.

The cab's impact against the guardrail was deafening in the sudden silence of the siren.

CHAPTER 9

The earth took him in a burning embrace. Doom plunged down through a maelstrom of lava. The land, in its agony, succumbed to currents of impossible violence. Heat, physical and sorcerous, cracked through the resistance of Doom's force field. His body began to burn, and so did his soul. All he could see was the furious storm of molten rock, the blinding orange of destruction. The vortex spun him until he had no sense of up or down. The pain savaged conscious thought.

He could fall here. He could surrender to the pain, and that surrender would bring an end. The duel would be over for another year.

If he surrendered, he was not Doom.

This is not defeat. This is victory.

The ley lines were reacting explosively to Purson's attack. The demon's power was supercharging the arena. This was what he needed.

Doom fought back the pain. He forced himself to think

clearly. He redirected almost all his armor's power to the force field, giving him a few more precious seconds before he would be overwhelmed. He felt the way the current was pulling him, and with the reserve power that remained, he fired against the drag with his jets. Sent a mystic blast in the same direction, and he shot forward. He stared into the blazing torment of the earth, staring it down, staring past it. He was not fighting for his life. He was racing toward his prey.

The lava released him, and Doom shot up into the night. The arena was intact, floating on the liquid surface of the lakebed. The pylons and the hill glowed even more brightly than the lava, the colors of the spectrum racing up and down the length of its arms, driven by spirals of lightning. Purson stood on the peak, his raging bear just below him on the slope. The demon roared when he saw Doom, and lashed out with another wave of hellfire.

Doom was faster this time. He fed more power to the jets, and he flew around the hill, just ahead of the wall of demonic power. The arena shuddered as the shockwave struck the ends of the pylons, absorbing even more energy. The brilliance of the glow intensified.

He flew faster, circling Purson. Doom jabbed at the demon with his own sorcerous fire, pouring fuel on Purson's anger and frustration.

"You are a coward!" the demon shouted. "You evade instead of fighting! By delaying your humiliation, you shall only compound it."

"Is that the future you see?" Doom responded. "Or simply the expression of your wishful thinking?"

Purson answered with another inarticulate roar and a wave

of hellfire. Doom put on another burst of speed, staying just ahead of the attack. The arena absorbed it again, now radiating a white so bright it stabbed the eye, painful even through Doom's darkened eye lenses. The demon did not appear to notice the changes in the arena. He was focused entirely on Doom, and he stayed on the peak of the hill, in the center of the silver disk.

Stay there, Purson. The Sator Square summons you, and you don't know it. Stay there, and I will take my prize from you.

Though the arena took in a great part of each of Purson's attacks, hellfire lingered beyond its edges, and the wall of flame grew higher and more ferocious with successive blasts. It contained the arena, sealing it off from the land beyond, and it began to close in.

"Your flight comes to an end," Purson snarled.

"Yes, it does," said Doom. The ring of hellfire was forcing him back toward the hill. It marched inwards, a constricting noose. In not much more than a few seconds, there would be nowhere to turn, and he would be within Purson's reach.

But the arena was ready. It trembled on the verge of eruption. It could not absorb any more. *Now*, Doom thought, and the arena answered his call. He became the lightning rod for its accumulated might. The earth's deep magic and the stored power of Hell lanced out at Doom from the ends of the five pylons. He did not hold it. Instead, he redirected it into a single concentrated bolt. In the split second that the power passed through his possession, he felt the uncoiling of temptation. *Strike at Purson*, it said. *Destroy the demon.* But he could not know if even this immensity of strength was enough against a king of Hell. He held true to the path he had set for himself, and he aimed the strike at the inscription on the platform.

"*SATOR AREPO TENET OPERA ROTAS!*" Doom shouted.

For a moment, the demon grinned.

You think I missed.

Then the silver disk turned starless black. The runes, flaring red, appeared to float in a perfect void. Purson's expression of triumph vanished. The bear screamed, and the viper writhed on the demon's arm. Purson tried to leap from the disk. He was held. Fangs bared in fury, he raised his arms to attack again. Then he froze, seized by the amplified summoning. Purson fell, and his right arm lay across the Sator Square, the runes now flowing over it like chains.

The power of Doom's attack ran down the hill and through the lengths of the pylons again, a feedback loop that threatened to tear the entire structure apart. The arena screamed too, and it discharged the energy once more. Again, Doom channeled it.

Again, temptation attacked, much stronger than before.

Purson is helpless. This is it. This is the moment that eluded you in every other duel. He is at your mercy. Finish him.

This time is different. This time is different. This time is different.

A fraction of a second turned into an eternity of hesitation. If Doom kept to his chosen course, he knew what would happen next. He *knew* he would lose. He would be deliberately squandering his advantage, one that might never come again.

And if he was wrong? If he tried to defeat Purson and failed? Then everything he and Helm had worked towards would be wasted.

Doom cried out, defying fate and raging against the pain that was only the promise it kept, and he struck. This was the pivot on which the battle turned, and that would determine whether hope would stay with him or be wrenched away.

He aimed the bolt at Purson's arm. The night flashed with annihilating brilliance. Thunder cracked, the sound of time snapping in half. When the light faded back to the angry crimson of the encroaching hellfire, Purson's arm had been severed at the elbow. Shrieking in pain and hatred, the demon tore himself away from the platform. The runes tightened around the severed arm. They became silver again, and the silver covered the limb, making it part of the platform.

Purson's lion jaw opened wide, and he breathed hellfire at Doom at the same time as the wall of flame reached the monarch of Latveria. The night disappeared as it had when he had fallen in the lava. Everything was fire and agony again, and he was falling. This time, his energy was depleted, and Doom knew he would not rise.

Verlak threw herself from the truck. She bounced off the guardrail and landed hard on the road, knocking the air from her lungs, paralyzing her momentarily with shock. She closed her eyes against the silence.

The truck exploded, shaking the cliff, sending a fireball roiling above the road. The sidewalk buckled and tossed Verlak into the air. Claws of heat passed over her. The windows of the houses facing the lake shattered, raining glass. The edge of the cliff gave way, collapsing into the lake, and a crevasse opened, gouging its way into the road. Ears ringing, head pounding, Verlak dragged in a strangled breath of air, and managed to crawl forward, away from the lakefront, crunching glass beneath her armored hands and knees.

The echoes of the explosion rolled away. Coughing on smoke and dust, Verlak struggled to her feet. She staggered and weaved until she could lean against the wall of a house. She shook her head, trying to clear it. When she started to hear again, she turned her earpiece back on. She listened in dread and hope to the cacophony of overlapping voices, then shouted for discipline. She took in the reports one at a time, and her knees went weak with relief. The Watch had acted in time. The damage from the explosions was contained. She wouldn't call it minimal, but primary targets had been preserved, and there had been no loss of life.

We were lucky.

She thought of the hospital. *Is Elsa still there?* Of course she was. She'd be helping with the wounded that would soon be arriving. Verlak wanted to see her, hold her, know that she was safe.

To the north-east, the sky flashed and roared. Doom was locked in combat.

Her duty to him and to Doomstadt on this night was not done yet.

She ordered a helicopter to her position, and radioed the teams that had been observing the Kavan estate. "Close in and attack," she said. "Raze that nest of traitors to the ground."

It took the helicopter five minutes to reach her, and another twenty to reach the grounds of the Kavan mansion. By then, the raid was over. The house was a guttering ruin. As the chopper descended, she saw some bodies laid out on the scorched grass in front of the building, and some prisoners being frogmarched toward waiting armored transports. She jumped to the ground with the rotors still spinning and ran to meet Kurt Genschow, who had led the raid and was standing a few yards from the smashed door of the house, going through the spoils of the attack.

"Fortunov?" Verlak asked as Genschow saluted.

"No sign of him, captain. We found an entrance in the basement to an underground tunnel system, but it had been collapsed before we arrived."

Verlak muttered a curse under her breath. "Tell me there are more prisoners than what I'm seeing." She counted less than a dozen. With the dead, there would have been about twenty defenders of the mansion.

Genschow shook his head. "That's all," he said. "The main force must have fled."

Where? Verlak wondered. *This feels wrong. They haven't fled. The main attack is yet to come.*

"We did find this," said Genschow. He unfolded a map. It showed the city and its environs in a hundred-mile radius.

Verlak took it from him. Red pencil marked the locations where the trucks had been found. Verlak breathed a bit more easily to see that there weren't any targets that hadn't been accounted for.

"We got them all," Genschow said.

"Maybe." She didn't trust her relief. Not with Fortunov missing. There was something else missing on the map too.

"What's wrong?" Genschow asked.

"The construction site." She glanced up as the sky flashed again with colors broken and raging. "Fortunov was heavily focused on it. We know he was. But nothing aimed there?"

"The coward wouldn't dare."

And if he had, he would most likely already be dead, as Doom had said. Still… "But I can't see him ignoring it completely. No target in the city would have any bearing on that location. I don't…" She stopped. She stared at the location of the arena. The implications of its geography sank in. "Oh no," she said, and ran for the helicopter, ordering a mass deployment of drones.

In the air again, she was about to try, against the odds, to contact Doom. But the sky burned, and the night roared. He would not be able to answer. Helm, then. She would try Helm. Maybe she was near enough to do some good. Maybe she could warn Doom.

Seefeld returned to where Fortunov waited, hidden behind the trees. "All the charges are set, Prince Rudolfo," he said. "Everything is ready."

"Well done, Emil. A good night's work." Fortunov stepped out from behind the trunk of the pine and broke cover, advancing to the edge of the cliff. To his right, the waters of the Kanof Valley Reservoir glistened with the reflected light of the battle to the south. Ahead of him was the gentle curve of the hydro-electric dam. To the left, at the base of the dam, eight hundred feet below, a fan of canals led the limited flow of water off into the cliffs, and from there to the irrigation systems in the plains to the east and west of the narrow mountain chain that bracketed the valley. The face of the dam was unmarked, a dark grey in the sodium lights that ran along the top. Seefeld and his team had rappelled up and down the height, planting their charges, and returned without being detected.

Fortunov turned the detonator over in his hands, savoring the anticipation now that the work was done, and all that remained was the pressure of his thumb on a button. The news from Doomstadt was not what he would have liked, but he had known better than to hope for too much. He had always conceived of the truck bombs as a distraction. This was the real strike, the one that had the chance of transforming Latveria.

Don't count on victory. But be prepared for the possibility.

"Where will the water go?" Seefeld asked, curious.

"Along its old course," said Fortunov. "Down the valley and to where there was once a lake, and where the usurper is now in battle, distracted." He smiled, looking at the distant strobing against the clouds. "And if it isn't stopped, I think it will flood the low-lying areas of Doomstadt."

"Who will stop it?"

"There is only one person who is responsible for stopping it," said Fortunov, still watching the brilliant pulses of combat.

"Can he?"

Fortunov shrugged. "That isn't for us to say. He fashioned himself as the savior of Latveria. Let him save it, or be exposed as the fraud he is." He paused, his thumb hovering over the detonator's button. "Do you know what I think, Emil? I think he's too preoccupied with his personal ritual at this moment to pay attention to the needs of his country."

Seefeld grinned. "I think you're right."

"Let's find out, shall we?" Fortunov pushed the button.

A vertical chain of explosions ripped up the center of the dam. Fortunov had purchased the demolition charges from

Advanced Idea Mechanics three years ago. He hadn't known then how he would use them. He had only known he wanted them in reserve. Now, in the perfection of their function, he wanted to see the hand of fate. The A.I.M. explosives punched through the entire width of the structure. The dam opened up like a gutted animal. The reservoir shuddered, then a wall of water, hundreds of feet high, roared through the valley.

The ground shook beneath Fortunov's feet. It felt like the shudder of a toppling throne.

PART II

UNDER HARROWS OF IRON

"... actions are our epochs: mine
Have made my days and nights imperishable..."
BYRON, MANFRED, II.i.52-3

CHAPTER 10

"YOU DARE? YOU DARE?"

Purson's outrage roared through the firestorm. It parted the flames as a tornado parts wheat, and the demon appeared before Doom, consumed by fury. He was ablaze. Flames circled his limbs and flashed outward from his mane. The viper and the bear had become creatures of fire, extensions of their master's rage. Purson was the source of the firestorm, the origin and lord of destruction.

"YOU DARE?"

Purson stared at his stump of an arm. The disbelief in his words was almost as great as his anger. Fire spouted from the wound, but the arm did not grow again. Inside its silver runic prison, the limb vibrated, trying to escape. Doom held it down with a whispered spell fueled by his will. That was the only strength he had left.

Hellfire washed over his prone form. The assault was unceasing. His force field and his sorcerous wards had crumbled almost completely. He had spent everything in his last assault. He had done what he had intended, and now the reckoning had come. The last of his reserves went to reinforcing the prison of the Sator Square.

The pain of the flames was transcendent. Agony forged from all the regrets of the past and the terrors of the future joined physical agony. Doom could not move.

Endure. Endure. Endure.

He always had. He always would.

"*YOU WILL SCREAM!*" Purson howled. "*I WILL HEAR YOU SCREAM!*"

Doom laughed. He laughed at the pain. He laughed at Purson's futile wrath. He laughed at the perversity that had led him to do what he knew would make him lose the duel. He laughed because it was the only action he still had the power to do, and he laughed because Purson was helpless before it.

Endure. Endure. Endure, and keep our prize.

It was Purson who screamed. Hell's firestorm became chaotic. The demon's adversary was defeated, unable to fight back, yet laughed as if victorious. Purson's rage went beyond words. He shrieked and danced, his firestorm of hellflame becoming chaotic. The blasts hammered Doom harder and harder, burning and crushing. They would have killed almost anyone else a hundred times over. But he lived, and he endured, and he laughed, because he knew, he *knew*, that Purson would find no satisfaction.

"*IF YOU WILL NOT SCREAM, THEN YOU WILL BE DESTROYED!*" Purson shouted.

"I don't think so," Doom said, and laughed again.

Purson roared. An apocalypse of hellfire came down on Doom. It was a storm of ending, of annihilation. The last of his shields fell before it. The storm would destroy him.

And then it passed. The flames vanished. Purson's scream of rage cut off, and its echo fell into silence. Doom's laughter weakened to a whisper, but it did not end. In defeating him, Purson had been cheated out of his full retaliation. Doom could no longer defend himself, and so the duel was over. Mephisto's rules were clear. The duel was not to the death. Hell was to be amused every year by Doom's humiliation.

You are not permitted to kill me, Purson. So your master has called you back. Without your arm.

Is this victory? Doom wondered. He couldn't tell. He could barely think.

He couldn't move. He couldn't rise. But he had his prize.

As he began the drift into unconsciousness, he thought he heard thunder in the distance. Thunder that would not stop.

Zargo heard the explosions go off, a chain of concussions booming around the city. From his vantage point in the tower, he could see the smoke and dust rising from four of the blast sites. And after the bombs, the sirens.

He could guess who was responsible for the explosions. Zargo wondered how much of a part he had had to play himself, without knowing.

It was after the bombs, with the battle still raging to the north, that the procession began. First in pairs and small groups, and then in greater numbers, the people came into the streets and began to walk north. Zargo watched them for just a few minutes before he headed down from the tower. By the time he reached the street, he was part of a crowd streaming toward the war in the sky. No one spoke, and Zargo didn't ask anyone what they were doing. He didn't have to. Now that he was part of the procession, he felt the same pull. There was something different this night, something that marked out this Midsummer from all the others. Instead of hiding and trying to shut out the terror of Doom's battle, they were going to bear witness.

What can we possibly see?

Zargo asked himself the question only once. The arena was miles away to the northeast. They could not walk there before everything was long over. There would be nothing to see even from outside the city walls. That didn't matter. It was the act of marching *as if* there were something to see that mattered.

They were all being called, but not by Doom. Perhaps the tug came from the tapestry of events. Perhaps, Zargo thought, it was the power of the ley lines, the power he had helped pull into a massive nexus, that was summoning them. He didn't know. It didn't matter. What mattered was that he answered the call.

The procession wound up through the streets of Old Town, growing larger all the time. It looped around the castle defenses, and at last out of the city walls, into the north-east. By then, the terrifying lights in the sky had ended. The night was quiet again.

Why are we here? Zargo asked himself. There was nothing to see. The night was calm once more.

Only he couldn't bring himself to leave. The pull was strong. It was like the tug he had experienced at the site of the arena. *You are a geomancer,* Helm had told him. It was a truth he did not want to accept, but he felt it now. The ley lines had called them all, and the people had answered, whether they were sensitives or not.

The moment Zargo was certain it was the ley lines that called, he jerked in sympathetic pain. The currents in the earth were thrashing in agony, creating a whirlpool of geomantic energy. Like a great ship going down and sucking everything nearby down with it, the lines were drawing the population of Doomstadt to their chaos. He didn't know how their agony would be manifested. He knew only that it would be terrible.

Fight it. Stop walking. Turn back.

He couldn't. He marched on, along with everyone else.

From the north-east came the deep rumble of something vast.

CHAPTER 11

The helicopter flew over the lakebed, rotors beating hard. Seated next to the pilot, Verlak leaned forward as if she could see further into the night.

"Shall I try the dam's control station again, captain?" the pilot asked.

"No. Lack of response is our answer. There's no one there who can speak to us." As soon as she had guessed Fortunov's real target, she had raised the full alarm.

"Do you think the bots will be there in time?" said the pilot, a compact bullet of a woman named Lodner. Along with drones, swarms of emergency repair bots were on their way to the Kanof Valley Dam.

"We should be so lucky," said Verlak. In her dreams, she had given the warning in time. In her dreams, Fortunov would not be able to damage the dam too severely.

The lakebed became narrower as the chopper sped north. The mountainsides drew in on either side, hulking masses of greater darkness. The clouds that had rolled in at sunset had shredded themselves with the end of Doom's battle, disintegrated by the conflict's final paroxysms. The stars were visible again, cold witnesses.

Verlak looked into the dark of the valley, hoping she would see nothing. Every second of nothing was a gift and a lie. But she knew she was too late.

The first sign of disaster was turbulence. The helicopter bucked up and down. Lodner cursed and pulled up higher, looking for stable air. Then Verlak heard the roar over the hammering of the rotors. A few moments later, she saw the blackness seethe with whitecaps. The valley was gone. An ocean was thundering by beneath the chopper, making for the arena, and then for Doomstadt.

"No," Verlak hissed. "No, no, no."

The chopper dropped sickeningly, then caught air and climbed again.

"Head back," Verlak told Lodner. "There's nothing we can do at the dam." She knew the worst, and it was the worst.

"What will we do at Doomstadt?" the pilot asked.

I don't know. "Whatever we can," Verlak said. Her answer sounded too close to *Nothing*.

Crouched low on the lakebed, Helm had watched Doom's duel with Purson with a mixture of terror, awe, and disbelief. The blows that Doom and the demon hurled at each other shook the ground. Seismic and psychic tremors rippled through the earth and Helm's soul. Her breath came in infrequent gasps. Hell had come for Doom, and he had fought it to a standstill. Knowing what Doom faced every year and seeing it was the difference between imagination and revelation. Helm had seen her fears made manifest, and seen the pain that could be inflicted upon them.

She lost sight of Doom in the cataclysm of Purson's final rage. But even as the demon smashed Doom into the platform, Helm had felt a fearsome exhilaration. Doom had cut off Purson's hand. They had their prize.

We can do it. We can defeat Hell. We can build the Harrower.

In the midst of the hellfire, she saw the path to her salvation.

When Purson fell back into Hell, she rose on unsteady legs. And then, before she could take a single step, Verlak was calling on the communicator Doom had given her when she had first arrived at the castle.

The moment of triumph evaporated before the face of onrushing disaster.

Helm sprinted towards the arena, and she called on the winds of Latveria. They answered, and a gale sprang up at her command. She spread her arms, and the winds picked her up. Her robe billowing, she flew to the top of the hill. "Be still," she said, and the wind obeyed, putting her down and dropping to a breeze, curling around her like a faithful cat. Doom was lying on his back, motionless. Helm called his name. She tried to shake him, but it was like trying to move a marble sarcophagus.

"Doom!" she shouted. There was thunder in the distance, thunder that came from the ground, and it was growing louder. "Awake! Latveria has need of you!"

The metal statue grunted. The eyes behind the mask blinked and focused on Helm. Bloodshot, they suddenly filled with iron. Somehow, the immobile expression of the mask seemed to mirror what she saw in the eyes. They were the embodiment of a will so immense, she only now began to see how little she had understood its power. The titanium mask was not really a mask at all. It was the true face of the man who wore it. No flesh could give full expression to a will so utterly beyond the human.

Doom stirred. He sat up, and the effort would have toppled cathedrals. "Tell me," he said, his voice coming to her through eons of exhaustion.

"Verlak says Fortunov is going to destroy the Kanof Dam."

Doom said nothing for a moment. He looked north, then growled. "The thunder," he rasped with new anger, and he stood. "Can you hold the water back?" he asked.

"I can delay it," Helm said. "I can't stop it. Not something that powerful. It will have to go somewhere."

"Somewhere," Doom repeated to himself, and grunted again. "Yes, I think it will. Very well. First fire, now water. This night will have its symmetries, won't it?"

Doom knelt and passed his hand over the Sator Square, muttering incantations. The runes melted away, the square bulged and the silver parted like a web, revealing the demon's forearm. The flesh had tightened and darkened around the bone, becoming a scaly gray. The limb was withered, mummified, as if its prison had held it for millennia. Doom picked up the arm and gave it to Helm. "Keep it safe," he said.

"What are you going to do?"

"Take a risk. If I'm wrong, we can't afford to lose what we have gained."

Helm slipped the arm through the rope tied around her robes. "Without you, this is useless," she said. "I can't complete the work on my own."

"But you will try," Doom said, and it was a command.

"I will try." Once again, she wondered how much free will she had in Doom's presence. She wondered how much anyone had.

The deep roar of the disaster drew closer. The horizon was still obscured by night, but Helm imagined she could see it move.

"Give me as much time as you can," said Doom. "Hold the water back in as narrow a form as possible."

"Understood."

A wind was picking up, blowing from the north, as the wall of water pushed the air ahead of it. Helm spoke to it, made it hers, and it lifted her up. Doom rose with her on his armor's jets. He began an incantation, and Helm shut her ears to it. The first syllables alone were enough to make her shudder. They were in a language that did not belong to humans, and to speak them now, so soon after what had happened in the arena, was a risk that bordered on madness.

Doom pulled back, and his voice became fainter. Helm closed her mind to what he was doing and concentrated on her task. Her sorcery was more sympathetic than Doom's. Where he had seized the ley lines and forced their power to serve him, she reached out to the currents, felt their pain, soothed as she could, and sought to heal the torture of the land. "Strength of the Earth," she called, "hear me and come to my aid. Let destruction end. Let me staunch your wounds."

She spread her arms. Phosphorescent spheres formed around her hands, grew in size and intensity, and then shot out, vibrating beams, extending her embrace around the entire width of the arena, linking her to the lines of the nexus.

She trembled with the power coursing through her frame, and with the elemental pain. The beams from her arms multiplied. Her embrace took the form of a lattice a thousand yards wide and high. It burned with the light of a dawn come early to this single spot of Latveria. False day illuminated the land, and now Helm saw the flood. A monstrous tide thundered over the lakebed, returning what had been lost and too much more. Its wrath smashed at the hillsides. Its head foamed with speed and fury. The valley was wider here than at the dam, but the monster was still twenty feet high.

Helm flew higher, and braced herself for the collision. As the water closed with the matrix of her embrace, the wave narrowed again. It climbed higher and higher, and then it hit, taking up the full height and breadth of the web of light.

She gasped. The impact almost shook control of the spell from her. The towering wall raged against the barrier. In seconds, the force of oncoming water was too strong, and Helm pulled back, taking the lattice with her. She tried to make her retreat a slow one, but the force was too immense. It pushed her back faster and faster. She didn't think she had done more than slow the speed of the flood by half. And when her spell collapsed, the wave it contained would be infinitely more lethal than it had been before.

Behind her, Doom continued to intone. He flew back too. Though the imprisoned wave roared, and Doom kept further and further behind, Helm still could hear fragments of his incantation. His metallic voice, grating with exhaustion and pain, spoke words of such power that the sound resonated over the land like the crack of an earthquake.

Helm focused her full concentration on maintaining the

barrier. She had to give Doom time to prepare his response, time to find more of his strength. She had seen Hell at work. She knew what they had to defeat. Her fears and hopes were greater than ever, and they fueled her determination to hold back the wave.

They were not enough. The water pushed her back and back, faster and faster. The disaster was racing over the land, eating up the miles, too few, that separated it from Doomstadt. Helm didn't know if she was slowing it down at all any longer, or if she was only preparing the greater destruction of the city. The land had been injured beyond her ability to heal it. Its pain demanded release. It strained her prison to the breaking point.

Helm could not call to Doom to know if he was ready. She had no energy to spare for speech. She couldn't hear him any longer, either. The wave pushed her with such force that her entire body, even her bones, rippled. She was flying backward so fast, the land was a blur.

How close was the city?

She didn't know. It didn't matter. She would hold until she couldn't, and Doom would be ready, or he would not be.

A little longer. Just a bit longer. Give him more of a chance. Give us both more of a chance.

The wave thundered. Her hold on the energies wavered. Her body was a tiny thing, a rag in a hurricane, too weak for the power she demanded of it.

One more second. One more second. One more second.

She shouted, pain exploded behind her eyes and the spell collapsed. Gasping, she flew on hurricane winds to the side, barely out of the way of the wave as it burst free.

Doom was a hundred yards behind her, positioned so that he was facing the center of the wave. Behind him, less than a quarter of a mile away, were the walls of Doomstadt. To Helm's horror, there were thousands of people gathered outside the walls, walking forward as if to meet the wave.

Why are you here? What are you doing? You fools! Run! Run!

She wanted to shout at them, to bellow warnings. She couldn't even move her lips.

Doom pointed at the wave, and Helm had a wild moment of faith that the power of the flood would submit to the power of his will alone. Then, as the light of true dawn at last spread over the city, a tear opened in the air behind Doom. It seemed to unfold from the billowing of his cape, a black aura that blossomed into a portal as great as the wave. Inside the portal was the void, but Helm looked away, knowing instinctively that there was not true emptiness there, and if she stared, she would see something she would regret.

Doom shot upwards. But he had more than a hundred feet to clear, and no time at all. The great wave slammed into him, taking Doom with it into the maw of unnatural night.

The portal closed in on itself a few minutes later, a carnivorous plant sealing its trap. It left behind a shallow lake before the city gates, and a mob of thousands crying out in fear and confusion.

Helm stayed by the shore until a helicopter landed and Verlak approached her.

"Where is he?" Verlak asked.

Helm pointed to the air where the portal had been. "Gone," she whispered.

The scale of her dread stopped all other speech.

CHAPTER 12

"Mark this occasion, comrades," said Natalya Rumyanova. "This could well be the last time we meet in a cave."

Vadim Shkurat rapped the table in approval. He was joined by several other lieutenants. Leonid Kutuzov muttered, "I hope you're right," but he and the officers seated closest to him looked unhappy.

Fortunov read the mood in the chamber before speaking. It was about what he had expected. The lieutenants who had lost the most troops to arrest and gunfire during the bombing attacks were the most displeased. They felt their influence diminished with respect to those who had come through with close to their full strength. He would have to deal with them now, and shore up their commitment to him. If that didn't work, he would know what weak links to remove from his chain of command.

He was standing at the head of the table, arms folded, his face in shadow. The lanterns on the table lit the other faces clearly enough for his purposes. He kept his features still. He didn't want his subordinates guessing at his feelings about the events of Midsummer Night, especially since, three days after the solstice, he wasn't sure of his own mind.

"You seem defeated rather than triumphant, Leonid," said Fortunov.

Kutuzov frowned, but looked a bit worried now. Even so, he did not back down. "May I speak freely, Prince Rudolfo?"

"That is why we are here." *So I will know whether I should be free of you.*

"Doom's forces routed us. Not a single truck detonated at its target."

"The fear they created was real, and that was the goal, not casualties," said Rumyanova. "If we had wanted to litter the streets with corpses, we would not have installed the warning sirens."

"I thought *chaos* was our goal," Kutuzov shot back. "Was it supposed to be that small and evanescent? Have the people taken to the streets? Is Doomstadt burning? Has our revolution come?"

"Yes, it has," Rumyanova said quietly.

Silence fell. Everyone waited for Fortunov to respond. When he said nothing, Shkurat stepped in. "You speak as if the destruction of the Kanof Dam never happened, Leonid."

"Yes, the attack none of us knew about."

Now Fortunov had to speak. "It was not for you know about," he said.

Kutuzov refused to be abashed. "The dam is already repaired. Doomstadt suffered no damage."

"And Doom is gone," said Rumyanova. "Or did you forget that small detail?"

"Is he?"

That was the question Fortunov had been asking himself for three days. It was because he couldn't answer it that he had said as little as possible at this council so far. *Let the others thrash the questions out. Maybe I'll see my way forward.*

"There is no sign he survived," said Shkurat.

"A corpse would be a good sign that he is dead. We don't have one."

"The days pass, and we remain a threat to the city," Rumyanova said. "The arrests the Watch made are pitiful compared to our real numbers. Would Doom choose to leave his power base vulnerable, day after day? I don't think so."

"We've thought he was dead before," said Kutuzov. "And been wrong."

Exactly. Damn you, Leonid, for articulating my fears.

"What are you proposing, then?" Rumyanova asked. "What's your plan, Leonid? Do nothing?" When Kutuzov didn't answer, she turned to Fortunov. "This is our moment, Prince Rudolfo. It must be. We struck, and Doom fell. We prepared for the opportunity, and now we have it."

She was right. These were exactly the circumstances his strategy had been designed to produce. Before Midsummer, he had barely allowed himself to imagine the possibility that the dam breach would take Doom out. Kutuzov was wrong about the operation's lack of success. It had been a stunning triumph.

It went perfectly. So it's too good to be true.

This could be Doom's trap. He could be waiting for me to show my hand. Attacking like Rumyanova wants us to do could be exactly what he wants too.

And what was the alternative? To do nothing? To hide in the caves indefinitely, fearing a return that might never happen? Was this what Doom had done to him, make him unable to act, too frozen by indecision to capitalize on his own victories?

He couldn't say that things were too good to be true. He couldn't afford to show that kind of weakness. And he couldn't afford to let Kutuzov raise that possibility.

"There is mourning and confusion in Doomstadt," Rumyanova said.

"But no chaos," Kutuzov interrupted petulantly.

"The order we see is brittle," said Rumyanova.

Shkurat nodded in agreement. "Where there is no crown, there is no head," he intoned.

Fortunov wasn't sure that really meant anything, but he grasped what Shkurat thought he was saying, and suddenly his choice was clear. There really wasn't a decision to be made. His fear was cowardly. Did he want the throne of Latveria or not?

I do. It is mine.

Then take it.

"Latveria is rudderless," he said. "Political inertia is the only thing holding the order together. It can't last."

"The people need their leader," said Rumyanova. "They need their rightful king."

"They need the order that was taken from them," Fortunov said, and that reminder of everything that would be restored seemed to placate Kutuzov and the others who agreed with him but had chosen to keep their thoughts to themselves. "It is up to us to return Latveria to its true self."

Shkurat banged the table again, and this time everyone joined in.

"Our forces are gathered," Fortunov went on. "We're ready." *Are we? Or are we delivering ourselves up to Doom?* He wanted to shake himself. He had struggled so long, and so hard, to reach this moment, he didn't trust its existence. "The order is given. It's time to restore Latveria."

Vassily Dubrov opened the door to the archives. Helm nodded a greeting to him, and he watched her walk slowly down the ramp. Midway to the floor of the hall, she stopped and stared blankly down the aisle she was crossing.

Dubrov approached, stopping a few paces back, so she would have to look up at him when they spoke. "Is there something I can assist with?" he asked, as carefully polite as he had been ever since Doom had first brought Helm to the archives.

Helm looked at him blankly for a moment. Then she blinked and shook her head. "No. No thank you, Vassily. I'll find my own way."

Dubrov was becoming well practiced in hiding his anger. He kept his face placid now, his resentment invisible. He hated her for having learned to navigate his domain so quickly. She had made it her own. It was a conquest he would never forgive. "If there is something I could locate for you ..." he offered. *Good little Vassily, helpful Vassily, obsequious Vassily, always there to be helpful, never to be appreciated.* Resentment and self-pity were a warm bath for his psyche.

"You're very kind," Helm said. "I'm afraid I don't really know what I need at this moment."

"We are all at a loss," Dubrov said. He congratulated himself on his convincing portrayal of sympathy. He had had three days to perfect it.

"We are, aren't we?" Helm sounded surprised to discover this applied to her.

"Do you know what you are going to do?"

"Not really, no. I'm trying to continue our work, even though I know I can't complete it on my own."

"If you would tell me what it entails, I might be able to assist," said Dubrov.

"No one can assist me in this. Without the genius of Doom, there is no hope of completing the work."

"Will you be leaving us, then?" Dubrov asked, shaping his tone of voice so the question sounded curious instead of eager.

"Not yet. I have to try. After what I've seen, and after what we've done, I have to keep trying, even if I know I'm going to fail." Helm paused. "Is this what he felt every year?" she whispered to herself, so quietly Dubrov could barely make out the words. Helm brought herself back to the present moment again, and said, "What about you, Vassily? What are you going to do?"

The question took him aback. It wasn't one he had asked himself. He rarely knew what was going on outside the castle. Days, and sometimes weeks, could go by with Doom not putting in an appearance in the archives. Before Helm's invasion, Dubrov had spent most of his days as the lord and master of a kingdom of one. The idea that Doom might really be gone had been an abstract one until now. The only consequence of Midsummer Night that had felt concrete was the effect it had had on Helm. She had been weakened.

She had no clear direction any longer. Dubrov had begun to imagine ways she might be induced, or forced, to leave. That was as far as he had thought.

What are you going to do now?

For the first time since he had taken on the mantle of archivist, he began to conceive of a world without Doom.

"I don't know," he said. "I suppose I will carry on as I always have, until I cannot any longer." The lie was convincing because it had been the truth until a few seconds ago.

Helm nodded. "I think that is true for so many of us." She started off down the aisle. She looked from side to side at the volumes on the shelves, but Dubrov didn't think she saw any of them.

What are you going to do now?

The question was an exciting one.

From the outside, Doomstadt Hospital was forbidding. Its brickwork dated back to the sixteenth century. Black with grime, it resembled a fortress. Its windows were small and gothically arched. Gargoyles stood sentry on its cornices, fanged jaws agape, wings spread as if about to leap into the air. Inside, the off-white, violet-tinged marble halls gleamed, their surfaces sterilized every few minutes by the passage of custodial bots. They were so thin in their construction, they were barely visible vertical lines passing along the walls and floors. They were collective entities that split apart to avoid contact with passing staff and patients, reforming to resume their cleansing. Whenever Verlak saw one go by, she thought for a moment it was an errant hair appearing for a moment at the corner of her eye.

One went by now in the Emergency waiting room. There were no patients there for the moment. The sudden influx of injured after the truck bombs had strained the hospital's generously staffed resources, but the organizational machinery of the hospital had operated at high gear, and the institution's atmosphere of calm had returned. That Orloff had come out to meet Verlak here instead of her consulting office was a sign that things were still some distance from being normal.

Orloff looked exhausted. She and the other specialists had, where possible, pitched in to help with the new arrivals. She had been working sixteen-hour days and longer since Midsummer. Verlak was matching her hour for hour. She worried, too, that Orloff thought the worst might be over. Verlak dreaded it was yet to come.

"I wish you would stay at the castle," Verlak said. "At least at night. We can bunk down there, and the trip back and forth from the castle to here is easier to secure than from home."

"Even though home is closer to the hospital."

"Home isn't safe."

"For us, or for anyone?"

"I don't know the extent of the threat," Verlak said. "What I do know is that I am a target, given my position, and therefore so are you."

"And how long do you want us staying at the castle?" Orloff asked.

"Until the crisis is over."

"Can you be sure it will be?"

Verlak didn't answer.

Orloff touched Verlak's cheek. "I understand. I really do. I'm not being stubborn just to make you worry."

Verlak leaned her faced into Oloff's palm, then nodded, resigned. "Being here is *your* calling."

"Yes," said Orloff. "It is."

"I need to know that you understand what's at risk, Elsa. If Doom is gone…"

"He might not be."

"By everything we hold dear, hope that he isn't. But if he is, then Fortunov will launch a coup. That's certain. If we can't stop him…" She trailed off, unable to find the words for her disgust.

"You'll stop Fortunov," said Orloff. "I believe in you."

Verlak sighed. "I wish I did. I'm not Latveria's savior. He's missing."

Fortunov's head brushed against the top of the disused sewer tunnel. He crouched lower, but his hair was slicked by fetid moisture. He coughed at the stench.

Rats. Rats in a warren. That's what we are.

It was not how he would have chosen to begin his assault. It was not the glorious crusade it should have been. In a world where justice was not a fool's dream, he would have led the charge through the gates of Doomstadt and advanced through to the castle, backed by the acclamation of the people. Perhaps somewhere there was a truly righteous universe where that was what was happening. But this was his reality, and he moved like a rat.

And at the end of his creeping, the rat would show how terrible his bite was.

The strike force had gathered in the cave complexes to the north of the city and traveled underground from there. It had taken years to dig the passages from the countryside to Doomstadt. Parts of the web had been compromised over time, but there had always been alternative routes that could be pierced. *Always have a contingency. Always have a way out.* Those were the lessons he had learned painfully in the years of his struggle against Doom.

Movement in the tunnel was awkward, between the crouched walk and crowding. Just a bit longer, though, and the rats would emerge on the surface and transform into heroes. There were hundreds of loyalists advancing through the network, patriotic blood flowing through parallel veins in the rock under Doomstadt.

Patriotic blood. That's a nice idea. Make sure you use that later. It will go over well. Stick with it and make it true.

There were plenty of troops who were the true sons and daughters of Latveria. But there were mercenaries too, hired from A.I.M. along with weapons. Not what should happen in a just universe. Needful for this one.

Seefeld walked just ahead of Fortunov. He had to bend so far down he was almost crawling. They had been in tunnels this low for more than an hour now. He had to have been in agony. He hadn't uttered a word of complaint, though. This man, Fortunov thought, was the stuff of heroes. This was loyalty. This was the true Latveria.

The line of marchers reached an intersection with a larger tunnel. Foul water streamed by in a canal. Seefeld paused at the mouth and shone his flashlight on a mark in fluorescent paint on the ceiling. "Almost there, Prince Rudolfo," he said.

"Good." He raised his voice just enough so the troops behind him could hear and pass the word. "We are minutes from destiny."

The army grew, fighters emerging from numerous small tunnels to gather in the main artery. Fortunov waited for his lieutenants to join him at the head of the line. They were covered in filth, as he was. Fortunov grimaced at the indignity of the advance, then pushed his anger aside when four soldiers came forward, carrying a coffin-shaped metal box between them. He stared at it eagerly. *This is my bite. This is my terrible bite.*

"The weapon is unharmed?" Fortunov asked.

One of the men nodded, unable to salute without dropping his share of the load. "Yes, my prince," he said. "We just ran a diagnostic check. All green lights."

Excellent. He ran his hand lightly over the case, thinking of the power within. *Enough reverie,* he told himself. *There will be time for such indulgences when victory is achieved.* "Keep up," he ordered the soldiers with the weapon, and moved on.

There was one more narrow passage to traverse, this one leading up from the main tunnel and through the floor of the warehouse that served as the muster point. Fortunov tensed during the slow process of gathering all the troops in the warehouse. This was the bottleneck, where an attack by the Watch would be most disastrous.

There was no attack, and by 1600 hours their warehouse was full, and Fortunov's army was ready. The building had once belonged to a vintner. Not the Kavans, but one of their rivals they had bought out and then gutted. The warehouse had been abandoned for years. Fortunov had never used it.

There had been no reason for the Watch to pay any attention to it. If any surveillance sweeps had gone inside, there was only a dusty, empty space.

Until now.

Now, when Fortunov received the signals from elsewhere in the city that the first phase of the attack had begun, the bay doors rose with a ratcheting snarl. Heavily armed troops charged into the street less than a mile from the outer wall of the castle. At the same time, concealed speakers in the roof of the warehouse blasted Fortunov's voice to Doomstadt.

"LATVERIANS, YOU ARE LIBERATED!"

Standing in the doorway, his soldiers streaming ahead of him, Fortunov waited for the cheers that would greet the news.

When the universe refused him justice again, he saw red.

CHAPTER 13

Beyond the portal was blackness, and the momentum of a fall. There was no time and no space in the blackness, but their perceptions persisted. So did the memory of sound, and though Doom could not see the deluge that had carried him though the portal, its roaring thunder resounded in his ears. Where there was no space, there was no air, yet he heard the water, and in his sense of himself, he was breathing.

Time did not exist, yet he fell for an eternity. The experience of time was marked by the attempt of his consciousness to grapple with where he was, and give meaning and shape to limbo. He began with the sense of falling, of being pushed down and down and down by the monstrous cataract. The belief in *down* implied the existence of directions. If there were directions, there was existence, a destination, the promise and threat of an end to the fall, of impact.

The sense of nowhere gradually became the sense of *somewhere*. And when Doom understood where he was, and where he was going, the darkness began to give way to light. Far away, in the perception of *below*, a blood-red glow appeared. It began as a smear in the black, a red void without form. Doom perceived it, and it drew his mind. It captured his thoughts. It grew bigger, and form appeared. The glow became a cloud riven by veins of brighter red that flowed around masses of darkness. The veins became flows of lava, and the darkness was the outlines of mountains.

Now he was falling to an endless landscape of eruptions, where in the beat of one thought the rivers of flowing lava seemed wide oceans and the mountains the size of worlds, and in the next thought the vastness was on a scale more easily graspable by the mind, though always defined by the horror of the sublime.

But he knew the truth of what lay below. And because he knew, the vistas defined themselves further. They did not change. Instead, they revealed themselves to him, taking on more and more shape as his thoughts drew him closer. There was a city in the lava. It was built on the mountains, and in the valleys, and in the midst of the lava seas. And some of the mountains were not mountains at all. They were pyramids, and there were towers spiking higher than peaks, and there were columns thousands of feet high.

And on the columns, things danced. They were not human, but their being was defined by human pain.

The more Doom perceived, the closer he came to the city. Perception drew him down to Hell, and the water came with him. The portal he had opened could have taken him anywhere, anywhen, beyond the initial nothing. But it was Hell that was closest to his thoughts, and it was Hell that had been just on the other side of the veil during his duel. He had understood the risk that came with tearing open the veil of reality again so soon after the first time. He had known where he would fall. He had told himself he would arrest the plunge and find his way back.

To find the way, he needed a path, a guide, some hint of the world he had left behind. There was nothing. There was only the vastness of the water, the great wave and great wall bearing down upon him. Here, where there was no here, where there was no space and no time, where the change from nothing to everything hinged on contingency, the water had become the idea of itself. It was the idea of millions of tons of water taking him with it on its destined journey. It occurred to him that this deluge was his gift to Hell. He was bringing a flood to quench the fire.

The thought was dangerous. It focused his attention even more firmly on the burning city. It rushed closer, vaster now. There were sounds, too, and smells. The sounds of drums, huge as despair, beating and beating and beating with command and reverberations that could shatter mountainsides. The tolling of bells, slow and heavy, resonant with the sorrow of cruelty. The blare of horns, defiant and defeated, triumphant and grieving. The choir of screams, billions strong. The stench of burning tar, of burning oil, of burning flesh.

The choking, suffocating, torturing grasp of Hell reaching up to claim him, to take him now and put an end to all bargaining and all hope.

You will not have me. I will come to take what does not belong to you. I will sour you, and the name of Doom will be the sound of fear in Hell. There will be no victory for you here.

But the water pushed down, and his thoughts had fastened themselves on the infernal, and plummeted faster, plunging toward the realm that became clearer and clearer in its hunger.

The Castle Guard operations center went from the drone of tense routine to the staccato rhythm of crisis. On a raised platform at the back of the chamber, Verlak looked out across the officers at their monitoring stations and the bank of screens that took up the entire north wall. The reports came quickly, called in short, clipped tones. At the same time, the screens filled with the images of the smoke and fighting.

The attacks had broken out with stopwatch simultaneity across the city. Squads of Fortunov rebels were attacking Guard barracks and the Doomstadt Rathauz. Others were setting up barricades along the major arteries, snarling traffic in all directions and impeding the movement of reinforcements. There were attacks, too, in Doomsburg and other smaller towns in Latveria. Fortunov was making his move, and making it everywhere and all at once.

"He can't think he's going to win," said Boris. He was standing a respectful half-step behind her. "Those aren't numbers that can withstand the Latverian Guard."

In a national crisis the castle was the nerve center, and with Doom absent, command fell to the captain of the Castle Guard. Verlak was getting her wish to confront Fortunov, and the thought was a bitter one.

Elsa believed in her. Doom did too, or he would not have given her this rank. Though the throne was empty, she would defend it to the last drop of her blood. But if Doom had fallen, who could stand?

She was glad of Boris' presence. His loyalty to Doom was made of an alloy stronger than titanium. So was his faith that Doom would return, and Verlak wanted the reassurance of that faith near her.

"They can't stop the Guard," Verlak said, "but they can slow us down."

"To what end?"

"To an end we can't see yet. These are all distractions, just like the truck bombs." And like the truck bombs, the attacks were distractions she could not ignore. She had to ensure the barracks held, that the Rathauz didn't burn. Wherever the traitors appeared, they had to be defeated. Necessity spread the responses of the Guard thin. "I think we can both guess what that end is likely to be, though."

"The castle," Boris grunted.

"If he wants Latveria…"

"And he does. The wretch doesn't know how to want anything else."

They didn't have to wait long to be proven correct. Surveillance cameras picked up the charge out of the warehouse.

"Captain!" one of the monitoring officers shouted.

"I see them," said Verlak.

"Vermin." Boris breathed heavily through his nose, barely containing his contempt and anger. "Of course the coward would wait until the master was absent."

"Coward or not, he's chosen his moment well." Verlak ran through counterattack options. Fortunov's strike force was a large one. It outnumbered the Guard stationed in the castle. Even so, on the face of it, the attack was an act of madness.

"Does he expect to besiege us?" Boris asked in disbelief, echoing her thoughts.

"No. He must know if this drags out, we'll crush him. He has to take the castle quickly, or not at all. So he must have a plan to do that."

"A plan, or a delusion."

"Let's make sure it is a delusion. I don't want his forces getting anywhere near the castle." The most powerful castle defenses could not be used by anyone except Doom. The resources she had access to would be more than strong enough, though.

The thought gave her no comfort. Fortunov wouldn't do this if he didn't believe he could win.

Verlak addressed the operations center. Her voice was calm, but her palms were sweating. Her gut told her that she had little time to react. Perhaps none at all. "I want a massed drone strike on the enemy. We take them down now."

Less than a minute later, the top row of screens displayed the attack drone views. The rooftops of Doomstadt flew by in crystalline black-and-white. Verlak traced the patterns of the roads with her eyes, counting the seconds before the drones had Fortunov's advance in view and decimated it.

She became aware of Boris' deep silence. "What are you thinking?" she asked the old man.

"I'm thinking that Fortunov must know that we can do this to him, and he would expect it."

"So am I. So am I."

The windows of the houses on Vandorf Street remained blank and shuttered. No one appeared at them. No one peered out of doorways. No one came out onto the street to cheer on the liberators, and to celebrate the fall of the tyrant. The speakers on the warehouse repeated Fortunov's pre-recorded exhortations. As he marched, Fortunov listened to his voice bounce over the roofs and down the narrow confines of Old Town. After a few blocks, he could no longer make out the words. The broadcast became a raucous noise, the rolling complaints of a murder of crows.

"Freedom for Latveria!" he shouted. "Doom has fallen!" His troops took up the chants.

The houses remained impassive. Their blank eyes stared over the heads of the shoulders, ignoring the shouts. Fortunov had the enraging sensation of marching through an empty city. The people, *his* people, the people it was his divine right to reign over, had their backs to him. They refused even to acknowledge his presence.

Fortunov glanced at the faces of his followers, and saw that the silence was wearing on them too. There was anger there, and mounting frustration.

"Where is everyone?" Seefeld asked.

"Hiding," said Shkurat, his face a rigid mask of grim purpose. "They have lived in fear of Doom for so long, they don't dare believe that change has come."

"They'll learn," Fortunov promised. "We'll make them understand."

Something whined in his ear. The whine became a high-pitched roar. He looked up and saw the Castle Guard's counterattack. Squadrons of drones, a swarm of metallic raptors, swept across the sky in wedge formations. The leading drones flew down the length of Fortunov's march, while the rear ones began to circle just ahead of Fortunov's position.

He whirled to the soldiers maneuvering the weapon's antigrav cart. "Trigger it now!" he ordered.

Above, the drones began their dive.

Resting on the antigrav cart, the top of the coffin split down its length and opened wide. Inside was a block of circuitry so dense it was almost featureless, its polished black surface reflecting the faint trace of intricate patterns in the sunlight. There was a single dark button in the center of its upward face. Fortunov reached in and hit it.

There was a click.

The weapon was the single most expensive piece of equipment he had purchased from A.I.M. It had taken almost as long to put together the funds for the device as it had to connect the caves outside Doomstadt to the sewers beneath it. The activation of something so crucial should have been marked by something more than a click. The sound was too small. It felt like a malfunction. With a spasm of fury, Fortunov thought he had been betrayed.

Then he realized the distant warehouse loudspeakers had gone quiet.

He looked up to watch the drones fall out of the sky.

CHAPTER 14

There was a small Latverian Guard barracks on the other side of the square from St Peter Church. Fortunov's rebels attacked it while a market was in full swing in the square. People streamed in panic through the church doors. On the porch, Zargo ushered them in. He didn't know how much protection he could offer them. He did know he had to try.

He stayed outside until the last of the shoppers and vendors were inside. Selfflagellating curiosity made him close the doors and remain a bit longer on the porch to watch the battle. There was little return fire from inside the barracks. Most of the soldiers must already have been deployed. Those who remained didn't stand a chance. Within minutes, the building was on fire. Flames raged out of the ground floor windows, and smoke enveloped the upper story with a billowing black shroud. The attackers then set to work demolishing the market stalls, constructing barricades at the north and south entrances to the square, blocking the main traffic routes in front of the church, and ensuring snarls for a dozen blocks in the vicinity.

The woman who led the rebels spotted Zargo. She was older than her troops, and her bearing was of one born and bred to the aristocracy, and who had never accepted the loss of her privilege. She walked up to the porch and grinned at him.

"Father Grigori," she said. "Why do you look so frightened? Why are the doors closed? Are you keeping the people locked inside?"

"You know I'm not," said Zargo.

"Then you should invite them out! Tell them, Father. Tell them that their liberation is at hand."

Zargo said nothing.

"No? I'm surprised, Father. Prince Rudolfo has told me a lot about you. Do you understand the role you have played? Thanks to you, Doom is gone. You are a hero of Latveria."

"I am not."

"You have the word of Natalya Rumyanova. Remember that. Prince Rudolfo will be generous with our heroes. So will I."

Zargo looked across the square at the fire. "You have no conception of heroism," he said. "There is none on display here."

Rumyanova's smile vanished. "There is always heroism when the rebel attempts to overthrow the oppressive power."

"Does that mean Doom was a hero when he overthrew King Vladimir?"

Rumyanova took one step up the porch. Her pistol was pointed at the ground, but the threat of her advance was unmistakable. "Be careful, Father Grigori," she said. "I remember heroes. I also remember traitors."

Zargo swallowed hard. He didn't answer, but he didn't flee inside. That was all the heroism he had the strength for. Rumyanova gave him a cobra's stare. Her lips pressed together in a twisted smile of contempt. Then she turned on her heel and headed back towards the barracks. "Think carefully," she called over her shoulder. "The change has come. Doom's order is finished. Don't begin a new era in error."

Zargo pulled the door open, slipped inside the church, and locked the entrance. If Rumyanova and her squad wanted inside, this barrier wouldn't stop them. The people in the church saw Zargo lock it, though, and that gave them comfort, even if there was none for him.

Comfort was his duty now. The comfort he did not deserve, but might be able to grant others.

He moved down the crowded nave, giving blessings, clasping hands and murmuring prayers. The thick walls of the church muffled the sound of distant gunfire. Zargo pushed away the thoughts of what the coming days would bring. The memory of what he had seen outside the walls of the city was so huge, it left no room for anything else to trouble him. The great wave he had walked towards still cast its shadow over him. And the sacrifice he and thousands with him had witnessed disturbed him with intimations of awe and the sublime. If Rumyanova had thought to taunt him by saying he was responsible for Doom's fall, she was days late. He had told Fortunov what the construction site was for. He had given the prince a target. He would have to atone, though he didn't know how, or how huge his crime truly was. Its repercussions were still rippling through Doomstadt.

The lights of the church went out. People murmured, and the alarm grew once those with watches and phones discovered that they had stopped working too. The late afternoon sun, streaming at an angle through the stained glass of the rose window, painted the nave red. The interior of St Peter glowed with the light of fire, and the touch of Hell.

The bells of the infernal city tolled faster. The drums boomed with new, eager hunger. The city shouted. It saw Doom. It saw him falling. It welcomed his arrival.

One of the immense columns was directly below him. He could make out the horned corners of its platform and the shapes of its revelers. He knew the texture of the stone, of the cracks that glinted with running blood, and the pale grey of the mortar of ground bones.

The damned and the demonic chanted his name in welcome. "*Doom. Doom. Doom.*" Hell mocked him. Its reality crystallized below him. The fullness of its being was ready now for the end of his descent. Space was real again, and so was time. He had seconds before eternity would begin.

No. My destiny does not end here, and not now.

He felt no fear. His cold, steel fury left no room for it.

Laughter swirled around him. Doom knew the voice. It was Mephisto's.

Hell's hunger would not be satisfied. With a roar of defiance, Doom turned his will away from the darkness and fire below him. He wrenched his thoughts from the shaping of his damnation and turned them to the water. He focused on the water, and then he could see it. The immense cataract reflected the infernal red. It roared too, its voice released into existence.

The water was the key. It had brought him through the portal. Its fall was defining his. But there was so much of it. He was falling with a river. He pictured its length. He pictured the flood stretching all the way back through the nothing and then to the real on the other side of the veil. He willed himself to see the water linking him back to the world.

He willed the end of his fall, and his was a will that could humble gods.

His descent slowed. The imminence of Hell's full reality diminished. The precision of mountains and spires lessened, becoming vague as his consciousness arrowed back through the deluge.

Hell screamed, and lost its grasp. Doom shot forward, in a new conception of *forward*. He rose over the cataract, and now he was the source of gravity, and the water, linked to him since it slammed him through the veil, followed.

The glow below faded, distance faded, space faded. Though he was in the nothing again, time had disappeared. Doom felt the same urgency as he had in his drop toward Hell. He had reestablished his link to the Latveria beyond the portal, and the danger to himself lost its importance. Fortunov had sent him here, and Fortunov was on the other side, with Latveria at his mercy.

Doom promised Hell a war, but it would have to wait. His anger and his will were one, on their wings he shot through limbo toward the promise of the real. The darkness weakened, became brittle, and began to draw back again. Light bloomed once more, the light that would be Doomstadt when he tore through the veil.

Faster. Faster.

Time in the world was slipping away, washed away by another deluge.

Faster. Faster.

The rage that was Doom's will hurtled toward the bleeding city.

Toward Fortunov.

There were no windows in the operations center. When the lights and screens blinked off, the room went pitch dark.

"Where's the backup power?" Verlak demanded.

"Gone too!" someone shouted. There was the noise of a button being hammered repeatedly.

"Everything's out," said another voice.

"EMP," Verlak realized. Confusion battled with horror. An electromagnetic pulse strong enough to disable the castle's power completely was something that should have required a nuclear airburst. But the castle was standing, and they were all still alive. Doomstadt was not an ash-filled crater.

If the power is out here, it's out everywhere. It's out at the hospital.

She cut off that train of thought before the consequences were too vivid in her mind's eye.

Stop Fortunov. Everything else comes after that, or there won't be an after.

There was a grind of metal, then weak grey light penetrated the operations center. Boris had made his way to the door and opened it. The hall beyond had windows.

"Get the power back," Verlak commanded the room. "There must be contingency generators whose shielding protected them from the pulse. Anyone with a weapon, you are with me. To the walls!"

Verlak ran into the twilight dimness of the hall, a half-dozen guards behind her. Outside, more troops were racing to reinforce the battlements. They were carrying pistols and automatic rifles, weapons that were rarely taken out of the castle's arsenals. They were primitive, imprecise, unworthy of Doom's army. The full impact of the EMP became clear to Verlak. At a stroke, Fortunov had taken out the most effective weapons that could be used against him.

Where did he get that technology? What price will his benefactor extract from Latveria if he takes the throne?

The sky was empty of drones. Instead, it was filled with smoke. Old Town was burning.

Verlak mounted the outer wall stairs three at a time. The battlements overlooked the moat and the ancient stone bridge that crossed it. The moat was deep as a gorge, and the water barely visible in its shadowed depths. It gave Verlak some satisfaction to think that the traitors would have plenty of time to scream before they hit the bottom.

On the other side of the moat, the guards on the outer wall were engaged in combat. They were clustered near the gate, sending down a steady rain of fire.

Until beam weapons swept the battlements clean.

And another melted the gate to slag.

The drones streaked down like meteors. Momentum and wings gave them an angle of descent when their engines cut out. The weight of their fuselage and armament dropped them fast. Fortunov ducked instinctively and pointlessly. The four drones on attack runs flew in eerie silence overhead, twenty feet above the heads of his troops, then slammed into the houses at the curve of Vandorf Street. They exploded. Fireballs spread over the road, and the house façades collapsed. Dust roiled up the street, and flames spread over the roofs of the adjoining buildings.

To the south, a chain of blasts like sharp thunder went off as the other drones hit the city.

"Doomstadt is bombing itself," Seefeld said with a grin.

"The people will rejoice when they see how suddenly we have ended the war," Shkurat promised.

They will be grateful, or I will know the reason why.

"The castle awaits us!" Fortunov shouted, and the assault raced upward.

Vandorf Street ended at an intersection with the ring road around the moat wall. The gate was straight ahead. Fortunov held back in the shelter of the houses and oversaw the installation of the other A.I.M. weapons. They had been held in crates protected by multiphasic force fields. The shields dropped when the EMP hit, but lasted a split second longer, protecting the energy weapons. There were two turret laser cannons and a heat mortar. Advanced Idea Mechanics mercenaries set up the tripods and installed the barrels of the cannons. They were slightly larger than heavy machine guns, and an order of magnitude more devastating. The heat mortar was a squat cylinder four feet long and a foot wide. Attached to its swiveling base, it looked like a Dobsonian telescope plated in steel.

The front lines of Fortunov's army crossed the ring road and engaged the castle defenders, while leaving the path to the gate clear. There was no shelter, and their advantage of greater numbers wouldn't last long. They did what they needed to, though, which was hold the attention of the Castle Guard long enough for the cannons to be prepared.

"Ready," one of the mercs said to Fortunov.

There was no respect for his position in the manner of these men. They were here because they liked war, and they liked being paid well to wage it. Fortunov didn't like having to work with them. He didn't like crawling, cap in hand, to A.I.M. He worried about what the end result of dealing with the technological thinktank would be. But the usurpation of the Latverian throne had to end. Toppling Doom's regime had no price.

"Then do what I pay you for," Fortunov said to the mercenaries.

Their grins were ugly, bloodthirsty. Two of them took the controls of the turret cannons. The other two operated the mortar.

The lasers opened up. Two continuously pulsing beams hit the top of the wall, starting on opposite sides of the gate, then moving toward each other, twin scythes cutting down the Guard. Enemy soldiers ducked beneath the battlements, and the mercs lowered their aim. The lasers went back and forth, slicing through the crenellations on the wall and through the men and women behind them.

At the heat mortar, one of the mercs tapped the other on the shoulder, who pulled a trigger mounted on the side of the weapon. The air between the mortar and the gate shimmered, and then the invisible charge slammed into the gate. Metal flashed incandescent and then exploded outward.

The way across the moat was clear.

"Bring the cannons forward," Fortunov ordered. "Cover the advance over the bridge."

Still grinning savagely, the mercenaries picked up the guns on their tripods and hauled them across the road. Shkurat led the charge through the melted wreckage of the gate. The Fortunov loyalists stormed across the bridge. The moat was so wide, the entire strike force was on the span before Shkurat could reach the far side. Fortunov stayed with the mercenaries at the gate, overseeing the laser fire. This was his artillery. He had neutralized the castle's main defenses, and now he would exterminate its defenders. He felt light-headed with exhilaration. The castle was going to fall.

Surrender, he willed the guard. *Why are you still fighting? There is no one left to demand your loyalty through fear.*

Shkurat had reached the gate on the other end of the bridge and was directing the installation of demolition charges. Another few moments, and the siege of the castle would turn into its invasion.

The light over the moat changed.

"What the...?" One of the mercs looked up, his finger pausing on the laser cannon's trigger.

Though the sky was cloudless, the sunlight dimmed, casting the moat into a prethunderstorm gloom. The air a hundred feet above the bridge trembled. It rippled. A line appeared, a floating crack running the whole length of the span. The crack spread wide, becoming a maw of darkness.

Doom flew out of the abyss.

Just beyond the extent of the maw, he hovered, arms folded, looking down on the Fortunov army in silent judgment.

"Shoot him!" Fortunov screamed at the mercenaries, knowing everything was already too little and too late.

The laser cannons swung to put Doom in their sights.

From the hole in the sky came the end of the world.

There was nothing, and then there was the wave. Fortunov's eyes saw water. They saw the massive wall that they had witnessed when he had blown the dam. But they saw the wave drop from the sky, and his mind refused the impossibility of the perspective.

From the troops on the bridge, there was a second of shocked stillness. They too could not process the sight of the flying river. Then they yelled in terror. Some opened fire on the water in their panic. Others ran back towards Fortunov. The hundreds of soldiers on the bridge turned from an attacking force into a routed mob. The crowd heaved with frantic movement, a huge serpent twisting in pain.

The water hit, endlessly, a monster beyond any conception of cataract, a vertical tsunami. Fortunov stumbled back and fell. With a shattering roar, the bridge collapsed. The river rammed it into the gorge of the moat. Fortunov scrabbled backwards away from the crumbling edge of the shattered span. Just a few feet ahead of him, the guns disappeared. So did the mercenaries, already crushed as they fell. A flood swept him up and carried him across the street. He fought to his feet and ran back down the street, into the dust and smoke of the drone impacts.

Behind him, the river he had unleashed poured down from the sky, filling the moat and drowning his dreams.

CHAPTER 15

In the dark, Dubrov touched the hilt of the dagger concealed in his robes.

Do I dare?

He would not have dared so many things a few days ago. He would not have dared *think* them. But his imagination had been freed from his chains when the impossible had occurred.

Do I dare?

He took a single step forward, then stopped. As ever, he had been shadowing Helm, keeping track of her movements through his realm. He was even with the latest aisle she had chosen to wander down when the lights went out. He had heard her startled jump, and then the exasperated sigh. There was no sound of footsteps. She was waiting, motionless, for the power to come back on.

She had been less than twenty feet from him when everything went dark. There were no obstacles between them.

He took another silent step, listening for her movement, for the sound of her breathing.

Dubrov had started carrying the dagger a couple of days after Helm's first visit to the archives. Just for the comfort, at first. Just to have a talisman, at first. That was all. She was a witch. He had to work in proximity to her. He deserved protection. The dagger gave it to him. It was one of the few heirlooms he had managed to hang onto after his family's collapse. The dagger was from the late sixteenth century. Its blade was silver. Its hilt was bronze, and engraved with minute lettering, a tight spiral of blessings.

After a week, just carrying the dagger wasn't enough. Dubrov read the *Daemonologie* of King James. He read the *Malleus Maleficarum*. Just for more protection. Just to be on his guard. To know what he needed to know. Because Helm was a witch.

He took another step and paused, listening. His left hand touched the books in the shelves next to him, guiding him. His right touched the dagger. He didn't pull it out. Not yet. He didn't know if he would. He wasn't committed.

He took another step.

Dubrov's ancestors would have already decided. They would have known what to do. And he knew what their decision would have been. They would not have suffered the witch to live.

The protection of knowledge ran deep in the Dubrov blood. So did the protection of others from dangerous knowledge. That meant, when necessary, destroying those with too much such knowledge. Arkady Dubrov had been the most important of the family's witchfinders. He had led the Latverian witch trials of the 1620s. He had suffered no witches to live. He had made them suffer instead.

When Dubrov thought of Arkady, he could smell the smoke from the burnings. He also smelled the mustiness of the lost past. The history of witchcraft in Latveria was a long one, a rich one, and the witches here, strong and proud, had also been able to fight back, and fight back hard, against the Arkady Dubrovs of their times. There were branches, too, of the Dubrovs that had embraced the dangerous knowledge, and become what their kin sought to destroy. Like so many families in Latveria, the tapestry of their history was woven with threads from both sides of the occult. Vassily Dubrov wasn't sure if Doom had engaged him because of the sorcerous Dubrovs, or because at some level it amused him to have the descendant of a former witchfinder in servitude.

Everything Dubrov had been reading, and preparing, had been a precaution only. Just for his protection. He would not do anything to anger Doom. Some sorcerers were so powerful they might as well be gods. Doing anything with the dagger was unthinkable.

So was the absence of Doom. Then the impossible happened, and Dubrov's imagination was liberated. And then the lights went out.

Something was changing in Latveria.

Dubrov took another step, listened. Finally, he heard Helm again. She was tapping a finger against book spines. She sounded bored, not worried. She didn't realize how serious a power failure in the archives was. She didn't know how impossible such a thing was.

The tapping gave Dubrov a sense of where Helm was. She was still some distance away. It wasn't too late to change his mind. He could turn back. He could also keep going without committing himself. So he did. Another step, utterly silent. Another wait, his breath slow and regular, though his heart was loud in his chest.

Don't rush. Don't make a mistake. Don't let her know you're there.

Maybe she already knows. She might be waiting. She's a witch.

No. She's distracted. She's been lost since Doom vanished. She's not paying attention. She doesn't think there's any reason to be on her guard.

His right hand clasped the dagger.

Another step.

The risk was so great, vertigo gnawed at him. She was powerful. If she realized he was there, and what he was thinking, she could destroy him like swatting an insect.

If she doesn't know, she can't hurt you. If she can't hear you, she won't know.

The dagger was protecting him. The dagger was for just this purpose. The dagger was for witches. She was strong, but she was human. She was flesh. The dagger would finish her.

The archives vibrated with a muffled thunder, barely audible but colossal. Dubrov froze. The sound might cover his approach, but he could not hear her finger tapping any longer. He wasn't sure where she was.

What is that? What is that?

The rumble was of something enormous. A cataclysm was unfolding above ground.

He's back.

Dubrov didn't question the sudden conviction. It was as if the being of the castle changed with the return of its master. Doom's presence was as certain as the sun in the sky.

Dubrov's knees trembled. What was he thinking?

Doom will know! Doom will know!

He let go of the dagger. He reached out so both his hands were touching bookshelves now. Utterly innocent, utterly harmless. Then he called out. "Are you nearby?" he asked. "Are you all right?"

"Vassily?" Helm asked. "Of course I am. Are you?" She whispered something, and an amber nimbus appeared around her, illuminating the aisle of shelves.

Dubrov cleared his dry throat and smiled.

"Is that better?" Helm asked. "Sorry. I should have done that sooner. I didn't think the lights would be out this long."

"They should not have gone out at all," Dubrov told her.

And then they were back on. Dubrov blinked, dazzled by the dim lighting after the perfect darkness. He felt exposed, as if the light was Doom's gaze. The dagger in his robe, so powerful in the dark, so strong with the tradition of centuries, seemed small, insignificant. As small and insignificant as Dubrov was.

Doom was back, but the chains didn't return to Dubrov's imagination. He was tired of being small. He was tired of being afraid. He had imagined a world without Doom, and he wanted that possibility back.

The bridge was already being repaired. Doom refused to let the castle bear the scars of Fortunov's attempted coup a moment longer than necessary. He would bury the man's folly in oblivion. The smoke was still rising from the burned houses where the drones had crashed, and the construction bots were hard at work creating a new span over the moat, which had never been fuller. Sluice gates were controlling the flow to Doom Lake, and the Kanof Valley Dam was whole again. Doom had sealed the veil again before all the water escaped from the beyond, containing the deluge to the moat. The flood was finally over.

The first thing Doom had done, before even landing, was run a diagnostic of the power blackout and tap into the deep, shielded generators of the castle, the ones only he had access to. Through them, power returned to the castle and then to the city. Now, while the Guard hunted for surviving elements of Fortunov's forces in the city, Doom walked with Verlak down the street from which the main attack had come.

They stopped beside the abandoned EMP device. Doom crouched, looking closely at the obsidian polish of the circuitry.

"This is the work of Advanced Idea Mechanics," he said. He straightened and looked down Vandorf Street at the wreckage of the crashes, and felt the throb of cold anger. "I will have to make corrections to the castle defenses."

"Perhaps if the Guard has access to some of the locked systems?" Verlak suggested.

Doom shook his head. "No. The adjustments will be to the defenses that are currently within your remit."

"The others might have allowed us to stop the attack sooner."

"That is not the issue, captain. Those defenses are not walled off from the Guard because I am infantilizing you. They're walled off to prevent their being taken over by our enemies. You understand the consequences if my own technology is turned against me?"

"I do, your Excellency."

"It has happened before."

"It has?"

"You would have been too young to be training for the Guard. But you are not too young to remember those few weeks when the Red Skull took over Latveria in my absence." The memory was a livid scar. He had been overconfident. He had defeated Fortunov's most concerted attack up to that moment, and the castle had been badly damaged. He had left during the reconstruction, never thinking another threat to Latveria would arise so quickly. He had wasted time in the *Riviera*, of all the pointless, ridiculous things to have done. He had observed the idle rich with contempt, oblivious to his own self-satisfied indulgence. And while he was gone, the Red Skull had come. He and his forces had seized the castle and all its defenses, and in a matter of days they had all of Latveria beneath the bootheel of fascism.

"I do remember," Verlak said, and she shuddered.

"I would have ended that dark time sooner if I had not been incapacitated by my creations. I will not allow that to happen to me or my country again."

"I understand," Verlak said with feeling. Turning back to the A.I.M. device, she said, "I'm surprised Fortunov could afford their help."

"I don't think he can. Even if he has managed to assemble the funds necessary to purchase these weapons, he can't afford the full price of dealing with A.I.M." Advanced Idea Mechanics did not supply terrorists and violent subversives with weaponry just for the asking. Their interest would always be in the overthrow of political sovereignty, and the establishment of their control. "If he thinks of them simply as resource providers, he is even more deluded than I had believed. Even if he thinks of them simply as dangerous allies, he is a fool. He will not reign without their help. He will be making himself their vassal. And for what? For this?" He gestured at the damage, at the rescue teams struggling to free the wounded and the dead from the rubble.

"You are referring to Fortunov in the present tense," Verlak said. "Do you think he's still alive?"

"Have we seen his body?" Doom asked.

"No," she admitted.

"You're thinking, captain, about all the corpses in the moat that will never be identified, no matter how thorough the dredging is."

"He could be among them."

"He could be," said Doom. "I don't think he is. Until we see him dead, we will assume he is alive and active." He thought with cold satisfaction about the annihilation of the enemy force on the bridge. "We can, though, consider his threat neutralized for the time being."

He started down the road toward the crash sites. Verlak walked swiftly to keep up with him. "I failed you," she said. "You entrusted Latveria's safety to my care, and I failed."

"You did not," said Doom. "You saved Doomstadt on Midsummer Night, and you kept order in my absence. You responded correctly to the attack. You did all that was within your power and your authority."

Verlak bowed her head in thanks. She did not look convinced. *Good.* Her personal need to make amends would forge her loyalty into an even stronger alloy.

"May I ask you something, your Excellency?" Verlak said.

"Go ahead."

"Was it chance that you returned at precisely the right time and place to destroy Fortunov's army at a stroke? Or did you know when and where he would be?"

"Neither," said Doom. "I never intended to be carried through the portal with the water in the first place. That happened because I had been weakened in battle. Fortunov did achieve a victory with that flood. It simply didn't last. I had planned to send the water to Hell, to insult its fires with a deluge. Instead, the water served a more useful purpose. It was not chance, planning, or fate that led me to the bridge, Captain Verlak. It was my will. My will led me to Fortunov."

Elsa Orloff stood back from the injured woman and let the paramedics load her into the ambulance. A fallen timber had broken the woman's leg and right arm. Orloff had applied emergency splints and stopped the bleeding. Everything she had done in the hours since the attacks had ended had been along the same lines. She was engaged in rapid field dressings, just enough to make it possible to transport the wounded without causing them more harm.

All medical staff not immediately needed at the hospital had been rushed to Vandorf Street. While the Guard and rescue workers dug people out of the shattered houses, Orloff performed triage and first aid. It was all anyone could do, and it didn't feel like enough.

The ambulance drove off. Orloff looked for the next patient, and there wasn't one. The digging went on, but for the moment, no other victims had been found. She hoped that was because there were no others beneath the rubble. There had been lulls before, though. She sat down on a chunk of broken masonry to catch her breath, and saw Doom approaching with Verlak. Orloff held her breath. She had seen Doom from a distance during Doom's Day parades, but never this close. He was a towering figure in his armor, but the closer he came, the bigger he seemed. He was somehow more real than anything else in the street, as if his being had a gravitational force greater than the Earth's. At the same time, he seemed a walking myth, a thing too extraordinary to be real.

Orloff scrambled to her feet and bowed as they reached her. Verlak began to introduce her. "This is…"

"Doctor Elsa Orloff," Doom said.

Orloff's eyes widened. "I am honored, your Excellency, that you know who I am."

"I have read your articles in *The Lancet Neurology*."

Orloff wondered if she should expect to wake soon from this dream. She looked up at the mask, at its iron grey as implacable as destiny, at its face that was the essence of command. "I… I'm flattered," she said. "They've been criticized for being too speculative."

"Their speculation is the reason they're interesting," said Doom. "You are not here in your specialist capacity, though, I see."

"This is where I'm needed."

"Good," said Doom. "You will do much for Latveria, Doctor Orloff. Now and in times to come."

Orloff felt her cheeks glow with pleasure. She bowed again, and Doom moved on. Verlak looked back to give her a grin and a raised eyebrow. Orloff was too flustered to respond. She was dizzy. She was bathing in the aura of Doom's approval. She understood in a new, visceral way, what drove Verlak.

However much Orloff had done in her life, it wasn't enough. It wasn't nearly enough. She needed to do more. She needed to serve the walking myth.

Zargo sat on the steps before the altar. The doors of the church were open. He watched and waited for the terrible figure to appear in the doorway. He was not going to be surprised this time, not by something that was inevitable. And Doom was inevitable.

It had been easy to tell that Doom had returned. There had been a long, drawn-out, roaring rumble from the direction of the castle. Moments later, the square had gone quiet. Zargo had opened the door a crack to see what had changed. The barricades were still up, and the Guard barracks smoldered. Rumyanova and her troops had disappeared. The disturbing pop of guns and the rattle of automatic weapons, which had been echoing from different locations across the city, had stopped. The coup was finished.

The people left the sanctuary of St Peter as soon as they were sure the fighting was over. Zargo had been sitting here since their departure, waiting for the reckoning. He tallied his sins ahead of Doom's judgment.

Zargo traced the line from his conversations with Fortunov to the catastrophe that had just ended. It didn't matter that Doom had known about the exchanges. What mattered was the result. The destruction of the Kanof Dam. The flood. The attempted overthrow. It had all happened because Fortunov had been able to take advantage of Doom's circumstances.

When the figure appeared at the door, blocking the light of the setting sun, Zargo realized he wasn't ready at all. His heart beat painfully. His legs were weak, though he managed to stand. He tried to look his reckoning in the face as it walked toward him, but the mask was too frightening, and he lowered his gaze. He braced himself.

"I…" he tried as Doom loomed over him.

Doom waited, then said, "You what?"

Zargo shook his head. There was no point. There was nothing he could say that Doom did not know.

"I agree," said Doom. "I have no patience for time-wasting discussions either. I know what you expected. I am here to tell you that you have been useful to me, and that your use has not ended yet."

Zargo looked up. "It hasn't?" He didn't know if that was hope or dread that made his voice quaver.

"Did you think your work was done?" Doom asked. "It is only just beginning. Rest well. The prologue of our labors is over. Tomorrow, we begin in earnest."

CHAPTER 16

After Doom left, Zargo watched the sunset from the porch, then began to close St Peter for the night. He locked the doors and began the rounds down the aisles and the choir, putting out the candles. He wasn't frightened as he had been, or despairing. He *was* uneasy. He didn't like how empty the church felt in Doom's absence, as if his arrival and departure brought and took something to and from the space. Whatever it was, it wasn't numinous. Zargo didn't have to remove that kind of heresy from his imagination at least. But it was a quality more than human, in the way the darkness of space was more than night.

He had just extinguished the last candle in the choir when he realized what the quality was. He had already known it when he was waiting for Doom to arrive. He just hadn't seen the truth fully. *Inevitable.* Doom was inevitable, yes, but he was more than that. He was *the* inevitable. His family name had been waiting for centuries for his arrival, so that the name and the word and the living being would exist as perfect, terrifying unity. The inevitable had entered this space, and then left it, and of course it felt empty now, just as the sky would if the moon abruptly vanished.

Zargo also felt uneasy because he felt pleased that he was still useful. The work on the ley lines had been invigorating, exciting. He had done what Doom had asked, and done it well, and he could not escape the pride and sense of accomplishment. He had turned his back on those studies. Doom had forced him to return to them, and then told him that they were more than his true calling. They were the expression of his identity. He should feel shame, burning shame, that he was a geomancer. Instead, the most he could summon was unease at the lack of shame.

You're eager to get back to work. Admit it.

Yes. I am. He would not compound his sins with lies.

He wanted to believe he could be true to his vows and to his self. He wanted to believe there could be reconciliation between the priest and the geomancer. For now, he would try not to think too deeply about the contradictions of doctrine and witchcraft, and the dangers to his soul that might open up.

He was about to turn off the lights when he saw one of the curtains of the confessional booth was drawn. There was someone inside.

He wondered how long they had been there. He was sure the curtains had been pulled back, and the booth empty, when he had been waiting for Doom. He hesitated, debating. *No guesses as to who might be there.*

If he was going to attack me, he would have done so already.

Zargo's hesitation vanished. The threat inside the booth

wasn't frightening as it might have been only a few hours ago. Zargo strode over to the booth and entered his side of the compartment. He sat down on the bench and sighed. "Why are you here?" he asked Fortunov when it became clear that the prince would not start the conversation.

"Neither for confession nor sanctuary, Father," said Fortunov. He sounded exhausted. The shadow on the other side of the lattice was slumped.

"Then what?" said Zargo. *Say your piece and leave my church.*

"I want to understand something."

Zargo heard genuine pain. "I'm listening," he said, startled.

"When it seemed that victory might be possible, when we marched on the castle, it was as if Doomstadt were deserted. I called on the people to join us, to rise up with us, and there was only silence."

"And you want to know why."

"*Yes!*" Fortunov cried in agony. "*Why?* Why did not a single person join us? Don't they want to be freed from Doom's tyranny?"

To replace it with yours? But that wasn't a question Fortunov would consider, and it was inadequate as a response. Zargo thought about what to say, and when he found his answer it gave him a deeper understanding of his own responses to Doom. "You've traveled outside Latveria, I assume," he said.

"I have. Especially in the days of my father's rule."

"You'll have been to Versailles."

"I have."

"Do you remember what Louis XIV was called?"

"*Le Roi Soleil.* The sun king. Yes, Father, I do remember. What is the point of your history quiz?"

"Be patient and you'll see. Why was Louis called the sun king?"

"Because his court was so magnificent."

"Yes, and he shone over his subjects. That is the point I want to emphasize. I want you to think about what that means, to shine over your subjects. When you were at Versailles, did you notice the king's emblem?"

"Yes..." Fortunov said slowly, drawing up memories. "Yes," he said again. "The king's head as a sun, golden beams radiating out."

"Exactly. And the magnificence of his court served a strategic political purpose. If you were a member of the nobility, and you wanted the king's favor, you had to pay court. And that was so ruinously expensive, you wound up entirely dependent on the king. And so power was utterly centralized, and everything revolved around the king. That is the truth expressed by that symbol, and by the name *sun king*. The light of the sun is its power. The power of the king is shown in the beams of gold. Everything, *everything* flows from the king. The nation becomes his reflection."

"I think I see where you are going with this," Fortunov murmured.

"I'll be explicit, all the same," said Zargo. "Doom is a sun king, even more fully than Louis XIV ever was. Latveria is a world power. How? Because of Doom, and *only* because of Doom. Latveria's strength and its wealth come from his inventions. And the beams of his sun touch every citizen. Universal basic income, free health care, free schooling, free universities, free training to the highest level of your calling – all of these things flow from Doom."

"*Free?*" Fortunov snarled.

"The price is obedience, yes," said Zargo. "And yes, Doom is feared." Zargo stopped himself from saying *Vladimir was feared and hated.* That would stop Fortunov from listening. *If you would just learn and give up, Prince Rudolfo. Walk away from what you can't ever win, and grant us peace.* "Even though Doom is feared," he said, "he also *is* Latveria in every sense that matters. I'm sorry, Prince Rudolfo, but that is something you will never be. No one can. Latveria will only ever have one sun king."

"The sun can be eclipsed," said Fortunov.

"Never for long."

"What about hereditary rights?" Fortunov demanded. "What about the rule of the rightful king?"

You listened, but you haven't heard. You fool. You deluded, arrogant fool. "Hereditary rights are a social convention," Zargo spoke gently, but he didn't deny himself the pleasure of using those words on Fortunov. They were his own little vengeance, and though that was wrong, he was human. He owed the prince for the weeks of terror he had experienced. "Those rights have no reality except what we choose to give them."

"That is blasphemy, Father!" said Fortunov. "I would have expected more from you. They are a divine right, and God will not permit them to be flouted indefinitely."

History seems to disagree with you, Zargo wanted to say. This time, it was something other than the need to make Fortunov listen that held him back. It was his own mistrust of history and its cruelties. He contented himself with, "You seem very certain."

"You should be too."

"The divine right of kings is not an article of my faith, Prince Rudolfo. It never will be, either." *The right imposed by a king with divine might is another story. I don't need faith to know that exists, and it isn't just a social construct. Everyone in Latveria knows its reality.*

"You are wrong, Father," Fortunov said. "You disappoint me."

"You asked me what I thought. I have told you. For your sake, if not for that of the country, you would be wise to listen." *I'm tired of being threatened by you.* If Fortunov decided to kill him, there was nothing he could do. No one would hear him if he called out. No one was close enough to help. The thought didn't bother him. Fortunov was defanged, if only temporarily.

"I will not give up," said Fortunov. "I will save Latveria whether it wants it or not."

"You are the one who needs saving," said Zargo. "Not the country."

There was no answer.

"Prince Rudolfo?"

The shadow on the lattice was gone.

Zargo stepped out of the confessional. The booth was deserted. The church doors were just swinging closed. Zargo went to lock them again.

"I don't believe you'll save anyone," he said to the absent prince. "I do believe that you might damn us all."

The laboratory purred to life when Doom and Helm entered, a faithful beast responding to its master. The recessed lighting flickered on, providing an even, shadowless illumination. The servo-arms extended slightly from the wall, ready for his commands.

"The power failure didn't damage anything?" Helm asked.

Doom saw the anxious look she gave the warding runes. "The generator in here is separate from the rest of the castle, and its shield can withstand something as primitive as an electromagnetic pulse. Don't worry. Even if the power had gone off, there isn't anything in here that would be disrupted. You have the arm?"

"I do," said Helm. She pulled it out of her robes. "I haven't been without it since Midsummer."

"That was a risk. If something had happened to you..."

"I know," Helm said with a visible shudder. "It seemed the least worst of risks. There was nowhere I would have trusted to store it."

"Agreed," said Doom. "You chose well. Still, I imagine your nights can't have been pleasant."

"I have not slept."

"Then you will tonight." He held out his hand, and Helm gave him the demon's forearm. Doom examined it, enjoying the luxury of having the time to do so. "The withering is no worse than it was initially," he said.

"No. The loss of the demon's essence at the moment of severing is all it has suffered."

"Any other effects, given the close contact you've been forced to have with it?"

"I sealed it away as much as I could." She held up a silk cloth embroidered with a magic circle and symbols of protection and imprisonment. "I don't think I dare use this again. It's tainted now."

Doom pointed to the wall opposite the entrance. Lead, silver, and iron shutters parted. The space beyond them pulsed red. "Place it in the incinerator."

"Even its ash can be fatal."

"There will be no ash. There will be nothing left at all."

Doom went back to his study of the arm while Helm disposed of the cloth and returned. He whispered an incantation, and the limb's veins glowed a dark violet. Its claws twitched. Doom reversed the spell, and the arm became quiescent again. *Good. It is subject to my commands now.*

"What do you think?" Helm asked. "Will it serve?"

"After what it took to acquire it, I would be displeased if it did not. But yes, I think it will. Despite its condition, its links to Hell are still strong. Dangerously so. Every one of our steps will have to be perfect."

After a moment, Helm said, "Do we dare carry on?"

Doom looked at her. "Is that a serious question?"

"I need to hear that we have no choice."

"Of course we don't."

"We could send the arm back to Hell."

"Accept defeat when we have already won so much?"

"I fear the consequences of our failure," Helm said.

Doom snorted. "Are you sanguine about the consequences of abandoning the work? Death and what comes after are no longer a concern for you after all?"

"They are. I wouldn't be here if they weren't."

"If you are here," said Doom, "then you are committed to the creation of the Harrower."

Helm nodded.

"I need to hear you say so," Doom told her.

"I am," she said. "I will not stop raising these questions, though. I *am* afraid. If you aren't, you should be."

"I am well aware of the risks we run."

"That's not what I said."

Doom held the arm over the silver pool. "Fear and I have been strangers since the end of my childhood. There will be no renewing of our acquaintance. I am on intimate terms with defeat, however, and with disaster." He grimaced, and the scar tissue on his face tightened. "Believe me, I have no intention of allowing them to make their presence known here."

The nanobot pool eddied beneath the demon arm.

"We are both here to end the consequences of the past," said Doom, "not to cast a deeper shadow over the future."

"Agreed," said Helm.

"There will be no more talk of fear?"

"Oh, there will be. There most certainly will be, because it is necessary."

"Perhaps," said Doom. "It can be a further safeguard against error."

"I am ready to begin," Helm added.

"You are resolute?"

"I am."

Doom recited the words of the Sator Square. Helm did too, in reverse order. The silver pool swirled from the outside in. The vortex at the center soon turned so quickly that a hole descended to the bottom of the pool. Doom and Helm each reversed the incantation. The spin was now so fast it was invisible. The pool seemed still again. The hole at the center became a pillar that rose four feet above the surface. The silver of the nanobots shivered with spidery fissures of night that came and went.

"Will it hold?" Helm asked.

"It will hold," said Doom. He had prepared the lab for this moment as completely as he had prepared the arena. *There will be no errors. There will be no defeat.*

With his left hand, he conducted the movement of a servo-arm. Every machine in the lab was reinforced by as much occult protection as they had technological precision. When the machine took the arm from Doom, no taint of the infernal could touch it. The servo-arm transported the limb over the pool and placed it on the silver pillar.

The arm sank into the column. The spinning of the nanobots slowed, and the column descended, spread out, and vanished. Soon the surface was an immaculate silver mirror again. There was no sign of the arm.

"Has it been contained?" Helm asked.

Doom smiled to himself. "More than that. It has been consumed. The Hell particles of Purson's arm are intermixed with the nanobots. There is no distinguishing them now."

The lighting darkened. A frigid breeze rose from the pool. The servo-arms trembled like aspen leaves. Doom whispered a command, and the lab's generator funneled more power to the wards. The breeze dropped, and the lights stabilized. On the surface of the pool, wards appeared and disappeared faintly.

"That seems barely contained," said Helm.

"The danger is real, yes. But so is the power." He leaned over the pool. "What was part of Purson is mine now," he said. "I have my piece of Hell to do with as I please." He reached over the pool and made a fist. The surface went black and tightened in response.

"And what will please you?" Helm asked quietly.

"To make Hell scream."

CHAPTER 17

The lake that had returned to the region around the arena was shallow and would not be there for long. It was already draining away down the riverbeds to Doom Lake, and with the Kanof Dam rebuilt, its lifeblood was cut off again. Knee-deep water lay sullenly around the upheavals in the landscape. Doom walked with Zargo along a ridge of lava that had congealed on a line a short distance to the west of the arena. The priest was staring wide-eyed at the scars the battle had left.

"Everything has changed," he said, awed.

"It has," Doom agreed. "Do you sense how profound those changes are?"

"I'm not sure I understand."

"You will."

He said nothing else for the time being. It was better that Zargo come to fuller knowledge on his own. *Let him take in the land at his pace.*

The lakebed looked as if it had been the center of a volcanic eruption. Lava was heaped in domes and ridges for miles around. Other formations suggested a fist had punched up through the earth's crust, with jagged outcroppings peeling back from deep wells. New hills of blackened rock had emerged, surrounding the one that had been the center of the arena.

Zargo stopped. He was looking at the arena and frowning. "What is it?" Doom asked.

"The arena," said Zargo. "Has its orientation changed?"

"It has," said Doom.

"The hill too?"

"You are observant." It was as if a giant hand had seized the arena and spun it. The structure bore scars of flame and sorcery. It had tilted too as it had started to sink into the molten land. Even its hill was tilted. The peak and its platform faced Doom and Zargo at an angle.

"It's the runes on the slope and on the pylons. Their lines are unbroken. But I'm sure this configuration was facing west when I was last here."

"It was," Doom said.

Zargo turned around slowly, awed into silence by the scale of the events that had transpired.

"Everything is different," he said at last.

Doom heard deeper knowledge behind the apparently banal understatement. "Go on," he said. *Follow your instincts. Do what I know you can do.*

"Everything *feels* different."

"Indeed. At what level?"

Zargo looked at the ground. The gesture was instinctive, even if he didn't realize it. Doom was pleased. The earth was speaking to the geomancer, and it was the geomancer, not the priest, who responded. "Every level," he murmured. He knelt and touched the ground, as if placing his hand on the flank of a wounded animal.

He caught what he was doing and stood up suddenly. He shook his head and took a couple of vague steps away.

The priest and the geomancer were at war with each other. The priest was trying to interfere with the geomancer's work. The priest would have to be defeated if Zargo was going to be any use to Doom. *A simple enough matter.*

"What is it that you wish me to do?" Zargo asked.

"I need you to find something for me."

"Find what? I found the ley lines for you here already."

"Have you?" Doom asked.

"Yes..." Zargo said uncertainly.

Ah. You're curious now. Good. "Can you feel them?"

Doom thought Zargo's show of reluctance was more for his own benefit than for Doom's. The priest closed his eyes and concentrated. After a few moments, his lids snapped open in surprise. "Where are they?" he asked. "They're not where they should be."

Now you're indignant. Something impossible has happened, and you want an answer. Excellent. Find the answer, then. Go looking. "They can't be far, can they?" Doom nudged.

Zargo walked down the lava with purpose now, his eyes half closed, his head turning from side to side like a dog on a scent. He scrambled down the ridge and waded out into the water. He moved with increasing energy, then came to a stop as suddenly as if a trap had snapped shut around his ankle. He looked back at Doom, the astonishment on his face almost comical. "I can feel one here." He looked back and forth, then stretched his arms out, fingers pointing. "It's running along this orientation. It hasn't just moved! Its direction has altered!"

Doom nodded. *And now you're excited. You won't resist the hunt now.* Zargo would have to take the bait and be committed to the search before he encountered the first of the real goals.

Zargo waded back to the ridge. "I'm not even sure if the line is even straight any longer." He pointed south-west. "Did I sense a curve over there?"

"Quite possibly," said Doom. "The Earth has suffered a trauma here. A deep one. The wounds will not heal quickly, or cleanly."

"So you want me to determine the new configurations of the ley lines?" He seemed quite reconciled to the idea of repeating a task he had accomplished once before.

"You must do that, yes," Doom told him. "But that is just the preliminary step to the true task."

"Which is what?"

"Just as the most intense heat and pressure, the deep pain of the Earth, produces diamonds, the equivalent agony of ley lines creates a particular formation. Let us call it a kind of lodestone." Doom gestured at the injuries of the battlefield. "The ground melted and transformed here, but not because of any natural causes. Sorcery, mine and Hell's, was the cause of the trauma. The occult energies of the Earth suffered. You have seen a hint of the result. The distortion of a ley line is no small thing. Where distortion has happened, there will be lodestones."

"And you want to gather them."

Doom chuckled dryly. "*Gather* is too simple a word, but

you grasp the principle. What we seek is much rarer than diamonds. They will not be scattered. There will be only one associated with each of the ley lines, and it will be located at the point of greatest injury. There will be five, one for each of the lines that formed the node."

"The node won't have the shape it did, if it even exists any longer," said Zargo.

"No, it won't. The arena forced the node on the lines. Though they did not intersect, the arena created the effect of an intersection between all five, and so the impact of what happened here was magnified for all the lines. There will have been considerable distortion."

Zargo thought for a moment. "I could perhaps work out the new trajectories of the ley lines. Then it would just be a question of excavation, wouldn't it?"

Doom folded his arms, looking down at Zargo in silence.

Zargo gazed up, hunching slightly as if expecting a blow. "Wouldn't it?" he asked again, his voice cracking.

"Would you dig up a ley line as if it were a power cable?" Doom asked.

"No," said Zargo.

"No," Doom repeated. "It would be absurd to try. The lodestones are not simple rocks. They have a material form, but it must be summoned. By a geomancer."

"I don't know anything about geomancy," Zargo said. "Not about its practice. All my studies at the Werner Academy were theoretical."

"Do not try my patience or question my judgment." *Obey me. Your doubts are too much like defiance.*

Zargo wilted before the metallic thunder of Doom's

warning. "I didn't mean..." he began.

Doom cut him off. "I do not make demands of incompetents. I choose my servants with care. They are always the right tools. The next objection that passes your lips will be treated as disobedience."

Zargo trembled and said nothing.

"We are clear, then."

Zargo nodded.

"You should be honored," said Doom. "I think you will understand, in time, the full enormity of what you are going to accomplish here. And you should be grateful. By my command, you are becoming what you were always meant to be. That cassock is not your calling, Grigori Zargo. It veils the truth from you. My voice is the one that calls, and you *will* answer. I know what you are, though you would deny it to yourself. You are a geomancer. You have a natural talent for that art greater than anyone alive in Latveria today. Today, you will learn what you can do. That is the command of Doom."

Zargo began his search with the ley line he had already located. He walked slowly through the water, the sun beating on the back of his neck. Every so often, he looked back at the arena's hill, and the figure of Doom on the peak, immovable as a monument. Zargo felt Doom's gaze more keenly than he did the sun.

He walked with his arms slightly forward, fingers spread. He had never paid much attention to geomantic dowsing techniques. He had a rough idea of the approach, but his only field experience had been during the construction of the arena. Then, though, he had charts to work from. He had known where the ley lines were from the start. He had felt them, yes, and once contact had been made, he had been able to maintain an instinctive connection to the lines no matter where he was on the construction site. But this was different. He didn't know where to look for the lodestones, or how he was supposed to raise them to the surface.

Doom said he would know, though. He didn't dare contradict the king again.

It's not just that. You know he's right.

I don't what him to be.

What you want doesn't matter.

Once he found the first line again, he found it hard to think about anything else. He felt the pain of the Earth. There was a throbbing in the stones like the pulse of a wounded finger. It beat through the ground and into his frame. He began to walk to the rhythm of the throb. The line held him to its course. He held his hands as if to offer comfort. He was too small a thing to give it, too weak, a creature of flesh instead of stone. The ley line demanded a witness to its pain, though, and so it held him, and screamed in his soul.

He walked on, sloshing through the water, his cassock and trousers and shoes soaked to ruin. The throbbing of the line led him around a curve, a curve that should have been impossible, and whose existence was a testament to the torture the Earth had suffered when Doom had done battle here.

Did he know what the consequences would be?

Of course he did. This is the second phase of his project, whatever it is, and he planned this from the start. He planned the pain of the Earth.

What was he fighting?

I don't think we need to know that. I really don't.

The curve changed direction suddenly. At the point of the angle, Zargo fell forward, gasping. He plunged beneath the water, and for a few moments the bottom of the lakebed held him as if it were a drowning man. He fought free and broke the surface, choking and coughing.

There was something down there. A massive concentration of pain. A tumor in the energy of the Earth.

Zargo didn't have to wonder if he'd found the lodestone. Carefully, he reached down, leaning over until his hands were under the water again. He pictured his fingers going down and down and down through stone. He pictured them closing around the knot of agony.

He didn't know what he was doing.

He knew absolutely what to do. He knew without being taught. He knew what to do as he knew how to breathe.

He had the ball of pain in his hands. He pulled it up, extracted it from the earth, and when he knew it was time, he closed his fingers, and they wrapped around a sphere of stone. He straightened and lifted it from the water.

The sphere was the crimson of blood, of murder. It was streaked with the black of rot and the white of bone. The streaks moved across the stone like worms, writhing as they sank beneath the surface and rose again.

Zargo tried to turn his head to call out to Doom. He couldn't. The lodestone held his gaze and drew it in. He couldn't lower the stone. His arms were locked in place. His vision greyed at the edges, and then began to smolder. The stone grew. The red intensified. It expanded until he could see nothing else. The world was on fire, and he tried to scream, but he could not open his mouth.

And the rot and bone took form, and he saw that there was more than just red. There were things in the burning realm that enveloped him. There were shapes, and though they were distant, he knew they were colossal.

There was a city.

Though he could not scream, he could hear screams.

He knew where he was.

Our Father… Our Father… Our Father…

The prayer would not come. It was not allowed to come.

And then, with a blink, he was free. He was standing thigh-deep in water under a noon sun. There was nothing in his hands.

Doom was beside him. He had taken the lodestone. He held it in one titanium gauntlet. He was speaking in a language that Zargo hoped he would never understand. A violet aura sprang up from his palm and surrounded the lodestone.

"Well done," said Doom. "Now you know what you are capable of. There are four more to find."

"What was that?" Zargo croaked. "What did I see?"

"You know very well what you saw."

"Hell." Zargo wrapped his arms around himself and squeezed, trembling. "I saw Hell." The words were monsters. They were never meant to have a meaning that wasn't metaphorical. The encounter with their reality made his faith seem the thinnest, most brittle of mental constructs. He was scared to reach for it for succor in case it shattered at his touch. "Four more stones," he said. He looked up, pleading for the sun to help. It seemed dimmer than it had been a few minutes ago. The heat on his face was merely warm now. "I can't," Zargo said. "Please, your Excellency, I can't do this. Please don't make me. Let the stones lie. This is unholy."

Doom grabbed him by his collar and lifted him high. "*Unholy?*" he snarled. "What do you know about *unholy*? You know *nothing* about Hell. One glimpse and you cower like a beaten cur. You claim to be a priest? This is your chance to bring the fight to your enemy. Haven't you been fighting against Hell since you took up your vows? Isn't that what you would claim. Then *rejoice!*" Doom spat the word as if the idea of rejoicing was beneath contempt. "Now you will *really* make war on Hell."

"I can't..." Zargo choked.

"Why not? Are you afraid?"

"Yes!"

Doom brought Zargo closer, until the awful mask filled his vision. "Fear me more than Hell," he commanded.

And Zargo did.

Doom let go, and Zargo splashed into the lake. "Go and obey," said Doom. "Fulfill your destiny."

Fear of Doom drove Zargo forward. He was trapped between terrors, but Doom was the greater. Doom was here, and had the power. Zargo dreaded finding the other lodestones, but he knew he would not hold them long. Perhaps if he averted his gaze before he held the stones, he would be spared the visions.

He didn't think any further ahead than that. There was no room in his chest for the fear of consequences.

Zargo found the second ley line a half-hour later, and the lodestone another thirty minutes after that. His curiosity and the half-ashamed pleasure in the discovery of his new skills were gone. It took the power of his terror of Doom to make him reach down for the stone. He closed his eyes this time, and kept them closed, squeezing tight when he felt the awful shape in his hands again. Eternal seconds passed between the raising of the stone and Doom arriving to take it from him. He didn't see the crimson and the fire in that time. He didn't see the materializing city. But he did hear the screams, and the tolling of dark bells.

Zargo didn't open his eyes until Doom had left him again. When he did, he rubbed them, because the impression that the day was getting darker was stronger. He wanted to be wrong, because there were no clouds, and the sun was still Midsummer-high.

After the third stone, with the bells still ringing in his ears, there was no longer any doubt. The region of the ley line node was in twilight. The sky was clear and grey, the sun bright but powerless.

With the fourth stone, shutting his eyes didn't help any longer. The vistas of Hell filled his mind, and he was a single heartbeat from joining in the choir of screams when Doom claimed the prize.

The sky was dark when Zargo located the last of the lodestones. There were no stars, just a cone of blackness surrounding the blinding, heatless, comfortless light of the sun. Small tremors ran through the ground, sending ripples like gooseflesh through the water. Zargo heard thunder, and it came from beneath the lake.

God, forgive me for what I am about to do. Have mercy on us all. Have mercy on me.

The helicopter that had brought him here took off. It hovered fifty feet up.

On the arena's canted hill, Doom waited.

The stone was beneath a mound of lava. Zargo planted his feet on the jumble of rock, held his breath and called the stone to the surface. As soon as he held it, the vision assaulted him. He didn't even know if his eyes were closed. Fire and darkness and torment swallowed him up, and he was sure he was lost. He fell into the maw of eternity, and there would never be any forgiveness.

Then the stone was gone from his hands, and he could open his eyes, but Hell had followed him into the day that had become night. The tremors were violent, and knocked him off his feet. He clung to the lava mound, afraid the world would shake free of him. In the light of a sun that was cold as the moon's, geysers erupted from the lake. Spurs of rock heaved, accusing fingers pointing at the sky. Steam billowed in thick clouds across the land. The runes on the arena were glowing, and the hill and pylons were tilting more. Molten red spread from beneath it, and across the lake. Lava ridges melted again, some sinking beneath the hissing water, others rising higher on magmatic pillars.

Zargo stared, prey before a snake, at the red tide spreading his way. Doom seized him and jetted up, away from the explosions. The helicopter was climbing higher, above the roiling heat. Doom shot towards it. When he drew level, he tossed Zargo into the open passenger compartment door. Zargo scrabbled on the floor and grabbed on to a seat, clutching with iron desperation.

Doom hovered a moment longer outside the helicopter.

He carried a lead case strapped over his shoulder, holding the five lodestones. "You have done well," he said.

"Done well?" Zargo cried. "What have I done? What have we done?" The entire lakebed for miles around the arena was molten now. The pylons were disappearing beneath the lava. The Earth screamed, and he was the one who had reopened the wound.

"Do not think this is Hell taking hold on this corner of the world," said Doom. "This is the fury of Hell's defeat." He flew off.

"I wish I could believe you," Zargo whispered. He pulled the helicopter's door shut and managed to climb into a seat. The pilot banked the aircraft away from the arena and set a course for Doomstadt. Before long, the sky was growing lighter again, and a minute later they were flying through the light of late afternoon.

Zargo looked back, half-expecting to see a dome of night enclosing the site of the arena. It was day there too, but the smoke and steam of the eruptions rose in grey columns.

Did I make war on Hell or release it?

He wondered if there was a difference between the two.

Hell has seen me. It knows me now.

Freed of the immediate terror of Doom and damnation, he turned to the fear of consequences. *They* would come for him, and for Latveria. Exhausted, he closed his eyes, then jerked them open again when all he could see in his mind's eye was the city of flame and torture.

So he leaned forward, and stared ahead, watching for Doomstadt to appear, and wondering what price he would be made to pay for what he had done.

CHAPTER 18

Summer turned into fall as the construction of the Harrower got underway. Fall became winter, and as far as Helm was concerned they were still only feeling their way through the preliminary steps. The slow pace didn't bother her. It was reassuring. They had months to go before Walpurgis Night. There was no reason to rush, and every reason to work as if they were trying to build a cathedral in a minefield. Doom planned, considered and reconsidered every step, and Helm was glad. The power they were building up was terrifying.

In the laboratory, the elements of the Harrower took shape. The lodestones were encased in retractable spheres of warded silver and lead. Servo-arms suspended them at five equidistant points over the nanobot pool. Two enormous electro-occult batteries faced each other across the same pool. Their bases were squat, fifteen-foot-high helical columns, with spirals of alternating gold and obsidian. A cluster of power coils branched out of the columns like the limbs of dead trees. Week by week, month by month, the batteries stored a bit more power, fed by technology and sorcery.

The primary focus of the work at this stage was the lodestones. Helm's side of the project was to make the lodestones resonate more sympathetically to her and Doom's magic. She had to remind them that they were of the Earth, that the taint of Hell was not natural to them. There was a delicate balance to achieve. She had to pull the stones away from their link to Hell without snapping it. Doom, meanwhile, focused the link and weaponized it.

"What Zargo retrieved allows Hell to strike at our world," he had said on the day they began their work. "Our task is to reverse the direction of the attack."

The process was so slow it could hardly even be called incremental. Every night, Doom opened the observatory, and they took detailed astronomical and astrological readings. These informed the next twenty-four hours of adjustments to the lodestones and the pool. Helm continued to consult the archives. Doom went more rarely. "I know too much of what is there already," he told her. "Better for your eyes and your perspective to see the same knowledge, and see the other interpretations that might help us."

In the lab, hours would pass where Doom seemed to not move at all. He stood on a podium at the edge of the pool, midway between two of the spheres, his head down in concentration, his arms outstretched. Strange energies passed between him and the five spheres and the pool, where the particles of the demon stirred but were held captive to his will.

The work was absorbing. During the day, Helm lost herself in it. Each minute was a step forward to the completion of the

Harrower was a step closer to the end of fear. During the day, she was glad to be involved. She was glad that she had agreed to join Doom.

At night, she had nightmares. Every night.

She told herself they were the distant attack of Hell, trying to turn her away from creating the weapon that would free her of its grasp forever.

For at least a day every week, and often more, Doom had Zargo brought to the castle. His instinctive understanding of the spheres was valuable, though Helm could see the work took a toll on him. Every time she saw him, he looked more drained and more frightened.

The first snows fell in November, and they stayed. By the end of the first week of December, the roofs of Doomstadt were under more than a foot of accumulation. Zargo was at the castle again, and Doom decreed he would stay there through the next day. Zargo accepted his fate without protest, though Helm saw the fire in his eyes dim still further.

She went looking for him shortly before midnight. His role for the night was done. Doom was still in the lab, and Helm would join him at the witching hour when the observatory opened.

Zargo wasn't in the sleeping quarters that had been assigned to him. The laboratory tower's courtyard was on the rooftop of the south wing of the castle, and that was where Helm found him. Wrapped in his winter coat, he leaned against the parapet at the southern end of the courtyard, looking out across the scattered lights of Doomstadt. A north wind was blowing. Snow slithered in serpentine patterns across the paving stones. Helm folded her arms inside her sleeves and joined Zargo. It was the first time they had been alone together since the work began.

"You carry a burden," Helm said without preamble.

Zargo gave her a twisted smile. "No one has ever accused me of being subtle."

"I would be happy to listen."

Zargo brushed the snow off a crenellation. "Do you know what happened when I raised the lodestones?"

"I do."

"Did you expect that?"

"I didn't know what would happen. When I heard, I was concerned, but I don't think I can say I was surprised."

"I envy you."

Helm put a hand on his shoulder. "Don't overestimate my sanguinity. I have my fears, too. Many of them."

"Doom said we're at war with Hell," said Zargo.

"Yes," Helm said. "We are."

"Do you really believe we can win?"

She raised her eyebrows, "Isn't that a given of your faith?"

"I never expected to summon it into the here and now," Zargo snapped.

"Sorry," she said. "I shouldn't have been facetious. Yes, we're at war with Hell, and yes, I think we can win. I wouldn't be here otherwise."

Zargo looked at her skeptically. "You believe you're here of your own choice?" he asked.

"Yes," Helm said, though with a hesitation that she hoped Zargo hadn't noticed.

"Then you are fortunate among Latverians."

"You are more fortunate than you think," Helm countered,

growing irritated with Zargo's self-pity.

"I don't think I am at all, so being more fortunate wouldn't take much."

"I've seen what you can do," said Helm. "Your talent is enormous. Doom is forcing you to be true to yourself. So yes, you *are* fortunate."

Zargo shook his head. "I have no desire to be a geomancer."

"You mean you fear being one."

"All right, yes, I am afraid of that. I'm not keen on damnation. Are you?"

Helm ignored the jab. "You shouldn't be afraid of what you are. You'll damage yourself through denial."

"You mean by pretending to be something I'm not? You think my calling as a priest is a sham?"

"That isn't what I meant," said Helm.

"That's what it sounded like to me."

"Because you see a contradiction where none exists."

Laughter burst out of Zargo as a pained bark. "In my capacity as a geomancer, I brought Hell to Earth. I'd say that conflicts with my ecclesiastical duties. I'd say that conflicts pretty badly."

"And breaking Hell's hold on us isn't a worthy endeavor for a priest?"

"That's what we're doing here, is it?"

"It is."

He shook his head again. "That isn't for us to do."

"How do you know? How do you know that isn't your destiny?"

"I don't," Zargo said. "But in the name of God, I would be hugely surprised to discover that is the case."

"I think you would sleep easier if you conceded that was a possibility."

"What about you?" Zargo asked. "Do you have doubts? What if this goes wrong?"

Helm thought about her nightmares. "That would be disastrous," she said. "It would be awful even beyond what I'm too scared to imagine."

"Yet you're willing to take the risk."

"I think what we hope to accomplish is worth the risk."

"Is that for you to decide?" said Zargo. "If things go wrong, the effects will not be limited to the laboratory."

"You don't understand," Helm said softly. "Of course it isn't for me to decide. It was decided last Walpurgis Night. *My* decision was to do everything I could to make sure there is no disaster, and that the hopes of the project are realized."

"Then you really are lucky." Zargo stared hopelessly into the night. "All I have are my fears."

The Tower and Chariot tavern huddled in on itself at the dead end of Meister Lane in Old Town. It wore its five hundred years heavily. The steeply gabled roof seemed to press the first floor into the sidewalk. Its timbers were blackened, and its façade had darkened from white to dirty grey centuries back. The windows were narrow, their leaded glass barely translucent enough to let the glow of the pub's fireplace leak out onto the street. To a passer-by, the patrons were the vaguest of shadows. For the patron, the outside world was a dark smudge.

Inside, there were only a few tables in the center of the floor. Booths of dark oak lined the walls, and they were what the regulars of the Tower and Chariot wanted. The backs of the benches were so high, they might as well have been walls. Lanterns hung from the ceiling, and the illumination was so dim that each booth was a well of shadows.

The Tower and Chariot was a place for people to be left alone. There would be the occasional group of two or three, but most of the patrons drank on their own, in the dark, private embrace of their booths.

Dubrov had been coming to the Tower and Chariot for years. He left the castle rarely, sometimes not at all for weeks at a time. When he did, it was to come here, to escape to the warmth of shadows and brandy. For the space of a few hours, he answered to no one.

He'd been coming more frequently since Helm had been in the archives. Once a week at first. Since the attempted coup, every night.

He sat in a corner booth, the one furthest from the door, and was finishing his third brandy when a man sat down on the bench opposite. He brushed snow off the shoulders of his coat, but didn't pull his hood back. In the gloom of the booth, his face was invisible.

"I didn't invite you to sit," said Dubrov.

"If you don't like what I have to say, I'll pay for the rest of your drinks tonight."

Dubrov snorted. "That might cost you a bright sum."

The man shrugged. "The offer stands."

Dubrov downed the rest of his brandy. "I'd like another drink now," he said.

"Go ahead."

Dubrov leaned out from the booth and signaled the

bartender. The man leaned back on the bench, in even deeper shadow when the drink came. Dubrov took a sip, breathing deeply from the snifter. "All right," he said. "What do you want?"

"I know who you are, Vassily Dubrov."

"I guessed you did. Otherwise why come talk to me?"

"You are the archivist of Castle Doom," the man went on.

"Again, good for you." He wished the other would hurry up, make his point, and leave.

"You are also from a noble family."

"I *was*," said Dubrov.

"You *are*," the man insisted. "Your rank and your wealth were stolen from you. What was stolen must be restored."

"Is that so?" Dubrov said, carefully noncommittal. If this was an agent of the Guard sounding him out for sedition, he was not going to be baited.

The man was silent for a few moments. He drummed his fingers, then said, "You could earn a huge reward by turning me in."

Dubrov choked on his brandy. He hadn't heard the voice in years, not since the speaker's father had been king, but now he recognized it. He stared across the table. He still couldn't make out the man's features. "Prince ..." he began softly, then stopped himself.

"Yes," said Fortunov.

"Why do you think I won't call for the Guard?" Dubrov asked.

"Because I believe you are, in the end, faithful to the oath your family swore to my father. I believe your family was always faithful. The connection to Maria von Helm was no fault of theirs."

"Whatever happened in the past, I'm also not a fool," Dubrov said. He didn't contradict Fortunov. He didn't agree, either. He was curious, though, to see where this was going. "What's going to happen to me if I don't call for the Guard?"

"Nothing. I can promise you that no one recognized me. Only you know who I am."

Dubrov sat quietly, thinking. The safe move would be to start shouting. Anything else from this point on would, as far as Doom was concerned, be treason. He had come very close, in the archives, to doing something irrevocable. Then, though, he had thought that Doom was gone. He was on the knife edge again now, only this time Doom was on the throne.

What was stolen must be restored. That was a fantasy he had never allowed himself to entertain. It was too painful, because it was too impossible. He wasn't even sure why he was feeling tempted. Fortunov had been routed. Dubrov would have to be delusional even to listen to the prince.

But Helm still roamed the archives. Dubrov's little fiefdom, his sole point of pride, had been taken from him, and turned over to the woman whose betrayal had sealed his family's doom.

He had had a glimpse of a world without Doom, and the dream wouldn't let him go.

"What are you asking of me?" he said. His heart pounded. With that sentence, he had committed a crime.

"I want to know what Doom is up to."

Dubrov snorted. "Is that all?"

"That construction in the lakebed had to serve a larger

purpose. I know that he convinced Maria von Helm to leave her seclusion and go the castle."

"That he did," Dubrov said bitterly.

"Why, though? What is going on?"

"I have no idea," Dubrov said, feeling both disappointment and relief. He hadn't sinned too greatly yet.

This encounter might still lead to nothing at all, and he would be safe. Safe, but trapped in a spiral of humiliation and resentment.

"I think you could find out," said Fortunov. "I think you could learn what Doom is trying to do, and I think you could tell me."

"That would mean looking in places I have no business being. That would mean taking a huge risk. Why would I do that?"

"Because it is the right thing to do."

Dubrov laughed. "You'll have to do better than that. And don't promise me the restoration of my family rights again. You're a hunted man without an army. Your promises are empty."

Fortunov leaned forward. "They aren't empty, because they're the word of your rightful king. And they aren't empty, because with your help I can change things."

"How?"

"That was a defeat on the moat bridge, but I'm not alone. The more we know, the better we can see how to take Doom down. We came close on Midsummer Night."

"You think so?"

"I'm sure of it. You are too. I can see it in your face. You saw what Latveria might be again. You saw the chance of your injustices overturned. Can you turn away from that possibility? Can you?"

Dubrov hadn't realized his face had betrayed him. He would have to be very careful about that back at the castle. Thinking that, he realized he had made up his mind. "Go on," he said. "I'm listening."

His brandy sat by his hand, ignored.

CHAPTER 19

The December solstice. The night after a series of sleepless nights. The night Dubrov had prayed would not come.

His quarters were a monastic cell, a blister attached to the uppermost level of the archives. The small window in its door looked into the amphitheater of shelves. The furniture was a cot, a desk and a wooden chair. Dubrov sat on the edge of the bed, staring at the locked bottom drawer of the desk. He had to unlock that drawer. He had to take a small metal case from inside. He could have used what was in the case any night since Fortunov had given it to him, a week after their first encounter in the Tower and Chariot. But he'd been too frightened.

He couldn't put things off any longer. The solstice was too important. He had read and understood enough of the materials of the archives to know that Doom and Helm wouldn't let the opportunity of the night pass them by.

Dubrov took a shuddering breath and got off the bed. He opened the drawer, took out the case and placed it on the desk. He raised the lid. Inside was a pair of gloves. They were silvery grey. They looked as if they were made of an extremely fine wire mesh. The material was a weave of circuitry.

"You want me to do *what?*" he had asked Fortunov that second night in the Tower and Chariot. Fortunov had just opened the case briefly and shown him the gloves. Dubrov jerked back from the case as if it held a serpent.

Fortunov pushed the box forward, forcing Dubrov to take it and conceal it on the bench beside him. "It's perfectly safe," the prince said. "They're simple to operate. I promise you won't fail."

"That's not the point! What if I'm seen?"

"Have you come up with another way of learning what's going on in that laboratory?"

"No," said Dubrov.

"Well then," said Fortunov, sounding like the soul of reason, "where does that leave us? Something is happening in the lab. You don't have access, and you have no way of getting through its door. There are no windows in the tower. The only opening is the observatory dome, and that's only when it's being used. Am I right? Because that's what you've been telling me."

"You're right," said Dubrov.

"So there we are. The only way to see inside the lab is to climb the tower and look inside. As for being seen…" Fortunov shrugged. "I can't help you there. You'll have to choose your moment well. You'll think of something."

"No." Dubrov shook his head. "No. It's too risky. I'm sorry, but I've done all I can."

"You haven't done *anything*," Fortunov snarled. "You've

done nothing except tell me about all the ways you *can't* get me the information I need. I'm showing you how you *can* do something. And you will."

"I can't."

"If you can't, you're of no use to me."

"I'm sorry. I wish I could do more."

"You just need encouragement, Vassily. A bit of a spur. So here it is. If you're of no use, then I don't see why an anonymous someone, working anonymously for an anonymous me, shouldn't make an anonymous call to the Guard and tell them what you've been up to."

"You would be killing me," Dubrov whispered, horrified. The anonymity of the caller wouldn't matter. The tip would be investigated. And Fortunov would no doubt make certain that damning evidence would be found.

"I would be tidying up loose ends, and sentencing an oath breaker to death. I don't want to do this. I want to see you regain your family's wealth. So take the gloves. Put them to use." Fortunov leaned forward so Dubrov could see him smile. "They'll uphold you in more than this."

And so, on the night of the solstice, Dubrov stared at the gloves and tried to will his hands to put them on. His arms hung at his sides, motionless. He stood like that for a long time, wishing he had never set foot in the Tower and Chariot.

At midnight, an alarm sounded across the castle. Three short blasts of a klaxon and a fourth long one blared through every hall and over the open spaces. Dubrov's mouth dried. Everyone in the castle knew the meaning of that signal. The laboratory and its tower were not just off limits for the night. All eyes were to be turned away from the tower. To be caught looking at the tower was to be subject to summary execution.

The alarm jolted Dubrov into motion. The ban on the tower extended all the way to its deepest foundations. In half an hour the alarm would sound the final warning. He, and everyone else in the tower who had not received orders to the contrary from Doom, had until then to vacate the premises.

It was rare to hear this alarm. Dubrov could think of only a handful of times that it had sounded during his residency at the castle. He had always obeyed immediately, and completely, and fearfully. The fear this time was worse, because the siren meant he was right about the solstice, and that he had to act.

He put the gloves on, cursing Fortunov. The prince had used his resentment of Doom to lure him in, and now used his fear of Doom to force him to act against Doom. If he wasn't so frightened, he would have admired Fortunov's deployment of irony.

Dubrov left his cell and took the elevator up to the exit level from the tower. He stepped out into the courtyard. He looked up at the dome and saw that it was open, the telescope jutting out to the heavens.

You can do this.

No, I can't.

All right, then. You have to do this.

He approached the tower wall. There was no moon, and the shadows were deep. He could almost believe he was invisible. He also felt extremely vulnerable. He turned around, but there was no one to see him.

What about cameras? It didn't mean anything that he couldn't spot any.

It doesn't matter. I'm dead if I'm caught, and I'm dead if I don't try.

Fortunov was forcing him to roll the dice.

He brought his hands together, as the prince had told him, and flexed his fingers against each other. The gloves activated. An antigrav field surrounded him. He felt buoyant, as if a single leap could take him straight to the observatory dome.

You'll think you can fly, Fortunov had said. *You can't. The field's effect is neutral. It's designed to keep you from falling. If you lose your grip, it will hold you at your position. That's all.*

He placed his hands against the wall, and the grip was instantly secure. He began to pull himself up. He started slowly, following Fortunov's instructions to the letter. *Don't rush. Your instinct will be to strain against your body weight, but it won't be there. Take it easy until you're used to what the gloves do.*

Fortunov had been right. His first pull was still too hard, and he rose so fast he almost flipped and did a handstand against the wall. He steadied himself, and kept his movements gentle, as if he were feeling the texture of the wall rather than climbing. Now he moved up smoothly. The rhythm came naturally. Going up the tower was as easy as walking. It was almost exhilarating. He would have enjoyed himself if he hadn't been so frightened of discovery.

The shade of his terror changed as he drew closer to the dome. He was becoming more and more afraid of what he would see. When he was just a foot below the lip of the telescope's opening, he paused. He didn't want to know. He didn't care about his titles. He just wanted to climb down.

Turn around now, and Fortunov will see me dead.

If he was going to risk destruction either way, it might as well be to regain what had been taken from his family.

Helm is in there.

The promise of vengeance gave him the last spur he needed.

The second siren came. Three short blasts and a long one again. The time of warnings was over.

Shrouded by the night, Dubrov raised himself by the last foot and looked down into the lab.

The night of the solstice filled the lab. The longest dark of the year poured in through the dome, and the nanobot pool shimmered deep black, reflecting the gaze of the telescope. Doom circled the lab, double-checking the settings. The veil between life and death had thinned again. It was thinner even than it had been on Midsummer Night. He could almost tear it with a gesture. The separate components that together formed the Harrower were humming, electrically and etherically. Everything was ready.

He was ready. The months had passed too slowly. If he could have triggered the machine sooner, he would have, but the days of strength and weakness of the veil between worlds were beyond his control. So he remained disciplined. He anticipated the test with an eager calm. Today, that machine would make its first, tentative probe of Hell. The step was decisive, its implications enormous. Calm, then, was all the more crucial.

Helm was running her own checks. Between the two of them, there would be no error. Zargo was following Doom like a reluctant dog, because he had not been told to do anything else.

Satisfied with the state of the machinery, Doom stopped in front of the control platform in front of the pool. It was on a raised dais. It looked like a pulpit with two long, hollow appendages spreading out like wings, pointing toward the lodestones on either side.

"You're running the test, then?" Zargo asked.

"I am." Doom tapped the panel in his gauntlet and triggered the preliminary warning klaxon. Zargo winced at the sound. "And you have thirty minutes to leave the castle."

"I can go?" The priest seemed to be expecting a lethal price for that boon.

"Do you wish to stay?" Doom asked.

"No," Zargo said with feeling.

"You don't wish to see the blow we will deal against Hell?"

"I fear what will happen when you try."

"Exactly," said Doom. "That is why I am sending you away now. You have been useful, but your work here is done. Your fear would be a hindrance to me."

Zargo turned to go, then paused, wrestling with himself. Finally, he looked back at Doom. "Will you allow me to speak frankly?" he said.

"Go ahead."

"I wish you would allow my fear to be a hindrance. I fear a lot of things, and I think many of them *should* be feared. I worry about where your lack of fear might take us, your Excellency." He looked at Helm as she joined them. "I think you're still capable of being afraid, Maria."

"I am, but I won't let that stand in the way of our work," said Helm.

"I wish you would." He shook his head. "I'm wishing for

too many things that won't be. So I will pray for all of us."

"Twenty-nine minutes," said Doom. *Go and be useless somewhere else.*

Zargo hurried from the lab. Doom waited until the doors had sealed themselves and reactivated their wards. "Are you ready?" he asked Helm.

"I am."

She had admitted to Zargo that she was afraid, but Doom heard her eagerness too. He felt calm. This was only a test of the Harrower's potential. They were not mounting the attack tonight. The only victory to expect was the evidence that they were on the right track. He was as determined as he had been on Midsummer, but he felt none of that night's anticipation of defeat.

When the last warning klaxon sounded, Doom said, "Let us begin." With the equanimity of a glacier, he stepped onto the control platform and inserted his arms into the extensions of the pulpit. Control surfaces wrapped around him up to the elbow. Connections were made, and there was a *click* inside his skull. The synaptic link was established. His mind was the Harrower's. It would respond to his thoughts like an extension of his body.

Helm took up her position opposite him. There was a control station for her too, but its only component was a lever, the failsafe shut down if the Harrower went wrong.

The batteries powered up. Dark red light moved up and down their coils, somnolent in its rhythms, waiting to be stirred into a serpent's anger.

Doom began by adjusting the telescope's orientation. He aimed it at coordinates that put the center of its view outside the constellations. He focused on what appeared to be a void. There was a target there, one that could not be seen by any telescope, only detected by its effects. Two years ago, he had located a black hole in intergalactic space. It had devoured all that had been near it. It had made itself alone, a monstrous void within the void, the nothing that devours, distorting space-time with its eternal scream of hunger.

The nanobot pool mirrored the emptiness of the black hole at its center. The silver edges of the pool rippled with potential.

Doom increased the flow of power, chanting as he did so. The words he spoke were from the Third Rite of Keseph Maa. No human culture had dared claim their language for more than three thousand years. It was worse than a dead language. It was a murderous one. It could not be shaped for any meanings that did not summon harm from carnivore depths.

He retracted the shielding spheres from around the lodestones, which began to glow. The pool trembled, except for at its center, which was so dark and so still there was no sign that it still existed at all. The batteries sparked with crimson lighting. The strikes leapt from the batteries to all five lodestones.

The pool cried out. The shriek was high enough to make ears bleed, profound enough to wound the soul. The silver flowed upward and created a loop fifteen feet high, anchored on the edges of the black center's periphery.

His tongue blistered from the words, Doom finished the recital of the Keseph Maa. The center of the pool dropped away. It did more than reflect the black hole. It became a hole itself, falling down forever, tunneling through the real and life and the veil and death, all the way down to the infernal fire. Beneath the top of the loop, a sphere of energy took shape. It was barely an inch in diameter at first. In less than a minute, it was a yard wide, hovering fifteen feet above the conduit to Hell.

Like an animal stabbed in the gut, Hell responded to the conduit's strike. It rose to confront its tormentors. Doom heard the bells again, the ones that had tolled to welcome his fall to damnation. They were distant, but their tone was clear and growing louder. The trumpets blared both challenge and mourning. The walls of the laboratory turned red, then began to thin. Stonework lost its opacity. Its being slowly melted away, changing it first into a screen, and then a window, and then something less than a film. Soon the laboratory tower would be gone.

No, Doom thought. *This is wrong.* The Harrower was meant to reach into Hell without summoning it.

Mesmerized, he saw a horizon. With each hammering toll of the bells, the shapes on that horizon took on definition. The city was coming. It had him surrounded. Then it would close in.

Helm's lips were moving. She was shouting. Doom couldn't hear her over the thundering of the trumpets.

Was she screaming?

No, the screams were rising from below.

With an effort, Doom concentrated on Helm, and he heard her.

"*Shut it down!*" she was yelling. "*Shut it down!*"

Yes, he realized. *Shut it down.*

Why wasn't she stopping it? She had the lever.

She was trying. She was triggering the failsafe again and again. It wasn't working. The surge of power along the connections was too strong to be interrupted.

The city grew taller and closer.

Doom forced the shields back over the lodestones. The controls fought him. Doom fought harder. He countered the Third Rite of Keseph Maa with the Whispered Banishment.

The crimson light of Hell flickered. The outlines of the laboratory tower returned.

Helm joined Doom's Banishment with her own. The ringing of the bells became discordant, the fanfare cut off. Doom commanded the batteries to shut down. His will traveled the synaptic links of the controls, and it was stronger than the hold Hell had taken on the Harrower.

The batteries went dark, and so few seconds later, so did the light of Hell.

The laboratory became real and solid again. The loop over the nanobot pool collapsed with a splash, and the infinite hole vanished. The surface returned to a placid hole again.

Doom stepped down from the platform. "Interesting," he said. *That was more dangerous than we had expected. There is much to learn here.* He was as calm as he had been before the test. There had been a struggle, and he had won it. *Hell rose, and was banished. All is well.*

Helm was leaning on the edge of the pool, her face drained of blood. "*Interesting?*" she said. "Oh, yes, I suppose it was that. Yes, that was *interesting*." She shuddered.

"This was a trial," Doom said. "A way of learning the corrections we needed to make. I think it would have been more worrying if everything had gone as we wished. I would not have trusted that result."

"I suppose," Helm said weakly. She cleared her throat and straightened. "But if we had not been able to stop the machine…"

"We did," said Doom. "That is what matters."

"What *did* go wrong?" Helm asked.

"Clearly we need to work on the defenses," Doom said. He circled the pool, examining the wards on the lodestone shields. "There's a balance of energies that needs work. There is too much of a summoning in the mix."

"Very much agreed." Helm looked like she needed a strong drink.

Doom concentrated on the center of the pool, considering the creation of the conduit. "We need the sending to have more force." He thought about his fall toward Hell. That was the momentum he had to harness. "The sending also has to be more focused, so that what is summoned is only what we choose."

"Can we do that?"

"Of course we can. This was a success. The principles of the machine are sound. We are not starting over. This is simply a matter of adjustment."

"A simple matter," Helm echoed, aghast.

Doom dismissed her doubts. They were misplaced. She didn't see what he did. Hell and triumph were within his grasp.

Dubrov didn't know how he had descended from the tower. He didn't know how he had made it back to his cell. He didn't want to know anything at all. Curled into a corner of the room, arms around his knees, he rocked back and forth, sobbing.

Stop him. Stop him. Stop him.

The thought was the only thing that was real. There was nothing else that mattered.

Stop him. Stop him. Stop him.

CHAPTER 20

By the end of January, the last of Doomstadt's scars from the Midsummer Night were healed. Though the land where the arena had been still smoked, a crust of solid lava had formed, and the flows had never reached as far as the city. The damage to Vandorf Street and elsewhere was repaired, and, more importantly, life in the neighborhoods most badly hit by Fortunov's attempted coup was close to normal again. That was the reason Doom gave for the proclamation that February 5 would be a celebration of the movable feast that was Doom's Day. The celebration would give thanks for the liberation of Latveria from the threat of Fortunov, and the restoration of order.

"The reason for the celebrations must be believable," Doom told Helm as they readied the Harrower for another form of trial. "The people must commit to the event as naturally as they would on Walpurgis Night. The experiment will be pointless otherwise."

There would be street festivals and a night of dancing and

music in the public square. There would also be a masked ball at Castle Doom.

"Isn't that pushing things?" Helm asked. "I'm not familiar with your social habits, but am I wrong in thinking that you haven't hosted this sort of thing often?"

"I never have," said Doom. "The last to be held in the castle was three months before the fall of Vladimir, over fifteen years ago. They were common during the rest of his reign."

"Won't the guests be suspicious?"

"Not these guests. They will see it simply as their due." He smiled in contempt at the thought. "An event long delayed."

The night came and proved him right. The great hall of the castle was given over to the ball. The immense chandelier shone more brightly than it ever had during his rule. On a platform to the north of the hall, next to the base of the grand staircase, an orchestra played a processional as the aristocracy of Latveria flowed in. The staircase led to an encircling gallery.

The original tapestries and portraits that had adorned the room were long gone, expunged with all traces of the Fortunov family. On the ground floor was a series of fifteenth century tapestries Doom had discovered. They were by the same hands that had woven *The Lady and the Unicorn*, though the theme was darker. *The Triumph of the Chimera* showed a knight's march to inevitable destruction beneath the claws of the monster. The patron for whom the work had been made had ordered it destroyed as soon as he had seen it. Someone had rescued the tapestries and hidden them in a cave in western Latveria for half a millennium. If the nobles who now passed by its panels took any kind of warning from it, they gave no sign.

In the gallery, the paintings were all modern. They were of Doom's ancestors, on the side of his mother and his father. No portraits had been made of them during their lifetimes. Doom's memories of his parents were vague, but Boris' were sharp, and he had overseen the work of the artists. For the other generations, though, there were no memories at all, and barely any names. Their portraits were abstract representations, somber collisions of planes and angles and colors that evoked an emotion or an idea that Doom had commanded the artists associate with the people long buried, long forgotten, and in their lifetimes ignored or worse.

Doom stood at the head of the staircase, looking down at the arriving guests. *How many of you are here because you feared not to come? How many out of curiosity? And how many because this is your right?* He suspected varying mixtures of all three emotions ran through the crowd below him. *You do like to believe you had a choice, don't you?* In they came, giddy in their finery and masks. Their gaiety was both forced and unrestrained. Their talk was loud, their laughter even louder, as if they could dispel whatever doubts and anxieties they felt with their braying.

The people in the streets are mine. All of you would turn against me given a chance. Very well, then. Until you damn yourselves by trying to turn a dream of betrayal into reality, make yourselves useful. Be my guinea pigs.

No one came up the stairs and tried to greet him. There was not that kind of courage in the hall. The guests saw him as they entered. They tried to avert their gaze and focus on each other, hailing each new arrival with too much enthusiasm.

But they kept glancing his way, tiny little risks despite the fear they might be turned to stone.

Their costumes were rich, elaborate, fantastical. They came as birds in dresses with five-foot trains of feathers, as cats in diamond-lined acrobat uniforms, as wolves in tuxedoes, as demons in doublets and capes of the seventeenth century. Some had only domino masks. One must have been close to suffocating in a white owl head so huge, the eyeholes were in the neck. They were a menagerie of bedlam, waiting for night and drink to deliver them to the instincts they told themselves they had mastered.

A guard closed the huge, floor-to-ceiling bronze doors to the hall. He looked up at Doom and nodded. All the guests had arrived. Doom signaled the orchestra's conductor. She brought the processional to a climax, and then the music to a sudden silence. Conversation died with the music. The crowed looked up at Doom, as if for judgment.

Doom stared down at them for a few long seconds, stretching their anxiety. "You are welcome to your revels," he said coldly, and that was all he said. After several more seconds, the orchestra began a waltz. Doom turned his back on the nobility and walked to the shadows in a corner of the gallery. A door of iron and of oak so dark it was black waited for him to depart. He was going to the lab to see that the trial was ready to begin. He would come back, though. He despised the idea of a ball, but he had a use for this one. In order to keep Hell from rising, the Harrower needed to be stronger. It needed more psychic energy. It would get that now. The modified Harrower would gather the energy generated by celebratory gatherings. On Walpurgis Night, that power would be even greater than tonight. The ball would give Doom the chance to perform a test under controlled conditions. He needed to see the impact of the psychic gathering. He needed to know if there would be side effects.

Before he left, however, there was one more task to complete. At the precise moment he had appointed, Verlak came up the stairs with the one guest who was no doubt genuinely confused about why she had been invited. Verlak was in full dress uniform, her helmet of gold and steel tucked under her arm. Elsa Orloff was in a black jacket and slacks, her simple arrogance at odds with the ostentation on display on the floor of the hall.

"You have no mask," Doom said to Orloff.

She did not apologize. "I have strong feelings about masks, your Excellency," she said. "I believe that for some, they are a truth. For others, they are a lie. If I wore one, it would be a lie, and I won't do that."

Doom nodded in approval. "Well said, doctor."

"May I ask, your Excellency, why you asked that I attend this event?"

Doom grinned behind his mask. "This is not something you would normally seek out?"

Verlak snorted before her wife could answer. "Not likely," she said.

"You are here, doctor," said Doom, "because I want to make use of your expertise."

A servant appeared at Orloff's shoulder, carrying a tray. Sitting on a small cushion in the center of it was a tiny earpiece. Orloff looked a question at Verlak, who nodded.

"I may need to communicate with you this evening,"

Doom said. She didn't need to know that the device was also a field dampener. Verlak, the guards, and the castle staff were wearing them as well.

Orloff took the earpiece and inserted it. "My expertise?" she asked Doom.

"You will observe the participants in the ball," he said. "You will note and evaluate anything you consider abnormal in their behavior."

"I see." Her confusion had given way to interest.

"At some point, and I leave when to your judgment, you will leave the ball long enough to observe the festivities on Vandorf Street."

"You want me to use the people there as a control group?"

"Essentially, yes."

"Is there something in particular I should be looking for?"

"I will be best served if you are not being guided by any prejudice."

"I understand, your Excellency. Thank you for the honor of this task. I won't fail you."

"I'm sure you won't," said Doom, and left them.

"I can't operate the machine as you do," said Helm. She was on the control platform in the laboratory, eyeing the sheaths waiting for her arms. "The Harrower is linked to your will, not mine."

"This is only a partial activation," Doom reminded her. "You are gathering power, not deploying it. We need to see how strong the sending can be made to be."

"I know," said Helm. "But if it slips from my grasp…"

"It won't. I know how strong you are."

"Your mother thought she was in control, too."

"You are not repeating her mistake," said Doom. "This is a controlled test. Its purpose is to prevent us from making a mistake when it really matters."

Helm nodded. She knew all of this. She just needed to hear Doom say it again. It was one thing when Doom operated the Harrower. Helm's dreams the night before had been of the machine breaking free from her and summoning Hell.

She and Doom had learned from the first trial, and the Harrower had new components. Four enormous psychic funnels, suspended halfway up the height of the lab by a titanium framework, pointed in the cardinal directions. Cables linked them to the batteries, and to three ten-foot tuning forks. The forks stood like iron trees around the nanobot pool, forming the points of an equilateral triangle. They would tune the psychic energy to the frequency the Harrower needed to surgically pierce the infernal world.

"I'm still worried about the possibility of feedback," she said. "There's going to be so much amplification." Having the observation dome open for the telescope broke the integrity of the lab's occult shielding. Some leakage of the psychic feedback was inevitable.

"Monitoring of that danger is well in hand," said Doom. "We'll know its extent before dawn."

Orloff stopped halfway down the grand staircase.

"What is it?" Verlak asked.

Orloff pointed. "The musicians are being given earpieces too." A pair of servants were distributing them to the orchestra, which had paused after the third waltz.

"So they are," said Verlak.

Orloff raised an eyebrow at her. "Doom thinks he might have to be in urgent contact with a second flautist?"

"You know what you need to know," said Verlak, touching her arm. "If he wants you to wear the earpiece, wear it. His reason may not be the one he tells you. That doesn't matter. Whatever the reason is, it's a good one."

Orloff brushed the outside of the device with her fingers. It sat comfortably in her ear. She was barely aware of its presence. Its sound transparency was perfect. *What is this really for?*

They went down the stairs to the floor of the great hall. The music started up again, and they danced. Verlak was on duty, but Doom had ordered her to be a visible part of the celebrations.

"Am I a cover for you, or you for me?" Orloff asked her as they turned around the floor.

"Both. We watch for different things, but we watch."

After another dance they made their way to the periphery of the hall. Tables lined the walls, and servants handed out drinks. They had avoided mingling so far, and the costumed aristocrats showed no inclination to speak to them. *We're the help, too*, Orloff thought. She took a scotch and sipped it slowly next to one of the Chimera tapestries. She watched the dancers closely.

"I don't like these people," she said.

"Nest of vipers," said Verlak. Her lip curled. "Look at them. Parading about like the castle belongs to them."

Orloff blinked. "Do you hear a hum?"

"No… Wait… Maybe. I'm not sure."

Orloff wasn't sure any more either. If she had heard it, she didn't now. She went back to watching the dancers. *My expertise. What is it about neuroscience that might become relevant here?* For the next half-hour, she and Verlak kept up casual appearances by alternating a single dance, and then a ten-minute pause by the wall.

Orloff began to see a change in the revelers. The conversations were becoming louder, almost frantic in their gaiety. The dancing was faster and more jagged. Though the orchestra was playing faster too, it seemed to be in response to the dancing rather than the other way around. The waltz was spinning by at an unnatural pace, just this side of nightmare.

"What are you thinking?" Verlak asked.

"That I need to make that visit to Vandorf Street." She didn't understand what she was seeing, but there was something happening in the great hall. As she and Verlak made their way to the doors, she wondered if she was going to see a control group, as she had suggested to Doom, or if she was going to see the street festival also showing signs of *losing* control.

Maybe that's what he wants me to verify.

The word *contagion* drifted through her thoughts. *A contagion in my field?* She grew more and more uneasy.

She and Verlak hurried from the hall, out of the castle and over the rebuilt moat bridge. They descended into Vandorf Street, and Orloff breathed a sigh of relief. The road had been closed to traffic, and food tents had been set up near the reconstructed houses to distribute Doom's bounty. There was dancing, and the ale was flowing freely.

"Looks normal to me," Verlak said.

"It is," said Orloff. "Let's go back."

They had been gone less than half an hour when they returned to the ball, and the changes were pronounced. The talk was louder yet, almost shouting. The dancers jerked and whirled, spinning marionettes.

What's wrong with them? Because something was wrong. Her unease returned.

Orloff and Verlak mounted the staircase to the gallery. The balustrades of the stairs were lined with revelers. The snatches of dialogue Orloff caught as they passed sounded like gossip shot out by machine guns. Everyone was talking. No one was listening.

The gallery was still empty, as if the fact that Doom had stood here barred the path to the guests. Orloff leaned over the oaken railing and watched the vortex of the ball.

"They should be exhausted," Verlak said.

They should be, but they're not. The energy of the ball was growing, as if the movements of each dancer fueled greater exertions from the others. Laughter, hard and brittle, built up like a thunderhead. The celebration pulsed with the warring beats of migraine and fibrillating heart. "'It was a voluptuous scene, that masquerade,'" Orloff said.

"I beg your pardon?"

"'*The Masque of the Red Death*.'"

Verlak grunted. "I can't decide if they're celebrating like tomorrow is the end of the world, or they're drunk on the victory of the castle hosting a ball again."

"Both, maybe," said Orloff. "They are drunk, but this a lot more than inebriation."

The huge doors opened again, and Doom entered the hall. Orloff was surprised to see him on the first floor. She shared a look with Verlak, who seemed just as startled. "He isn't going to... *mingle*, is he?" Orloff asked in disbelief.

"If he does, the sun is going to rise in the west tomorrow," said Verlak. "This is more of his experiment, whatever it is. You're providing data for him."

Is this right, what I'm doing? Once the question arose, she couldn't put it aside.

What's the alternative? Leave? Shout for everything to stop?

The options felt as absurd as trying to flout Doom's will.

Is this right? I don't know.

A weak answer, and the one she would have to live with.

From the moment Doom arrived, the energy in the hall climbed vertiginously. Orloff's arms prickled with gooseflesh. The dance became frenzied. He moved up and down the room, and the reactions to his passage were all spikes of emotion, whether fear or desperate sycophancy. Doom was the center of the ball, no matter where he was in the room. Every masked celebrant reacted to his presence, his proximity or his distance.

"He holds 'illimitable dominion over all,'" Orloff quoted Poe again, awed by the power Doom wielded by the simple act of *being*.

The dances were beyond wild now. The music no longer resembled a waltz. It was just a hammering stab of strings, mimicking the seizure-like spasms of the spinning couples.

"I'd be wondering if I should be arranging for ambulances," Verlak said, "if I thought Doom cared about any of these people."

"They might need them yet," Orloff said, only half paying attention. New symptoms were presenting in the people

Doom went closest to. He had come to the staircase now and was climbing it slowly, a majesty of armor and mask as weighty as death among the crowd of meaningless costumes. Orloff had a better view of the revelers on the stairs, and she saw the symptoms clearly in them. A woman in a dog mask and a man wearing a moon face tried to talk to Doom. All they got out, during the brief second he paused to look at them, was a shouted gabble of "Your Excellency your Excellency your Excellency." When Doom left them, the woman's arms dropped limp. Even though Orloff couldn't see her face, she seemed vague, making quarter turns where she stood, back and forth, purposeless. Her companion started swatting at phantoms in the air. He was breathing hard and whining anxiously. There were others near them behaving similarly.

Doom reached the top of the stairs and turned to look down at the ball. He stayed there, motionless, the presiding shadow, as the celebration worked itself to higher and higher pitches of hysteria.

Orloff wondered if she was meant to speak to him and say what she was observing. She took half a step, but Verlak took her arm.

"No. He'll call you when he wants you."

The dance went on, and on, and on. The energy built higher and higher. Orloff halfexpected a mass case of spontaneous human combustion. The maelstrom swallowed the hours in its fury. Then Doom cocked his head slightly, as if engaged in a private conversation. He looked up, and the orchestra stopped.

The dancers froze.

The castle's tower bells struck the hour of two. The reverberations of the bells faded away, leaving the silence of the grave in the hall. The assembled nobility of Latveria stared at the king, panting like dogs.

"The ball is finished," Doom announced. "Remove your masks and leave."

All did as he commanded.

Orloff hurried down the stairs to observe the guests more closely as they left. They were drenched in sweat and haggard with exhaustion. They spoke with each other normally, though. They sounded like any other crowd after a social event that had been, they thought, satisfactory. Orloff had expected at least a few of them to collapse before they even made it to the doors. No one did. The nobility departed, their voices fading away. It was as if there had been nothing abnormal about the ball.

Weak with relief, Orloff rejoined Doom and Verlak at the head of the stairs.

"What are your conclusions, doctor?" Doom asked.

"The people in this room were clearly under some form of influence."

"And those on Vandorf Street?"

"No. The effect was limited to the castle. Possibly to this room." She glanced at the musicians putting away their instruments. "It was also limited to the guests."

"Quite," said Doom. "You may, incidentally, remove your earpiece now."

Orloff had forgotten she was wearing it. She took it out just as a servant arrived to retrieve it from her.

"I can't say *what* was affecting the dancers," Orloff

continued. "But I was seeing increasing cognitive impairment as the night wore on. There was a significant loss of coherence and precise motor function. Everyone was getting energy from somewhere." She paused. "Those of us wearing earpieces, though, were not affected." She waited.

"Quite," said Doom.

Don't push. "I have no definite conclusions," Orloff said carefully. "None of what I saw made any medical sense."

"There is much in the world that does not," said Doom. "Yet it exists. I am not troubled by your lack of conclusions, doctor. How did Latveria's glorious nobility seem to you after the ball? Was there any sign of lasting impairment?"

"I would have to run tests to be certain."

"Which I'm sure they would be delighted to let you do," Verlak put in.

"No doubt. At a glance, though, there seemed to be no lingering effects. It surprises me to say this, but I think it's likely none of them will wake in the morning with anything worse than a hangover."

Doom nodded. "Good," he said.

Orloff found it hard to believe he was satisfied that the welfare of his guests was assured. She had the impression she had been watching a sideshow while the main event went on elsewhere.

"You are a valuable resource, Doctor Orloff," Doom continued.

"If I may…" said Orloff.

"Yes?"

"You read my articles, so you know that I'm interested in transmittable neurological effects. What I saw tonight…"

"I thought it would intrigue you. Circumstances do not permit me telling you more at this time. However, I think we will work more closely in the future."

Doom left them. Orloff remained still after he had passed through the gallery exit. After a minute, Verlak took her hand.

"What just happened?" Orloff whispered to her wife.

"That was your destiny being decided."

In the laboratory, Helm stepped carefully away from the control of the Harrower and sat down on a bench next to the wall. She took deep, slow breaths, feeling herself grow calm. She smiled in spite of herself.

Doom finished his inspection of the components, then strode over to where she rested.

"That went well," she said.

"It did. The machine is intact. I see no sign of ruptures of any kind."

"It felt right," said Helm. "It felt good."

"How far did you take the build-up?"

"To the limit."

"Excellent. The psychic feedback was minimal and contained. Those wearing field dampeners were not affected at all."

"And we were feeding on the psychic energy of the entire castle?" Helm asked.

"We were, as on Walpurgis Night we shall feed on the entire city, in the confidence that we will be in complete control of the Harrower and its effects. It will be strong enough to hold back Hell."

Helm leaned back, exhausted. She pictured the unwitting test subjects Doom had brought into the castle. "Do you know," she said, "I've often wondered why you allowed so many families of the old regime to linger, pretending to themselves that they still matter."

"Now you know. The aristocracy has its uses, and the advantage of being disposable."

Doom turned back to the Harrower. "Our work is not yet done," he said. "But our time is."

CHAPTER 21

Stop him. Stop him.

The command, the desperate need, filled Dubrov's existence. It was all he thought about during the day, except when he was using all his terrified concentration to appear normal. At night, when he no longer had to maintain a façade, the command took over completely. His nightmares were an endless reliving of what he had seen in the laboratory.

He considered himself lucky in only one respect. Doom had not sent for him once in weeks, not since the night of the solstice, nor come to the archives. The lab held Doom's attention. If Dubrov had faced Doom, he would have given himself away. He didn't have to interact with Helm when she came to the archives, and that was a blessing too. She was just as responsible as Doom for bringing about the end of the world.

Stop him. Stop him.

Nothing else mattered. This was the most important task of his existence. There was even someone who was waiting for Dubrov to bring news of Doom's project. There was something precise Dubrov had to do. But he couldn't bring himself to do it. He was too frightened to do *anything*. He moved through his days like a zombie, curled into a quivering ball at night, and he did nothing. If he put a step wrong, if his thoughts made him sigh, Doom would see, and Doom would know. Through the last days of December and January, Dubrov tried to withdraw into a numb darkness. If the world faded from him entirely, then everything would be gone, including the need to act.

The night of the masked ball, he failed once and for all to make that retreat. Something thrummed through the castle, and he knew that the machine had been activated again. He cowered in his cell, back against the wall, sweat pouring down his face and neck, soaking his clothes. His heart beat like a rattling train. The terror built up until he screamed himself hoarse. The terror ended abruptly at two in the morning. He collapsed, his strings cut.

Stop him. Stop him.

He had been frozen, but time had marched on. Hell was coming, and soon.

When?

Dubrov took his first action the next day. As he pushed the cart through the aisles, replacing the latest documents and books that Helm had consulted, he looked at them himself, flipping through with the hope of finding clues as to when the disaster would come.

He found that Helm was interested in dates too. She had examined a number of ancient astrological almanacs. In one of them, she had forgotten a scrap of paper. Dubrov couldn't understand her scrawl of runes, but she had marked the page in the almanac that dealt with April 30.

"Walpurgis Night," Dubrov whispered, then clapped his hand over his mouth. Motionless, he imagined his words scuttling up the bowl of the archives and up the tower to the laboratory.

He hears everything.

That night, he took his second action. Despite his terror, despite his certainty that he would be caught, he went out to drink at the Tower and Chariot. Though it took a Herculean effort to do even that, and then to act like all was normal and that he wasn't checking to see if he was followed, Fortunov did not appear. Dubrov returned to the castle convinced that he would not have the strength to try again. But two nights later, the thought of what would happen if he did nothing was so awful that he tried again. Still no Fortunov.

Dubrov wept. He despaired. Three nights later, he tried once more. This time, two hours and four brandies after he'd sat down in his booth, Fortunov arrived.

"I had expected to hear from you long before this," the prince said. "You tried my patience. I thought you were hiding, and was about to teach you a lesson."

"I've been here three nights in a row."

"I know. I have been watching to see that you were not hoping to betray me. And your presence now happens only after weeks of absence."

"I was too frightened."

"Of Doom? Then you weren't scared enough about what I might do to you."

Dubrov suddenly saw Fortunov's threat for the posturing

it was. The prince might still be able to destroy someone as insignificant as Dubrov, and what a sad triumph that would be. Fortunov was not the power he wanted others to think he was. Dubrov prayed that he was still just strong enough to make the crucial difference now. "I was scared of you," Dubrov said, bolstered by drink, "but I don't care about what you can do to me any more." He leaned forward. "You have to stop him. I don't know if I can help you at all, but you have to stop him. Even if you die. Nothing else matters."

Dubrov couldn't see Fortunov's face inside its hood. He couldn't tell if his appeal was making an impression.

"What are you talking about?" Fortunov asked. "What is he doing?"

"He's raising Hell."

"That's nothing new. He…" Fortunov paused. "You mean that literally," he said quietly.

Dubrov nodded. He sat back, ready to weep again. The prince was listening. There might be hope.

"Why would he do that?" Fortunov asked. "What can he possibly hope to gain?"

"Why does he do anything?" Dubrov shot back. "His reasons are his own, but I know what I saw."

"Tell me," said Fortunov. "Tell me everything."

Dubrov told him. He relived the nightmare on the tower so that Fortunov would understand. If he felt a tenth of the fear Dubrov did, then that would feel like a victory.

When Dubrov finished speaking, Fortunov was quiet for a very long time.

Zargo's eyes snapped open. He rolled over in bed and fumbled for his watch on the bedside table. The green digits told him that it was not quite three in the morning. He sighed. There would be no more sleep tonight, even less than the night before.

He surrendered to the insomnia, got out of bed and dressed. He wondered if he was being punished for having slept relatively well when he had been working with Doom and Helm.

That is the least of my sins. And this is the least of my penance.

He left the rectory and went down the stairs to the church. Moonlight through the stained glass windows gave him just enough light to move through the familiar space of the nave to the altar, where he lit the candles and knelt.

Fortunov's voice came out of the dark. "You still have the audacity to pray?"

Zargo stood up, interested to note that he was neither surprised nor startled by Fortunov's presence. *Did I sense he would be here? Or am I beyond caring?*

Fortunov stepped into the circle of illumination thrown out by the candles. He looked different. He was angry, but something had drained the arrogance from him. He was frightened. Zargo had never seen fear in the prince.

"I am *trying* to pray," Zargo said. "That is something that should come naturally to a priest, don't you think? It hasn't, lately."

"You haven't been to the castle lately, either."

"No. My work there is done, thank God."

"Thank God? *Thank God?*" Fortunov took a step forward, his hands clenched into trembling fists. "How *dare* you speak those words? I know what you've been doing up there."

Fortunov looked up at the vaults of the church. "The very stones of Saint Peter should fall and crush you for what you've done." He jabbed a finger into Zargo's chest, making him stumble. "How can you defile that cassock by wearing it after what you've done?"

"What have I done?" Zargo asked, fearing the answer.

"You summon Hell and then ask that question?"

"Summon… Has it happened?" He turned to the windows, expecting the moonlight to have turned red.

"Not yet," said Fortunov. "Are you disappointed?"

"No!" Zargo exclaimed. "No! It's not supposed to happen at all."

"But it already has, almost. And it clearly will, if Doom finishes his work."

"No," Zargo said again. "That's not what he's trying to do at all."

"How do you know? Because he told you? Or because you understood what you were doing?"

I didn't understand, not really.

I don't think Doom lies, but I think you do, Prince Rudolfo.

But if Doom doesn't lie, he does withhold the truth, doesn't he?

The thoughts and the guilt and the confusion tumbled through Zargo's mind. He despised Fortunov, yet the man's anger was hitting home. All Zargo's wounds of shame bled anew.

"What were you thinking?" Fortunov demanded.

Before Zargo could catch himself, he said, "I was doing what Doom commanded."

Fortunov gave him a look of frigid contempt. "You were only following orders," he said quietly.

Zargo rounded on him, furious at himself and at the prince's hypocrisy. "I won't take lessons in morality from you! How many thousands would have died if Doom hadn't stopped the flood you unleashed?"

"How many brave sons and daughters of Latveria did he kill with it?" Fortunov returned.

"That isn't even good sophistry," said Zargo. "But that does tell me how much you value civilian life."

"The flood was never intended to kill civilians."

"That makes it all right, then."

"Is this how you justify yourself?" said Fortunov, frustrated. "By confronting me with my sins? I have done what I have done. *So have you.* You have helped bring Hell to Latveria, and I won't believe that you knew nothing about what you were doing."

Zargo didn't answer.

"How could you have done this?" Fortunov asked with genuine pain. "You, a priest."

Zargo winced. "I don't know if I am one any longer."

"Look at what Doom has done to you. How could you not wish his overthrow?"

Zargo looked at the crucifix on the altar for help. The icon was silent. It gave him no comfort. He sighed. He was tired of thinking, tired of doubting, tired of being afraid. Tired of the blows that would not stop coming. "I don't even know what I wish any more," he said. "My wishes do not matter."

"Your actions do," said Fortunov. "Atone for them. Get me into the castle."

Zargo shook his head.

"You cannot refuse." Fortunov seemed astounded that

Zargo could even consider saying no. "This is your duty as a priest."

"What did I just say?" Zargo asked.

"If you don't…"

Zargo raised his hand, interrupting Fortunov's empty threat. "I'll tell you why I'm not going to help you. I don't know what the things I did will lead to. I am afraid of what Doom is doing. That's why I was sent away. I'm terrified. But there's one thing I *do* know. Doom has nothing but hatred for Hell. He isn't seeking to raise it. Are there dangers in his project? Terrible ones? Clearly. Can we prevent them? How? By stopping him? How? When? There's too much we don't know. I won't help you bring another, worse disaster on Latveria."

Fortunov glared. "I should have expected that from someone who betrayed his vows. You won't even admit to yourself that you've been working to destroy our country."

The words stung. Fortunov wouldn't know a moral high ground if he was airlifted to it, but the words stung all the same. Zargo responded defensively. "I *did* expect this from someone whose pole star is his own power and glory. Your concern for Latveria is a veil, and it's a pretty transparent one."

To Zargo's surprise, Fortunov didn't disagree. "Maybe," he said softly. "I always believed that what I wanted and what was best for Latveria were the same thing. I still believe that. What I want no longer matters, though. Doom has to be stopped. I will stop him if I die in the attempt. At least I'll know I died doing the right thing. That's more than you'll be able to say. I should feel sorry for you." He walked away, out of the candlelight. From the darkness he called back, "Farewell, priest. If your sins let you sleep, then I will too."

The prince's footsteps faded. There was the sound of the church door opening and closing, then silence.

Zargo started to kneel again, then changed his mind. He blew out the candles and headed back to the vestry to sit and wait for the dawn.

Doom would want to know about this visit.

No. Zargo had done what Doom expected of him, and his reward had been to no longer know who he was, and whether anything he did was for good or ill. The wounds of shame bled and bled and bled. Fortunov and Doom deserved each other. He would keep his silence and let them damn themselves. Anything else he did would only further his own damnation.

CHAPTER 22

April 30. The afternoon before Walpurgis Night. The Harrower was complete.

The final adjustments done, the last of the wards inscribed, Doom and Helm stepped away from the machines. Doom surveyed the laboratory with satisfaction. *This is my sword. This is the weapon of my mother's deliverance.* The Harrower filled the lab, a conglomeration of monolithic devices and webs of interconnections that did not look like a coherent whole. Yet every time it was active, either partly or at the somnolent level Doom permitted it when he activated the entire system, it created a sense of completeness. The transformation was a psychic one, but no less real than the move from the tangle of the human nervous system to the sentient being it powered.

Helm seemed limp, her energy suddenly drained from her. She moved unsteadily out of the lab, and Doom followed her outside the tower. She stopped in the center of the courtyard and turned her face to the sun. Arms spread, palms up, she breathed deeply, seeking strength from nature. Doom waited until she lowered her arms, then joined her. She looked up at him, her face as drawn as it had been before she came outside.

"The night of our triumph is at hand," said Doom. "Why do you look defeated?"

"Because this is the hour of the triumph of my doubts," said Helm.

"You should have left them in your cave. That was the last chance to have them."

"I know." Her smile was bitter and wry. "Yet they followed me, and they're having their moment. As long as there was work to do on the Harrower, the time of its activation was put off."

"It was always going to be tonight."

"Oh, I know that, but my fears are liars. If we never finished it, we would never have to risk using it."

The idea was nonsensical for Doom. The march from the last Walpurgis Night to this one had been maddeningly slow. Helm had her own critical investment in the Harrower being finished and being successful. She should have been eager for the moment he unleashed it. "Tonight, we strike our blow," he said. "Tonight will be an end to your fears."

"Then they're at their strongest before they die," said Helm.

Fortunov thought of the passage as the last tunnel. It was barely a tunnel, more of a zigzagging crack in the bedrock. But it was the last. The last one discovered, the last one worked on, the last resort. It was the most preciously guarded secret of the entire network. If everything else failed, the last tunnel offered the chance of one more roll of the dice, one more stab of the blade at the heart of Doom's power.

The passage was separate from the sewers and disused mines beneath Doomstadt. It was accessible only through the basement of an abandoned house on the east side of Old Town. The split in the earth in the cellar floor was the one part of the passage that Fortunov had commanded to be improved. It was a descent, in stages, that went down for several hundred feet. He had had knotted ropes put in to make the climb a little less dangerous. After the descent, the passage was more or less horizontal. Other fissures led off from it, all to dead ends. The main passage was barely wide enough for one person at a time to squeeze through. It changed direction so many times that it didn't seem to go anywhere at all. When Fortunov had explored it, he had come close to giving up. A hunch had kept him going forward, and he had found a miracle.

Fortunov led Rumyanova and their squad through the last tunnel toward the miracle. They began their descent in the pre-dawn hours of April 30. Night had fallen by the time they emerged. Rumyanova gasped when she realized where they were.

"And all this time," she said, "Doom has had no idea."

"It seems fated, doesn't it?" said Fortunov.

The last tunnel had taken them west, below the moat around Castle Doom, and brought them to a ledge in the castle mount twenty feet above the water.

"Doom can't know every geological fracture," said Fortunov. "Until tonight, it didn't matter." To get into the castle from here, he needed help from the inside.

"Where to now?" Rumyanova asked. "This ledge doesn't extend far."

"It extends far enough," said Fortunov. He inched his way

along it, balancing carefully so the weapon on his back didn't pull him over. Just before the ledge disappeared into the cliff wall, he stopped. He uncoiled the length of rope from around his waist. There was a metallic case at its end. When he tapped it, an articulated grappling hook extended, its claws flexing like a spider's legs. He looked up, straining to see in the darkness. Finally, he made out the outline of an effluent pipe ten feet up. He spun the rope, built up momentum and threw. On the fourth attempt, he got the A.I.M.-manufactured hook inside the pipe. Its telescoping claw shot out wider, gripping the interior. Sensors determined how far the hook was from the edge, and how much space there was for someone to enter. The hook scrabbled forward five feet, then stopped again.

Fortunov pulled on the rope. It was secure. He climbed up and crawled inside the pipe. He grabbed the hook, retracted its claws, moved past the device, then opened it again. He jerked the rope to signal Rumyanova.

One by one, the squad climbed up into the pipe. It was four feet in diameter. They were going to have to crawl. It felt spacious after the last tunnel.

Fortunov touched his forehead, turning on the light strip he wore. It was a relief to be able to see again.

Rumyanova rapped the pipe. "This is dry," she said. "Completely."

"Disused," said Fortunov.

"Then how do you know we can even get into the castle this way? It might have been blocked off decades ago."

"It has been."

"Then why are we here?"

"Because the person who knows it's been blocked also knows that we're in it, and will open the way for us."

For the first time since his father was deposed, Fortunov was going to be *inside* the castle. *I am striking at you from your very heart, Doom.* He grinned fiercely.

Behind the throne room of Castle Doom, reached by a single door that opened to no one except Doom, was the Garden of Absence. It was a small green space, surrounded on all sides by windowless walls. Here, Doom's privacy was absolute.

A single yew tree reigned over the center of a low, grassy mound. Beneath the twisting branches were two seven-foot obelisks of black, polished granite. The monuments were featureless. There was nothing to indicate what they commemorated. There was no need. They were for the eyes of Doom alone.

Doom stopped before the left-hand obelisk. "Mother," he said.

Her remains were not here. Nor did his father rest beneath the right-hand stone. The blank faces of the obelisks reflected the absence of the dead. The bodies of his parents had been destroyed when he was a small child. There were no relics to find, no traces of their existence to preserve. Doom had created the Garden of Absence as a tribute, a place for meditation, and a physical incarnation of the total erasure of two human beings.

It was an erasure that had led to the fall of a king and the transformation of a country.

"Tonight, Mother, I will find you," Doom said. "I will free you."

He let the promise hang in the evening air for a time. Then he said, "Tonight, I will unleash a power that will reach down into Hell. It will scrape the Infernal. It will tear the damned from its grasp. It will find you, Mother. If I could tell you of this kind of power, what would you think? If you could use it, would you?" He looked up through the branches of the yew at the stars coming out in the deepening violet of the sky. In the streets of Doomstadt, the Walpurgis Night celebrations would just be starting, igniting the first embers of the psychic fire he would seize.

"The power you chose in desperation escaped your control. It killed every child in your village. That was not your crime, Mother. Mephisto betrayed you. He cursed you with something you could not wield. You and those children were both his victims."

He paused again. "I know what could happen if the Harrower slips its leash. The crime *will* be mine, because I took this power, and I chose to wield it, and the horror I will release will be ten thousand times yours. But it will not happen. I have made sure of that. Tonight marks the end of my failure and the end of your penance."

Did he have any doubts?

No. He did not. The doubts had been there on Midsummer Night, in the duel Mephisto had created to make Doom lose faith in himself year after year. About the Harrower, he had never had any doubt.

There. He had marked the moment. He had made his promise. It was time to begin.

Dubrov pulled the case out from under his cot, opened it, and assembled the weapon. Fortunov was right. It went together easily. Any fool could do it. In Dubrov's mind's eye, he saw armies of chaos wielding these guns, and he shuddered.

Don't think about that. How A.I.M. distributes death is not our problem. If this weapon helps save Latveria from Hell, then that's all that matters.

The pistol and trigger clicked into place on one end of the barrel. The stock went on next, and that was it. A green line lit up along the barrel. The gun was ready to fire. The whole thing was only eighteen inches long. It was hard to believe that it was powerful enough to do what Fortunov had promised it would.

Dubrov checked his watch. He was about to find out.

He moved his cot away from the exterior wall of his cell. He had gone through the old schematics of the castle's plumbing. The work went back centuries, and had been overhauled many times. Some of the older pipes had not been removed. They had simply been disconnected from the rebuilt systems. In one of them, Fortunov and his team were crawling. Dubrov had to bring them into the castle proper.

He pulled the trigger. An intense green beam shot out and burned into the wall.

As a child, Dubrov had sometimes amused himself in the summer by taking discarded documents onto the cobbled drive in front of his parents' mansion and using a magnifying glass to burn holes in them. One time, he had held the concentrated dot of sunlight on the center of a sheet for longer than usual. The brown aura of the burn had spread gradually at first, like he was used to. Suddenly, the hole widened. He stared, unable to understand what he was seeing, as the entire center of the sheet disappeared. Then the flames licked up.

That old memory, forgotten for decades, returned. For a moment, he was ten years old again, as the wall disintegrated around the beam in exactly the way the paper had burned. He held the trigger down for less than five seconds, and already there was a perfectly circular hole six feet wide.

Dubrov released the trigger. There was a faint smell of ozone in the cell. He took the headband light Fortunov had given him, turned it on and looked through the hole. On the other side were massive pipes and conduits. He went back into the cell. Fortunov had given him an earpiece too, which he put in now. Then he put the climbing gloves on again. With the disintegrator strapped over his shoulder, he held his breath and leapt out of the cell.

The gloves justified his faith again. The jump was more like walking across empty air. He crossed a six-foot gap, and the gloves latched onto the pipe across from him.

"Four down," he muttered to himself. He climbed downwards into a huge vault of blackness within the castle foundations. He felt like an insect clambering down the relics of giants. The first two pipes, easily ten feet in diameter, vibrated with the rush of water inside them. The next one was quiet, and so was the fourth. There he waited, caught between boredom and fear.

He had been there maybe half an hour when his earpiece began to ping. Fortunov was within fifty feet of the device's twin. The transmission was so narrow, it was almost impossible for any scan to pick up the signal passing between the two.

Cautiously, Dubrov took his right hand away from the pipe. His left held him in place. He felt perfectly steady. He raised the disintegrator and seared a long hole open in the upper portion of the pipe.

Fortunov appeared in the gap a few minutes later. "How far?" he whispered.

Dubrov pointed up. Light shone from the interior of his cell, less than fifty feet away. "Does everyone have gloves?" he said.

"Do you have any idea how much those cost?" Fortunov hissed.

"I'm sorry, I didn't realize…"

Fortunov produced a rope and a flexing grappling hook. Dubrov caught his toss.

"Take the hook up to the cell," he said. "Fix it anywhere. We'll do the rest."

Five minutes later, the entire team was in his cell.

"Stop him," said Dubrov. Speaking against Doom felt even more momentous than getting the rebels into the archives. He trembled between terror and excitement. "Stop him!" he said again.

"We will," Fortunov promised. "And you're coming with us."

"Five minutes to tower warning," the security center operator announced.

Verlak watched the banks of surveillance screens from her command post. In just over half an hour, all the cameras would be turned away from the laboratory tower again. Until that moment came, she had doubled surveillance over the castle. Drones flew over walls, scanning the entire exterior for any unauthorized movement. The castle's curfew had begun at sunset. There should be no one outside. Only servo-guards were on the ramparts.

Doom had not told Verlak what he and Helm had been working on, but she sensed the culmination had arrived. It was Walpurgis Night, Doom was cloistered in the laboratory, and the tower was about to become forbidden to sight again. The air vibrated with anticipation. Something huge was in motion. She would do everything in her power to see that her king achieved his goal.

The views across the screens were quiet. Nothing moved that wasn't supposed to.

"Tower warning," said the operator. The klaxons sounded their three short and one long blast.

Another fifteen minutes went past. No one left the castle. Nothing popped up on the screens. Nothing triggered a sensor. The night was quiet.

Verlak's shoulders grew tense. Her body was waiting for an explosion. The calm was a lie.

Ten minutes before the screens showing the exterior of the laboratory went blank, one of the technicians jerked with surprise in his seat. A red light flashed on his console.

"What is it?" Verlak asked.

"There's a rupture in one of the effluent discharge pipes, captain." He shook his head at the display. "It's not even used any more."

"Then nothing should have ruptured it," Verlak said. "Where exactly is the breach?"

The tech put the schematic up on one of the wall screens.

Verlak's jaw tightened. The warning pulse of light was even with the upper level of the archive.

"Initiate lockdown," she ordered. "No movement between any of the wings." She marched out of the control center, five guards at her heels. Though the tower was forbidden to all, she had the authority to enter it if the taboo cordon had been breached. She did not do so lightly, and she descended to the archives furious that anyone would defy Doom so blatantly.

She was also wary. She could think of only one person who would dare do this, though she couldn't fathom how Fortunov might have entered the lower depths of the castle.

The archives were quiet when they arrived. Only the security lights were on. The amphitheater was a sea of darkness. Guns drawn, Verlak and her team entered on the uppermost tier, level with Dubrov's quarters on the other side. Verlak held up a fist. Motionless, the team waited, listening.

No sounds in the archives, no movement.

Verlak pointed, and she led the team in silence along the outside wall, making for Dubrov's cell. They stopped just to the left of the door. The window there was dark.

No lights. A bit early for Dubrov to be asleep.

She nodded. One of the guards, Melchior, padded ahead, readied a flash-bang grenade, and grasped the door handle. He started to turn it.

The final klaxon warnings sounded.

The wall exploded with a muffled blast.

The dome of the laboratory opened. The nanobot swarm

assembled the telescope, and the mirror turned to the coordinates of the black hole. Doom was about to take hold of the controls of the Harrower. That was when he hesitated.

Something's wrong.

The instinct held him fast. The sense of warning was strong, palpable. He listened. Something had caught his attention, but it was gone now.

"What is it?" Helm asked, in position at the failsafe.

"Did you hear anything?"

"The dome opening."

"Nothing else?"

"No. Is something wrong?"

Doom ran another diagnostic sweep of the lab and the Harrower. Power flowed and was stored where it should be. He muttered an incantation, and the wards in the huge chamber responded, glowing faintly silver. No seals or protective circles were broken.

He waited, listening again. Nothing.

Why am I hesitating? Am I looking for a reason not to proceed?

The idea disgusted him. If the hesitation was a manifestation of latent doubts, it was shameful. "Nothing is wrong," he said to Helm. "Our moment has arrived." He stepped onto the platform and reached into the control sheaths. "Ready?" he asked.

"Ready." She began to murmur her incantations of protection.

Doom activated the Harrower. The silver pool began its spin. The central reflected void became intense, and then real. The unshielded lodestones pulsed with light, and the loop of nanobots began to form over the pool. There was a hollow sound, like wind and thunder being pulled down into the room – the psychic funnels gathering energy for the Walpurgis Night celebrations across Doomstadt. A still deeper hum resonated below all the other noises, so profound it seemed to come up from the bones. It was the sound of the great tuning forks, shaping the energy into the force it needed to be.

Bit by bit, Doom turned up the power, turning the Harrower into the extension of his will.

"Now," he said. "Now. Let us teach Hell to fear."

CHAPTER 23

The explosion sent Verlak flying. There was no flame, only the sudden eruption of stone and the blow of a giant's hand hurling her across the bowl of the archives. She smashed into bookshelves, heard wood crack, heard bone crack, heard the fall of stone, and then she was down, her head hammering from the concussion, her vision smeared by pain and dust. Her left forearm was broken. Blood poured down the side of her head. Shelves and books tumbled in a low angle over her.

She was too stunned to move, but could just make out, through the leaning rubble, the other side of the archive. She had landed two-thirds of the way down the amphitheater. The entire interior wall of Dubrov's cell had been blown apart. Two of her guards, the ones who had been at the door and immediately behind her, were dead, crushed under masonry. She had been lucky to be thrown this far.

Lucky. She still couldn't move. She could barely think.

Fortunov emerged with five other traitors. Dubrov brought

up the rear. Struggling to breathe, Verlak concentrated her hate on the rebels. The dust-filled dimness of the archives made it hard to see the faces, but she focused on them, and as her ringing brain began to work again she drew their identities from her mental database. She recognized Natalya Rumyanova first, and then her known associates fell into place. Carla Ratoff, Josef Heitz, Hans Cass, Friedrich Benedikt. Traitors all. If hate alone were strong enough, she would already have killed them all.

And Dubrov. Dubrov, given the sacred trust of the archives. Dubrov, the worm in the heart of the castle. Death was too good for him, though it would have to do.

Verlak realized that only seconds had elapsed since the blast. Fortunov's team had taken just a few steps down from the cell. They were sweeping the wreckage with their forehead lights, checking for survivors. They carried assault rifles, except for Dubrov, who held something she didn't recognize, but looked highly advanced. He cradled it like it was made of porcelain.

Gently, Verlak got her right arm moving. She still held her pistol. She moved it up slowly, quietly, careful not to give away her position. She had lost her earpiece in the explosion. She had no way of getting a warning out. Her only option was to stop Fortunov here. She hoped she wasn't the sole survivor of her team.

She didn't have a good shot. She couldn't take down all six before one of them blasted her. She had to get out from under the wreckage. Clenching her teeth, refusing herself the luxury of even a hiss of pain, she dragged herself forward.

Fortunov's team were a few rows down from the cell,

walking over fallen bookshelves. Verlak's last two guards came around a bookcase that was still standing. They fired first, but they were still stunned from the explosion, and their aim was off. Fortunov and the others cut them down with a coordinated hail of bullets.

The murder of her guards gave Verlak her chance. Fortunov's guns were all facing away from her. So was his team's concentration. Hate and guilt burning in her chest, Verlak shoved herself forward with her knees and lunged out of the wreckage. She lurched to her feet and ran to her left, up the slope, racing for the shelter of the standing shelves. As she turned into the aisle, she looked back.

Dubrov had spotted her. Their eyes met. She promised him death. He responded with terror.

"*Over there!*" he yelled, and he opened fire with his weapon.

The disintegrator's beam swept wildly over the archives. Dubrov sliced through the priceless books and documents that had been his jealously prized possessions for years. Shelves split in two and collapsed. Books turned into swirling edges of paper. Dubrov had no aim at all, and he vaporized portions of the floor. Shelves went down like dominoes into the craters.

Verlak sprinted down the aisle and up into the next one as archives fell down around her. A tumbling wall of books clipped her left arm, and she screamed silently at the quasar flash of pain. She hit a ramp, shot up to the next aisle, and ran back down it while the beam from Dubrov's weapon chased where she had been, kept going the wrong way, and leveled another portion of the archive. He couldn't see her. He was shooting everywhere.

The lethal green beam shot back and forth, not holding long enough on any target to build its momentum of annihilation. If Dubrov had held the gun steady and turned slowly, he would have wielded an end-times scythe across the archive. Instead, he wasted the intensity of the beam, cutting wildly and without purpose.

"Stop it!" Fortunov was yelling. "Stop it, you idiot!"

Verlak crouched down. The disintegration storm was happening thirty yards from her. She paused in the dark, getting her breath.

The beam stopped its mad dance.

"Look what you've done!" Fortunov raged. "You drained the battery!"

"Give me another," Dubrov begged.

Verlak heard a slap, and the clatter of metal hitting the floor.

"We don't have another!"

"It took six months of smuggling to get enough for the initial payment for that," Rumyanova said.

"I'm sorry," said Dubrov, sounding miserable. "I didn't know. But that was–"

"I know who it was," Fortunov snapped. "Here. Take this."

"I don't know how to use a pistol."

"Maybe not, but there's less damage for you to do." There was a pause. "Are you amused, Captain Verlak?" Fortunov called out.

I am, a bit.

"Enjoy this while you can!" the prince warned.

"We can't let her raise the alarm," Rumyanova said.

"I know we can't. You and Heitz stay here. Kill her or keep her pinned down. Just don't let her get by you. We'll go on."

"Me too?" Dubrov asked.

"No, not *you too*," said Fortunov. "You're staying here too. Help undo what you've done."

"Will you stop him?"

"I will," Fortunov promised, a fraction more gently.

Running footsteps then, Fortunov, Ratoff and Benedikt crossing the archives and taking the exit to the tower.

Stop him. Only one person they could mean. So, they were heading for the laboratory. She had to catch up. Her lips pulled back in a snarl of frustration. She had no illusions about how well she could take on three armed foes with a broken arm.

"She's helpless if we just guard the door," Heitz said.

"You think so?" Dubrov asked. "The captain of the Castle Guard? You don't think she's already almost on us?"

"We can't risk it," said Rumyanova. "Flush her out and kill her."

Verlak heard them move into the archives. Their footsteps drew apart. They had split up, she thought. One was starting from the topmost aisle, the other from the bottom. They would be on a ramp, checking each aisle in turn, moving together again, and then heading to the next quadrant to repeat the search.

Still crouching, Verlak moved quietly toward the sound of the steps. *Let's cut to the chase.* She stopped ten feet in from the end of her aisle, deep in shadow. The ramp ahead of her was the one Rumyanova and Heitz were on. She lay down, right arm forward, pistol aimed up, and waited. It was the traitor coming up that would get to her first.

The footsteps were quiet, careful. *You think you're hunting me. Keep thinking that.*

The beams of the forehead lights were visible now, swinging back and forth as the enemy checked the aisles on both sides.

Hurry up. The pain in her arm stabbed and burned, and felt cold at the same time. She was worried she might go into shock.

Heitz swung into the aisle. Verlak fired into the dazzling glare of his light. It went out and he fell, shot through the head. Verlak jumped up and sprinted back the way she had come, racing to outrun the agony as her arm jounced and swung. Behind her, bullets dug into the books at the entrance to the aisle, Rumyanova firing blind, and making the mistake of holding her position.

You may have taken well to the life of a guerrilla. But you were born and trained into nobility. You should not be dueling with me.

Verlak reached the other end of the aisle before Rumyanova stopped firing and made her move. Verlak spun right and pounded back down the aisle one row uphill from where she'd been. The firing stopped, and she heard Rumyanova start to run.

Verlak slowed, aimed her pistol straight ahead.

Running steps. So close.

Verlak pulled the trigger, five times in quick succession. Rumyanova couldn't stop in time and ran into the line of fire. A bullet caught her in the right shoulder. It whirled her around and she staggered back, her light facing Verlak and jouncing up and down. Verlak shot it out too, and put Rumyanova down.

She stopped moving and caught her breath. She waited for Dubrov to react, and he did exactly what she expected. He panicked. As soon as he saw his defenders die, he screamed and shot at everything and nothing with his pistol. Verlak waited him out.

She felt light-headed. She made herself breathe slowly and steadily. *Keep going. Stop Fortunov.*

Dubrov's clip emptied. He kept pulling the trigger, a *click click click* of fear.

Verlak stepped out of the aisle. He was at the top of the ramp, aiming his useless weapon at her.

"I had to!" he sobbed. "You don't understand!"

She didn't answer. He turned to run. She shot him before he took the first step.

Exhaustion and pain tried to force her down now. She resisted and forced herself up the ramp, and then along the top tier to the exit from the archives. Fortunov only had a head start of a minute or two. It felt like years.

The lift from the archives to the laboratory level had been disabled. She had to take the stairs. There were hundreds of them, rising in a spiral inside the tower's outer wall.

Hissing in pain and frustration, she began the climb.

Time was slippery. Every step was a hard-fought battle against futility and defeat. She kept going. She had her duty, and it was as unyielding as the stone that surrounded her.

But then the screams came, screams that were not human, screams that filled the tower and tore the mind, screams that came from a darkness far beyond night.

The screams were the voice of a triumphant power. They brought their darkness with them, and they hammered her down. She fell to her knees, clawing against an enemy she could not fight.

The dark and the screams swallowed her.

The Harrower reached full strength. The sphere of energy beneath the top of the silver loop formed, and became a constant beam firing down the black hole at the center of the nanobot pool's vortex. It reached the infernal depths, but this time Hell could not rise in response. Crimson shadows moved up the laboratory walls, but the stones remained solid.

Doom smiled. "I have you at bay," he growled. He flexed his right hand. He curled his fingers into claws. Far below the veil of death, the blade of his attack responded. The harrowing of Hell began. Doom could not see the overturning of the matter of Mephisto's realm, but he could sense it. The ground of Hell trembled. The cities of Hell shook. And the chains of Hell broke.

The first of the souls rose from the depths. The silver loop shimmered, and faces appeared on its surface. They were vague in their features, trace memories of the human shape, though their torment was clear and deep, as if etched in steel. The damned passed through the circuit of the loop, and because they were not his mother, the other end of the loop sent them back to their chains of fire. The howls of the souls Doppler-shifted as they traveled the loop, the cries of pain turning into pleas and then despair as the Harrower lifted them from Hell and plunged them down again.

Doom's will guided the Harrower. He didn't need a map. He didn't need to look upon the panoramas of Hell and search for a direction. There was only one direction, and that was toward his mother's imprisoned soul. *Find her*, he commanded. *Free her.* The Harrower obeyed. It carved its long furrows into Hell, and Hell could not resist. The longer the Harrower moved over the lands and through the cities like the claws of an earthquake, the more control Doom had over it, and the closer he could bring it to the single soul that was its true target.

The souls rose and fell in a continuous river of pain through the loop. Doom saw them more clearly than he did anything else in the lab. The physical world was an ill-defined phantom. More than half his consciousness was with the Harrower's blade in Hell, and he reveled in the taste of revenge. He could see Helm working to maintain the wards of protection. She was only a dozen yards away, yet they were separated by universes. He thought he could talk if he had to, but his body was distanced from him too, except for those actions needed to guide and power the Harrower.

Hell bled. Its humiliation grew. The river of souls streamed through Doom's hands. The Harrower drew closer to his mother. He could almost sense her. Another few seconds and it would not be his will alone that called the Harrower. It would be her voice, emerging from its silence.

The next sound Doom heard was not his mother's call. It was the crash of the laboratory door flying off its hinges.

Fortunov, Ratoff and Benedikt came out of the elevator, locked its controls and ran across the hall to the laboratory. The space was clear. There were no guards. Verlak had not managed to raise the alarm.

Ratoff went up to the door. She hesitated. A web of runes engraved in the metal was glowing a soft silver, the light intensifying and diminishing with slow beats, as if the door itself were breathing.

"It's his sorcery, Carla," Fortunov said. "This is what we've come to destroy. Pray we're not too late."

"I don't see Hell," said Ratoff. "So we're not." Reassured, she placed their remaining kinetic charge against the door. The base of the hemispherical explosive fixed itself to the surface with molecular adhesive. She withdrew a few yards along with Fortunov and Benedikt. She presented the detonator to Fortunov.

He shook his head. "The honor is yours."

They had used the same kind of explosive in Dubrov's cell, planting it on the door and waiting for Verlak's guards to try to open it. He had guessed the breaching of the pipe might trigger a sensor somewhere, and he had needed to win with a single blow if he wanted to keep his attack secret. The kinetic charge shattered the wall with a massive discharge of force and little sound. The archives were too deep in the foundations for the shattering of stone to be heard elsewhere in the castle.

Ratoff thumbed the detonator. There was a bright flash from the back of the charge, and the door flew inwards, cartwheeling and crashing against the walls.

Fortunov didn't have to give the order. The three rebels ran forward as one, guns at the ready. They crossed the threshold into a chamber of shifting red shadows and strobing energy discharges. Pain itself seemed to be crying out from the center of the laboratory. Fortunov stumbled, assaulted by the blast and pound of the fusion of machinery and sorcery. And there was a hum, so deep and low, no earth tremor could equal it. The hum made his soul vibrate, and terror filled his chest.

His eyes widened, trying to take in the full evil of what they saw. Monolithic blocks of machinery towered over him and poured their energy into the atrocity in the center of the lab. Fortunov saw Doom at the controls, and he saw the silver pool, and he saw the looping despair of the damned, and he knew that everything Dubrov had feared was true, and that it might already be too late.

The witch of Mount Sivàr was at the near side of the pool. She had turned as the doors blew in. Her eyes blazed. "*NO!*" she roared. Her hand shot out, and lightning flashed from it, striking Ratoff and turning her to ash.

Doom's titanium skull of a face looked at Fortunov, and his rage made the air ripple.

Fortunov felt himself on the fulcrum of destiny. The weight of a single decision turned a fraction of a second into an eternity. He knew before his finger tightened on the trigger of his assault rifle that he would not have the chance for a second action.

Doom's arms were held by the components of his machine. In this single moment in time, he could not attack. Fortunov could shoot him first.

But the bullets would not penetrate that armor. Fortunov's attack would lead to nothing.

Shooting Helm would lead nowhere too. She was not the heart of the machine. She was not the one who was raising Hell.

It was not Doom that Fortunov had come for. He understood that now. It was the machine. He had to kill the machine. He had one chance, one choice, and if he was wrong, then Latveria was doomed.

And when he knew he had to kill the machine, he knew where to fire. It was the hum, the deep hum of damnation, that showed him what he must do. He aimed his gun at one of the huge tuning forks.

Time resumed. Half a second after Helm incinerated Ratoff, Fortunov opened fire on the tuning forks. The bullets hammered its tines. The hum turned into a screech, as high and unending as the hum had been low. The machine flew out of tune and out of control. Fortunov staggered under the assault of the cluster of supernova flashes that filled the lab. An explosion hurled Doom against the back wall. The silver loop broke free of its anchor in the pool. Instead of a loop, it became a whip, thrashing back and forth. The instant that the cycle of rise and fall from Hell broke, no further souls appeared.

Other things came.

They screamed, but their screams were of hunger, of triumph and of annihilation.

PART III

THE WALPURGIS CRUCIBLE

"though I wore the form,
I had no sympathy with breathing flesh"

BYRON, MANFRED, II.II.56-7

CHAPTER 24

Vortex. Whirlwind. Demonstorm.

The end of Doom's dream of hope.

The whiplash of the loop unleashed them. Creatures of claws and fangs, of wings and scales, of burning eyes and slithering tongues. No two were alike. They carried the nightmare traces and distorted memories of the human and the animal. They were patchwork creations, but they were also complete wholes, individually and collectively, a unity of evil. Hell had not risen to Latveria, but its army had, and the tornado of demons burst through the dome of the laboratory, spreading over the sky.

Fortunov's last accomplice was screaming. He was frozen, his arms limp, his jaw straining wide in horror. He didn't even move when a demon with the body of a vulture and the head of a serpent snatched him up. It carried his writhing form up past the telescope, hovered with him for a moment just above the dome, then tore him apart with a screeching laugh. It wheeled away, joining its brethren in the great revel of Walpurgis Night.

Doom rose in fury. The Harrower thundered in its madness. Helm was struggling with the failsafe, shouting spells of banishment, but again the mechanism they had designed to prevent disaster did nothing. It would have worked against Hell straining to be released. It could do nothing when the Harrower was damaged from the outside.

His first instinct was to try to get it back under control, but already the demon swarm was falling on Doomstadt. Even if he tamed the Harrower, that would not stop the slaughter that was about to transpire.

Fortunov had backed up to the exit of the lab, staring in horror at the demon geyser. The creatures shot up from the depths and did not even glance at the laboratory. The call of freedom was so strong. They raced, screaming with delight, out to the promise of the untrammeled feast.

"*YOU DID THIS!*" Doom roared at him, and Fortunov shrank away. *The worm. The miserable, damnable worm.* He wanted to vent his wrath on the prince and tear him to pieces, but he forced himself to stay rational. *Latveria needs its savior in this moment, not another vengeful spirit. And it needs every warrior it can find.*

"How can I stop it?" Fortunov pleaded.

"Fight any way you can, you wretch! In material form they can be hurt, though not destroyed. You wanted to save Latveria? Go, then! Go and fight for it until you die."

Fortunov ran. At the same time, Helm abandoned the failsafe and arrived at Doom's side.

"Can we reverse this?" she asked.

"No. We can try to end the flow, but..." He looked up. The sky was changing. That wasn't night up there any longer. It was a cloud of demons. There were hundreds already, circling in wider and wider spirals as they chose their first prey. *My mother's crime is now mine a hundredfold.* She had tried to save her people and unleashed horror instead. He had tried to save her, and now the demonstorm could destroy all of Latveria.

"Go," Helm said, understanding what he needed to do. "Give me control of the Harrower."

"It's fatally out of tune," said Doom. Magic burned round the tines of the damaged tuning fork. It was beyond repair. "The psychic energy in the city is now already so huge there is no way of depriving the Harrower of power."

"Then we have to try to rein it in. Go and stop the demons. I will try to hold it back until you return."

"You're going to try to do more than that," said Doom, seeing what Helm had not even fully admitted to herself. *Save her, Helm, and my debt to you will be eternal.*

"Yes," she said, fear and determination at war with each other. "I have to try. I have to know she and I can still be free."

"Do what you can."

"And you."

He feared neither would be enough. He fired up his jets and flew up, into the night, into the storm, into war.

The year had come round again, and brought with it the dark refrain.

The repetition of ritual. The repetition of fears.

Repetition as endless rehearsal.

And so:

The bonfires of Latveria burned high on Walpurgis Night. They burned in the market squares of Doomstadt. They

burned before the churches of St Peter and St Blaise. They
burned on the rooftop of the Werner Academy. And the
people danced around the bonfires. Arms linked, faces turned
upward to see the flames strike at the night, they danced and
they chanted.

Only this night came the end of repetition, the goal of
rehearsal. All rehearsal must, at the last, give way to the
performance.

And so:

Walpurgis Night in Latveria. Walpurgis Night in all its
glory, in the fulfillment of the promise. No longer the night
when the veil was thin. Now the night when the veil was rent,
its tatters the rags of a shroud in a hurricane.

The theatrical fears gave way to their terrible truths. There
were demons in the streets of Doomstadt, but there were no
gargoyles to chase them away.

The Harrower had begun its work at the start of the witching
hour. The costumed terrors had finished their carnival in the
streets by then. They had played their games, gathered their
pyro-wands, thrown them into the bonfires, rejoiced, and
then gone home to sleep. The other rituals carried on, and
at the height of the witching hour, the red light erupted from
Castle Doom, and the demons returned to the streets.

At the bonfire in Vandorf Street, the dancers paused in their
rounds. At first, they thought they saw lightning. At first, they
thought they heard thunder. But should thunder scream?
Should lightning be like blood, and should the clouds be hot
like the sun?

The sky rained demons on the dancers. Fear descended
with talons and fangs, wings of leather and feathers of flesh.

The demons formed a circle around the people, and they danced too. The circle tightened, and the dance became more frenzied. The demons sang, drowning out the few voices that still tried to recall the rituals of protection. There would be no protection in Vandorf Street this night. There was only feasting.

Hell embraced the dark and sleeping houses of Doomstadt. The demons scuttled over the walls and over the roofs. Their hoofs clattered on tiles. Their nails skittered on walls. Their fingers tapped, tapped, tapped on windows with the sound of dead branches in streets with no trees. They laughed quietly with each other, amused to play at being patient.

In the houses, if anyone had been sleeping, they woke. The people heard the sounds. They heard the hint of laughter. They tried to believe they heard the play of wind, the rattle of rain, the games of old timbers and foundations settling. They turned on lights to make the fears vanish. But the lights dimmed and went out. The fears took form. Shadows moved over the windows, uncertain shapes like the waving of red moonlight through huge leaves. Some people, seeing the world crack before them, acted as if the determined refusal of terrors would banish them. They threw open curtains to prove to themselves that there was nothing there.

At every parted curtain there was a face at the window. A face that smiled. A face that laughed. A face that snarled. A face pale as the moon. A face crimson as blood. A face with horns. A face that melted. A face of glass.

For every set of eyes that looked out in the hope of disbelief, a face answered with the proof that all fears were justified, because all nightmares were real.

Then, because the truth was out, and terror in the houses could not be greater, the monsters smashed the windows and came inside.

All over Doomstadt, Walpurgis Night in all its glory. The fulfillment of every dark promise.

Orloff had begun the craniotomy shortly before the first of the warning klaxons from the castle. She had heard the blasts only faintly in the surgery. She knew what they were, and they were irrelevant to her here. With no windows, there was no chance anyone would gaze at the tower and be turned into a pillar of salt. She was deep into the procedure by the time the final warning sounded. She had removed the bone flap. The patient's brain was exposed to her, and the lesion she had to remove was easy to see. It was the procedure to deal with a wound of that size that raised the complications.

It was ridiculously late to be operating, too. But the patient had been seizing. It was act now or not at all.

The lights dimmed. Orloff froze. There suddenly was not enough light for her to make an incision. One second later and she would have already been cutting. She stepped back from the patient. The lights brightened again. She waited to see if they would fluctuate.

"Should we continue?" Anton Berger asked.

"Let's wait a minute," she told the assisting surgeon. "Lothar," she said to the nurse, "call the power plant. Ask them if we can rely on the lighting. Just in case we want to do something like save a life."

While Lothar Hellmer picked up the phone, Orloff bent down to look at the lesion again. She worked through the cut she would have to make, practicing in her head so precisely that when she performed the surgery, she would be repeating an action already familiar. The light remained steady.

"They say things should be fine," Hellmer reported.

"That's good of them," Orloff said without looking up. "All right then, let's put our faith in the gods of illumination and get started."

The lights flickered again.

The lesion squirmed.

Orloff blinked. She hadn't seen that.

The lesion squirmed again. It wriggled, a red worm. It crawled down the exposed brain, growing as it went. It reached the edge of the skull and crawled over it.

"What's wrong?" Berger asked.

Orloff couldn't move.

Berger joined her. He gasped.

The lesion grew longer, its tail twisting back and forth over the surface of the brain. The entire grey matter twitched, and then again, more violently.

Orloff took a step back.

The lights dimmed and stayed that way. They threw the room into grainy brown twilight.

The brain burst free of the skull, its convolutions separating out into a grasping tangle of red tendrils. They wrapped themselves around Berger's arm. He screamed and tried to pull away. The brain kept coming and coming and coming out of the head, and it wasn't a brain any more. It was a cord, a rope of muscle. The patient's body contracted in on itself, skin cracking, bones slithering. The head split wide, and the python muscle emerging reared up, taking on mass and shape. The tendrils holding Berger were the end of an arm. At the top of the mass, a rounded shape formed. Redness parted in a slit, revealing perfectly white and perfectly human teeth. They chattered.

Orloff grabbed a scalpel and slashed at the demon's grip. The blade cut through the wet muscle, freeing Berger. She lunged forward, refusing to believe what she was seeing and doing. "Run!" she yelled. The demon clacked its teeth but reared back from her attacks. Berger and Hellmer yanked the surgery door open and fled into the corridor beyond. Orloff slashed once more at the horror and then ran too. The demon gabbled at her. She could hear a tongue forming inside that mouth. There would be speech in another second, and if she heard its words, she didn't think she would survive.

She slammed the door behind her as the demon lunged. It pounded against the door with a liquid thump.

Run, Orloff had told the others. *Run*, her instincts shouted. *Run where?*

What about the patients? What about those who can't run?

She couldn't move. She held the door closed. The demon slammed against it again, mocking her. There was nothing she could do except hold this line.

The frontier rushed past her. Gray-brown light filled the corridor. Motes swarmed in front of her eyes like hungry flies. People were fleeing to nowhere. Lines like veins of ink spread over the ceiling, the walls, the floor. The corridor rippled. It shuddered beneath Orloff's feet like taut flesh. Fissures opened in the ceiling, and blood spattered to the floor like rain.

The ink veins thickened. They burst free of the walls

and ceiling, and became black tentacles that whipped out and grasped their fleeing prey. Orloff shouted in terror and frustration. She couldn't save anyone. She couldn't save herself.

The door turned warm and slick to the touch. She backed away. The corridor began to contract. She was insignificant prey in the belly of the monster that had once been the hospital.

From above, there was the distant boom of an explosion. The floor shook, this time as if in pain. The tentacles went limp, dropping their victims. On the other side of the door, the demon stopped moving.

Amplified into thunder, the voice of Doom roared over the hospital, rattling the windows, the sound so ferocious that the demonic hold on the building weakened, and the lights brightened.

"*LATVERIA IS MINE!*"

There was another explosion. The thing that gripped the hospital screamed in fury. Orloff fell to her knees, hands over her ears. The shriek seemed to be cutting through her, shredding her being. She thought she would fly to pieces, leaves in the wind. The demon in the surgery howled. And then the tentacles withdrew, the veins retracted, and the walls became walls again.

The lights flickered once more and became stable. Orloff pulled herself up. She stood in a hallway slicked with blood, filled with the dead and the injured. From outside, she heard a new storm as Doom's challenge was answered.

Doom flew down from the castle, into the plague of demons.

They were everywhere, hundreds and hundreds of them, a cloudburst of evil over the entire city. The futility of his task did not make him pause. It fueled his rage. He did not think about the Harrower and the imprisoned soul of his mother. He saw his city in the grip of an invading force, and he fell on the demons with an anger beyond Hell's.

He streaked over Vandorf Street, too late to prevent the slaughter. He brought retribution instead. He attacked the demons below with a dual strike of concussive and mystical blasts. The first shattered the physical bodies of the demons. The second incinerated their hold on the world, shredded them and hurled them back through the torn veil.

Doom swooped up at the end of the street and met a vulture-winged horror head-on. It had human arms, and each hand wielded a flaming sword. It brought the blades in from both sides. They glanced off Doom's force field. He hit the demon's head with both blasts at once, exploding its skull, and the body fell away, disintegrating as it spiraled toward the ground.

He rose higher, stealing a few seconds to look down at the whole of the city. He could not be everywhere at once. He had to choose his targets wisely.

There was a cluster of demons over the hospital. Doom swooped toward the greater concentration of enemies and civilians. He sent his voice booming across the city, reclaiming what was his, and exterminated a handful of flying demons over the roof. These were not champions of Hell. They were its foot soldiers and its winged infantry. He had fought their rulers, and individually they could not withstand him.

But in their hundreds…

He dismissed the thought. Midsummer belonged to Hell. Walpurgis Night belonged to him. There would be no defeat. He would grind the enemy to dust.

A collective of demons had fused together, a coral reef of the infernal surrounding the hospital and transforming it. A mass of writhing, struggling vines, black and red and thorned, covered the exterior. Doom shot down to street level, then rose up, destroying the vines over the front of the hospital, and then ripping them apart over the roof. A score of demons screamed in pain and anger. He pulled back, out of the reach of the vines.

Wounded, maddened, the demons released the hospital and came after him. The form rose from the roof. It was legion, and it was a coherent whole. It had the shape of a monstrous centipede, clawed legs lining its plated flanks. Giant fangs gaped in an eyeless skull. Hellfire spewed from the maw, and Doom jerked suddenly in the air. The edge of the flame brushed against his force field, and for a moment his energy began to smolder and burn. Doom shot up faster yet, sailing over the top of the creature's head, and fired the blasts from his palms down at the center of the skull, shouting a spell of exorcism at the same time.

The serpentine horror split down the middle, then shattered into a rain of black glass. Below, the lights of the hospital came back on.

One small part of the city saved, at least for the moment.

A tiny victory in the midst of a deluge. More meaningful than the vengeance in Vandorf. It wasn't enough. It was a drop in the ocean. He had to bring down the demons faster than they could arrive.

Doom looked back at the castle, and the eruption from Hell continued without pause. Helm did not have the Harrower under control. Her attempt might be futile. He had to let her try. If there was even a chance she would succeed, there might be more than ashes to salvage from the night.

To the east, demons flocked together. There were even more of them than had taken the hospital. They formed a cyclone over the towers of St Peter Church.

CHAPTER 25

Zargo spent Walpurgis Night awake again, watching the celebrations in the square from the church. That much was the same as he had done for years. Everything else was different. He wasn't angered by the ritual this time. He was frustrated, but with himself. He felt worse than he ever had. Until this year, he had been drunk on sanctimonious judgment. Until this year, he hadn't felt divided, uncertain of his own morality, of his path in life and of his own identity.

He stayed in the shadow of the church porch, watched, and was torn by doubts and fears.

Ilona Sandor spotted him when she arrived for the bonfire and approached him. "It was nice seeing you at the Academy again," she said. "I'm sorry you weren't there longer."

"I was called away to other duties."

"Can you tell me what they were?"

"I really wish I could." It would have been a relief to speak to someone who wasn't Doom, Helm or Fortunov.

"I understand," said Sandor. "Will you join us tonight? You look like you could use a celebration."

Zargo laughed sadly. "Oh, you're right about that. But no. Thank you, Ilona."

"Still no truck with us hypocrites?"

"That isn't it at all. I'm the one who would be a hypocrite, but I don't even know to which side of myself."

"Don't overestimate how certain anyone is of themselves."

"You're right, I shouldn't." He shook his head. "Even so, I'm not good company tonight. I'll stay here." He was too frightened to think about dancing.

As the night wore on, he didn't move from his position. He felt increasingly like a sentinel. His attention went back and forth between the bonfire and the castle. He watched the dancers and envied them, wishing he could reconcile his faith and what Doom said he truly was. He watched the castle and worried.

Did I do the right thing?

What thing? The help you gave Doom? Or when you did nothing at all after Fortunov asked for your help?

I don't know. Every choice, every action, and every moment of silence all seemed to point toward disaster.

Sins of commission and sins of omission. He had plenty of both on his conscience, and he didn't even know which was which, and whether he had made a single right decision in his entire life.

There was one decision he had made about tonight. He would not turn away from the reckoning. Whether Doom or Fortunov was in the right, Zargo would bear witness to what he had brought about. So when the witching hour began, and the final warning sounded from the castle, he did not look away. He fixed his gaze on the castle. It was time for the reckoning.

The minutes ticked by, and he thought about what Fortunov had said and what he might be doing. He wasn't sure whether to hope Fortunov stopped Doom or Doom prevailed. All he wanted was for the night to lead to dawn and nothing else, a Walpurgis Night like any other. He wanted to see the sunlight of the first day of May and simply feel tired. That was what he tried to pray for. But as long as he looked at the castle, he couldn't pray.

The center tower of the castle shone like blood, and then the roof erupted. A cloud burst up from the dome and spread out, wider and wider, coming to cover Doomstadt. No, not a cloud. It was filled with lightning and fire.

Minutes later, the night had wings.

Fortunov was right, Zargo thought, and he despaired.

The celebration in the square became a riot of screams. Demons snatched people and carried them off. The emissaries of Hell landed in the midst of the bonfire and sent waves of flame washing over the dancers.

I made this happen, Zargo thought, his heart squeezed by guilt and horror. *I found the ley lines. I helped him. I did this.* He had succumbed to the old temptation of witchcraft, and now the innocents were reaping his whirlwind.

He had to help however he could.

"Here!" Zargo shouted. "Over here!"

Many of the people in the square were already running for the church. He held the doors open for the stampede. Most of the dancers in the rings closest to the bonfire never made it. They burned, or were broken, or were devoured. Dog-like snarls, the croaking of crows and the hoarse shouting of infernal praise drowned out the screams. The Walpurgis

Night celebration fell before a much older revel.

Zargo slammed and bolted the church doors behind the last of the refugees. He turned around to find his terrified flock looking at him with desperation, Sandor among them.

They need me to tell them this is a sanctuary.

He needed to be able tell them just that. Only he was frightened it might be a lie.

Outside, the screeches and laughter of the demons grew louder and louder. Zargo had the awful conviction of being at the center of a massive storm. The image of the church lifted from its foundations by Hell's vortex would not leave his mind.

Don't wallow. Do your duty. Help these people. Help them for as long as you can.

"Let us pray," he said. "We will strengthen these walls with our faith."

That almost sounds believable.

Sobbing, the people moved into the pews and kneeled. Many of them clutched the backs of the pews in front of them as if the thick wood, chipped and polished by the centuries, were a relic and a shield. If they held on hard enough, the demons would not be able to haul them away.

Zargo moved to the altar and led the prayers. He felt exposed, and the space of the nave seemed horribly vast. Given the chance, he would have crouched in a pew as well. He longed for the illusion of security that came with a small space to hide, an embrace of wood to keep out the monsters.

Claws scraped along the stained glass windows. Though it was night, red light shone through them and silhouetted shapes with wings and horns.

Zargo raised his voice, and the people responded. They shouted the prayers. Their voices filled the spaces between the pillars and beneath the vaults. For a few minutes, the noises of the demons became a harsh background, merely the roar of a hurricane instead of the voice of Hell.

The shapes crawled over the windows, but they did not smash the glass. Hope flared in Zargo's heart. A year ago, he would never have doubted that St Peter *was* a sanctuary. He would have proclaimed to his future self that no demon could enter the sanctified space. He raised his voice even higher in praise. His congregation bowed their heads and did not look at the things on the windows.

Zargo experienced a full minute of hope.

The strain told. They couldn't keep their voices at that level for long. The prayers went quiet, and the laughter outside the church, dark and bloody, filled the spaces instead. The candles wavered, and the shadows stirred. The scraping on the windows went on and on, the sound spine-twisting in its intensity.

The bells of the church began to ring. Zargo's breath caught in mid-prayer. He looked up, as if he could see through the roof and know what had crawled into the towers. The bells clanged, and they were out of tune. They rang as if their clappers were bone. The peals were a call, a summons, and a mockery. They were a proclamation that the church was no sanctuary, that the horrors outside its walls were not held at bay, but were simply choosing the moment of their invasion.

"Don't listen!" Zargo shouted. "Stay strong! That sound is a lie!"

You're the liar. Will you tell your flock more encouraging lies while they're torn apart?

He would have liked to tell himself that the voice in his head was not his, and that the thoughts had been put there by a demon. It was his voice, though. His doubts.

"What's that?" said Sandor. She lifted her head and looked towards the door.

Zargo heard it too. Between the bells, between the snarls and the laughter of the demons, the stuttering bursts of automatic rifle fire. It drew closer to the church. A demon screeched with rage, and something heavy smacked into the pavement outside.

Zargo ran down the nave to the door. The gunfire came closer yet. He paused with his hand on the bolt.

"Are you going to unlock it?" Sandor asked.

"No!" a half-dozen people shouted at once.

Zargo held up a hand for silence. He listened.

The firing was even closer. More demons yelled in anger, and Zargo heard pain too.

The door trembled as something massively strong stuck it. "*No more games,*" a voice snarled on the other side. "*Tired of games.*" A voice of snakes. A voice of rot. "*I want in!*" The demon smashed at the doors, and the frame began to crack.

Zargo jumped back at the sudden, very loud burst of gunfire. The demon howled. The gun kept going, and there were thuds, as if a stream of nails were slamming into flesh. There was a long, loud hiss, and then the *fwump* of an implosion. The doors radiated sudden heat.

And then there was a very human knocking. "Let me in!" Fortunov.

Zargo threw the bolt back. The handle was hot to the touch as he pulled one of the doors open. Fortunov rushed in and helped Zargo shut and lock the door again. The prince's dark fatigues were torn. His face was burned, and something had raked him across the chest. He was breathing heavily, and his eyes darted like a rabbit's over the church interior. He had the drawn look of someone who had seen too much, too quickly.

"What's happened?" Zargo asked. "Did Doom…?"

Fortunov shook his head, still trying to catch his breath. "This is my doing. I was wrong. Oh God, Father, I was wrong. I tried to stop him, and…" He trailed off, haggard with guilt.

"You came from the castle."

"Yes." Fortunov took another magazine from his belt and reloaded.

"You're shooting demons?"

"All the way down from the castle." Fortunov leaned against the wall and turned his eyes to the absent heavens. "Doom was right. They can be hurt. Put enough bullets in them and they vanish. Back to Hell, I guess. It takes a lot, though."

"How much ammunition do you have?"

"Some. Not enough. There must be at least twenty crawling over the church. I can't destroy all of them."

The bells rang and rang with oppressive, unending mockery.

"Maybe they can't come inside," said Zargo. "It would take nothing to smash the windows. They haven't done that."

"I don't know. The one I just shot wasn't worried about holy ground. It wanted inside. It was going to break your doors to splinters, Father."

"What are they waiting for?" Zargo wondered.

"They're waiting for something. They'll come inside when they're ready, I promise you that."

"I wish you were wrong again."

"So do I."

"What do we do?" Zargo asked.

Fortunov sagged a bit more. "I really hoped you would tell me."

"You didn't come to rescue us?"

"I wanted to. I've been fighting the demons all the way down from the castle. But they're so many. They're everywhere. We've already lost."

"No," said Zargo. He glanced back at the watching congregation. The noise of the demons was so loud, he thought they might not have heard what Fortunov said. "Keep your defeatism to yourself. That helps no one."

Fortunov didn't appear to hear him. "I wanted to save the church. I thought, if I could do that one thing, that would be some redemption. Too many, though. Too many."

"We fight them how we can, then," said Zargo. "Do you have any other weapons?"

"A pistol. Only a few rounds left."

"Keep it. You're probably the only one who can shoot straight. We'll pray. That *must* count for something. You shoot the ones who try break in. We hang on." He willed Fortunov not to ask what would happen if the demons all came in at once.

"Hang on?" Fortunov asked. "For how long?"

"For as long as we can."

A roar of demonic laughter met his words. Clustered shapes beat at the windows in their mirth. Huge fists hammered at the doors again. Fortunov faced the doors, weapon ready. Zargo took up a position just behind and to his side.

What do you think you can do?

I don't know. But I won't run. I will protect my flock from Hell.

He was angry now, as well as afraid. Angry at the terror that had taken Doomstadt. Angry that he had helped bring it about. No more. *Here I stand.* As he thought the words, he had the sudden image of himself as a statue, a pillar, rooted with foundations that grew from the bedrock below. His determination had the strength of the Earth.

The doors shattered. A demon lurched into the opening. It had the shape of a horse, its body covered in black metal plates. Between them glowed the red of lava. Its jaws were lined with hooked teeth. It reared back, its hooves like granite blocks. Smoke billowed from its nostrils.

Fortunov opened fire. The bullet punched into the armor of the demon. It snarled and lunged forward. Fortunov backed up quickly, still shooting. Chunks of the beast flew into the air. Boiling blood ran down its chest and flanks. It slowed for a moment, leaning into the bullets as if into a stiff wind. Then it charged.

Zargo had not backed up with Fortunov. He held his ground. He *held* it, and was immovable. He raised his arms. "*Begone!*" he shouted at the demon, and five feet away from him, the demon hit an invisible barrier. There was a flare of reddish-brown light, and the demon staggered back, its limbs sprawling.

Fortunov pressed the advantage, sending a long burst of bullets into the demon's head. The skull burst open. The air around the monster shimmered, and then the body collapsed violently on itself. The implosion made Zargo's ears pop, and the short, powerful gust of wind yanked him forward a step.

The demon was gone, leaving behind a slick of blood that bubbled and steamed.

"How did you do that?" Fortunov asked.

"I don't really know." *Earth magic*, he thought, wishing it had been otherwise. He should have faced the demon down with a cross. *I truly am no priest.*

He had acted instinctively, and he had no idea how to repeat the attack.

Spindly things, long legs like spiders and bodies like porcelain dolls, dropped down from the wall and into the doorway. They giggled like clowns. Their jaws chattered like castanets. Fortunov ran at them, shooting into their central mass. They were more fragile than the other demon and they came apart easily, spider legs spinning away, doll-faces shattering into white shrapnel. They cried as they fell back through the cracks in the real and down to Hell, and the sound was the wailing of cats. It lingered in the church after they were gone, sinking into the heart, and touching the soul with the cold finger of guilt.

Their weeping took its toll on everyone in the church. People lowered their heads and wept too. They were afraid, and they were grieving too for everyone they could not save. Zargo realized that Fortunov's easy destruction of the demons had not been a victory at all.

Even so, there was a lull. No other demons appeared in the doorway. The laughter and the snarls were more distant. Zargo and Fortunov looked at each other.

"Retreating?" Fortunov asked.

"Why would they?"

They walked slowly to the doorway. They paused just inside and looked out. Bodies covered the square, arranged into symbols that hurt the eye and stabbed the mind. Claws had gouged the paving stones. The bonfire was scattered. Flames licked out of the windows of the houses surrounding the square. There were no demons to be seen.

A huge wind roared, powerful as a jet engine.

Zargo and Fortunov stepped through the doorway and past the porch. They looked up.

"Lord, have mercy upon us," Zargo croaked in horror.

Hundreds of demons had formed a maelstrom over the church. They were the night, and the night was churning. The spiral was descending slowly, though the demons whirled at a mad speed. The attack was leisurely because the demons were savoring the moment.

"We can't stop that," Fortunov whispered.

"They know it," said Zargo. "They want us to know it. They want us to despair."

"I am."

Zargo grabbed Fortunov by the arm and pulled him back inside the church. "Don't tell the others," he said. "Don't let them despair too. Don't feed the demons."

Fortunov looked at him hopelessly, but he said nothing. He faced the doorway as if he could hold off what was coming.

As if the demons sensed that their witnesses would not spread terror among the prey, the roar of the cyclone became deafening. The windows rattled. The walls and floor vibrated.

"What is happening?" a man shouted. "What is happening? What is happening? What is happening?" He didn't want an answer. His fear came out in a yell that pleaded for the happening to cease.

The roar descended. Shapes whipped past the red light in the windows. The roar swallowed the church. Fortunov shouted something that Zargo couldn't hear.

The stained glass window exploded, and demons flew in triumph into the church. Their screeching laughter was the lightning in the thunder of the cyclone roar. They swooped low over the congregation and scooped up victims in their talons. Fortunov fired wildly. There were too many targets. He was shooting into a hurricane, and he screamed at the futility of his gesture. Zargo screamed his denial. He reached up at the demons as if he could drag them from the air, but the flash of power he had used before had deserted him.

The church filled with the demonic swarm.

Then two blasts of force blazed through the window. They tore demons apart and incinerated them at the same time. They cut through the swarm like a scythe.

And now it was the demons, and not the people, who were screaming.

CHAPTER 26

Doom hovered in the circle of the shattered window. Energy auras crackled around his fists. The demons in the church shrieked at him and pulled back toward the other side of the nave. Outside, the whirlwind of shapes howled in rage, but did not approach.

Zargo stared at the cloaked figure floating where the stained glass had been, and saw majesty as dark and terrible as it was overwhelming. For the first time, he saw Doom at war, his power unleashed. He trembled as if before a prophecy fulfilled. The rituals of Walpurgis Night rushed before his mind's eye. He saw the mock combat of the costumed gargoyles chasing the demons down the streets. He looked at Doom, at the being of armor, and the mask, the unmoving mask of iron wrath, and he beheld the lord of gargoyles. He believed now that all the centuries of ritual had been rehearsals for this night. Every child that had donned the mask of Latveria's defenders had been preparing the way for this moment. Every bonfire and firework had been the mimicry of the war to come.

He saw the sublime in its darkest form, and it overwhelmed him. He couldn't breathe. He trembled in fear, and felt he could not stand. He shivered, ecstatic, and felt that he might fly.

The demons released their prey. The massed numbers in the church flew at Doom as one. He shot forward to meet them, a single knight hurtling to meet an army, and the army dreaded his impact. The beams blazed again from his gauntlets. They tore into the swarm and burned the demons away. Doom passed through the demons, cut the swarm down. He doubled back, and now he was the pursuer. The surviving horrors screamed at him and fled the church, rejoining the great mass of the cyclone. The roar of the vortex diminished. Punctuated by screams, it retreated, pulling back higher above the church, but not departing.

Not with so much prey in one place.

Doom landed in the center of the nave. "All of you except Zargo and Fortunov, be ready to leave at my command. Gather near the doorway."

Zargo's congregation rose at once. What Doom decreed, they obeyed. Even in the midst of the demon storm, they did not hesitate. His will was absolute.

Fortunov objected as they moved past him toward the open doorway. "You'll be sending them to the slaughter."

Doom turned to Fortunov. Zargo felt the contempt radiating from behind the mask, and Fortunov flinched. "We will not," Doom said, "because the demons will be held here, at the church."

"How will we do that?" Zargo asked.

"Not *we*." Though Doom was twenty feet away, it was as

if he were right in front of Zargo, looming over him like the shadow of fate. "*You*," Doom said. "You will hold them."

"I don't understand."

"Yes, you do. You may not wish to, but you do."

"He hurt one earlier," Fortunov said. "But he couldn't do it again."

"He will now," said Doom. "Come here," he said to Zargo.

Zargo walked down the nave until he was just a few feet from Doom.

"You will obey," Doom said.

"I will," said Zargo, and he would. Still awed, he gave himself completely to Doom. There had never been a choice. Obedience had always been the only possibility. Zargo understood. The epiphany was complete. If Doom said he could hold the demons here, then he could.

"Be what you are," said Doom.

"What I did before, it was geomancy," said Zargo. "But I don't know how to do it deliberately." He wasn't challenging Doom. He was pleading for help. "How did it happen?"

"Why do you think St Peter Church has such a hold on you?"

Zargo shuddered. In the breath before Doom spoke again, he saw the construction of his life collapse, the façade he had believed in fall to ruin, revealing the truth behind. He would have given anything not to hear Doom's next words. *Please. Leave me with something. Don't take it all away. Please. I'm begging. Please.*

No god or tyrant gave him mercy.

"The church is built over another node," said Doom.

Zargo stared down at the marble floor.

"Feel the ley lines," said Doom. "Feel their intersection."

Zargo did. With vision that went beyond sight, he looked past the ephemeral floor and deep into the ground. In the darkness of rock there was a light, pulsing and flowing, and another, paths of the Earth's life force running under his feet.

"Reach down," said Doom.

As he had at the site of the Midsummer arena, Zargo put out his hands and sent his grasp down into the ground.

"Take that power."

The voice of Doom could not be disobeyed. The words it spoke shaped reality. Doom told Zargo to seize the power, so he did. There were no questions about how he might do it. If Doom gave the order, then it could be done.

Zargo held the current of the ley lines. He was not searching for a lodestone this time. He opened himself to the power and it flowed through him, a fire in his veins, lightning in his mind, exhilaration in his soul.

He wept, eyes unblinking. He wept as the self he had wanted to be disintegrated. He became what he had always been. He surrendered to destiny and he surrendered to Doom, because they were one and the same. *We are all his tools.*

But some tools could perform miracles.

"Hold the power fast," said Doom.

"I am," said Zargo. "*I am!*" he shouted with brutal joy.

"Now reach up. Reach up and hold the demons with the power of the Earth. Show them the cost of taking material form. Teach them gravity."

Zargo obeyed, and in his obedience he could perform the impossible, and he became Doom's weapon. Light that no one saw but him sprang from his fingers. It lanced outward in a webbed cone. It shot out past the roof of the church. His eyes beyond vision saw it grow, climbing higher and higher in the sky, until it enveloped the cyclone of demons. They did not see the light either. They did not see the net that closed around them. Zargo saw it without seeing. He knew the full texture of the web, because it was part of him, as he was part of the Earth.

"Seize them," said Doom.

Zargo pulled the net tight. He pulled the net down.

The demons howled. They were caught in the trap. They had gathered at the church to feast on the fear of a concentrated mass of prey. They had rejoiced in their carnival of fear, and had been ready at last to finish the prey. But then the destroyer had come, and their prey was taken from them. And while they circled in rage, gathering their numbers for an overwhelming assault, a force seized them. Zargo laughed with joy at the frenzied struggle against his net. He heard and felt the dismay of Hell, and he rejoiced.

"Do not give in to a transport of sensation." Doom's voice broke through his mounting ecstasy. "Be disciplined, or Hell will make use of you."

The command was given, and Zargo obeyed. He focused on keeping his grip on the net. For the moment, the demons were still responding in confusion.

"Now," Doom said to the congregation. "Leave now, all of you. Run to your homes. Lock the doors, shutter the windows, and do not look outside. Do not give the demons more to feast on by witnessing their acts."

The people rushed out the door and into the night. They scattered as soon as they hit the square. The demons saw their prey escaping, and they strained against the net. The Earth held them in the cone of their cyclone. They were matter now, and for as long as Zargo sustained the net, they couldn't break free any more than they could achieve escape velocity with the beating of their wings.

The collective shriek of rage slashed through the church, tearing open fissures in the vaults and pillars. Fortunov crouched and raised his gun, aiming at the ceiling. Doom stood beside Zargo, the glow around his metal fists becoming bright again. The air crackled with barely restrained destruction.

Zargo held tight to his net. Hideous strength strained against it, and then came down all at once, too fast for him to shout a warning. The roof of the church shattered. Blocks of masonry plummeted into the nave and flew off into the night, caught by the hurricane wind. Zargo stared up into the center of the cyclone, and Hell's legion came for their jailer.

At the moment of their descent, Doom raised his hands. He shouted an invocation. The words made Zargo's ears bleed. The center of the space above the nave exploded. Fire bloomed, fire that was destroyer and banishment. It consumed the demons that plunged through it. Crumbling bodies came out the other side, and screams of pain disappeared into the cracks of the night.

The swarm of demons lost direction. Confusion reigned. Attacking horrors collided with retreating monsters. Fortunov fired into their midst. The wounds he inflicted threw more demons off their course, and there were more collisions.

Doom flew up into the swarm and began his slaughter.

Helm stepped onto the platform. She put her arms into the

controls. She felt the strain immediately. The device was constructed for Doom's stature, and it did not adjust for her. The Harrower seized her arms, and it made the links. Helm had braced herself to be hurled back, rejected by the wailing, writhing machine. She had not expected its eagerness. It wanted her in its dance, and the synaptic link formed with snap of a steel trap.

Helm was the machine now. Its power surged through her, wild and screaming. The taste of blood filled her mouth, and that was the only point of contact she still had with her body. Her consciousness rode the storm of the Harrower, and she tried to calm it. She tried to seize the energy. If she could not direct the deluge, she would try to contain it behind a dam and finally shut it down.

The power was too foreign to her, too different from her own strength. It was imprinted with Doom's character, as an artist's brushstrokes marked ownership of a canvas regardless of the image. The force that animated the Harrower was so destructive, so shaped by a will untempered by generosity or care, and was carved by lightning. Helm wielded the forces of the elements, but she did so through sympathy, by flowing with their currents and embracing them. This was not a power that would respond to her that way. The Harrower had the fury of its creator, and would not be tamed.

The doubt assailed her when she could least afford it. *Would we ever have succeeded? Was the Harrower flawed to its core?*

She fell deeper into the union with the machine. All sense of the material world disappeared. Her vision was the Harrower's. Its blade still ripped into the ground of Hell, and where Hell bled demons surged up and burst into the reality of Doomstadt. Helm saw the realm of her nightmares. She saw what Doom had wrought in the search for Cynthia's soul. Towers had been toppled and iron walls breached. If Helm had shaped the Harrower, it would have been gossamer net cast over the infernal, its movements like fog, leaving the landscape of torture to its sleep until it found Cynthia and snatched her away. Doom's Harrower had come with vengeance, tearing open Mephisto's kingdom, laying waste and bringing a new kind of ruin.

Every time she tried to regain control of the blade, it whipped away from her. Over and over again, she thought she almost had it. With each attempt, she melded herself more completely with the machine, until she was trying to contain the whiplashing impulses of her own mind.

Finally, she had it.

Shut it down.

But it still could work. We might still free Cynthia.

Maybe she could direct it. Maybe she could still win.

She had the blade. She held the conduit, and so she held a current of demons in her grip. They sensed her. They knew that someone else had become the Harrower. They paused in their flight up to the world, and they gazed at her.

Hell gazed at her.

It saw her, and knew who she was.

Helm faced her worst fear. This was the terror that had stalked her since the night of Cynthia's fall. To be marked by Hell as its possession, to know that what she did in her life made no difference, that her damnation was preordained, that was the source of all her dread. All her nightmares were variations of that single great one. Her retreat to the mountain top had been her flight from Hell. Doom had convinced her to fight. He had shown her the possibility of winning. He had made her believe that destiny.

She had believed this even as she had witnessed Doom tell Zargo that there could be no running from destiny. She had believed in her own free will, and that she was making choices that would save her.

She had believed she was free while she worked in tandem with Doom.

She had shackled her fate to the works of the man who *was* his name, in every sense, in every possible and unthinkable way.

She realized all these things as she confronted her worst fear. She fought the terror and forced it down. She faced Hell, and she did not surrender.

There was victory in that. There was also the truth that came with the realizations. The truth was that she was lost.

The machine could not be controlled again, not by her, not by Doom, not by any mortal.

Hell had possession.

The demons flew up. Instead of ripping through the veil and into the world, they came for her. The full current of the Harrower surged into her, and then back out, and then through again. The circuit closed around her. In the laboratory, a universe away from her consciousness, the silver loop reformed. One end remained in the nanobot pool, conducting Hell's power upward. The other struck like a serpent and fastened itself to the back of Helm's neck. The power surged through her being. She saw infinity. Temptation, desperation, and the insanity of hope made her reach for it. Infinity seized her as the Harrower had, and the demons arrived. They poured into her being, a possession by thousands.

Helm saw her danger at the last, and she tried to withdraw, to disconnect herself from the Harrower. Her body threw itself back, straining to pull free of the controls. They would not let her go. The effort was too late. In her despair, as her self eroded and claws wrapped around her soul, she saw that everything had been too late from the moment she and Cynthia von Doom had fallen into Mephisto's trap.

She cried out. In warning and defiance and grief, with the last act of her body and her sorcery and her soul, she cried out to Doom. The shout exploded from the laboratory. It shook the castle and its rock. It sounded across all of Latveria. It reached the crown of Mount Sivàr. The mountain trembled in its grief, and the peak collapsed, burying the cave that was her home forever, the rockslide rumbling and echoing down the mountainside with the thunder of mourning.

Her cry was done. The possession was complete. She became the Harrower.

Helm took what was hers. She took the power of a thousand demons.

She...

No.

It.

The Harrower took what belonged to it. The Harrower had one of its creators. She had grasped infinity, unaware that infinity was taking her, because the Harrower was the infinite. It had her. It had her sentience, the coherence of a human being. It used her as its core, and came into the full maturity of its powers. No other demons flew out of the laboratory to join the invasion of Doomstadt. The Harrower looked upon the attacks on the city as the buzzing of flies. It felt contempt for the lack of ambition of its inferiors. It was the true collective of demons. The legions in the city could act in concert for moments in time, to achieve a single end, and then they would split apart again, following the hungers of individual appetites. The Harrower was the many made one. It was indivisible. It was the great champion.

It used Helm's body to speak its first words. "Myself am Hell."

The Harrower turned its gaze onto the world. It learned the measure of its physical being. It was a unity of demons, and it was also a machine. The technology that had given it life was its flesh, the matter of its body. The Harrower's body was not to its liking. It was a network of parts, constructed to have no existence outside the space of the laboratory.

That was not enough. The Harrower would not be a prisoner. It would stride the Earth. It began to reshape its matter into a body that would reflect its new unity.

At the same time, it explored the currents of its technological power. It found more currents and more facets of its identity. It traced the fingerprints of its creator. It was Doom's machine, and so it knew him well. It followed the currents outside of the lab. The construct broke through the occult wards, and the demon defeated the physical barriers.

The Harrower spread its grasp into Castle Doom and seized everything. Already, the swarm of demons inside the church had thinned. The ones that remained kept trying to attack Zargo, but Doom cut them down before they could get near. Even the worm Fortunov's gunfire, well placed, was maiming enough to make a difference. The greater mass of demons had retreated to the outside, trying to escape Doom.

Helm's cry crashed the night. Moments later, the sensors in Doom's armor issued a warning tone. He had lost his connection to the castle defenses.

Doom shot up through the roof, a meteor of fire and sorcery. He passed through the demons like a flamethrower decimating infantry. He rose high and left the demon vortex behind, still struggling in Zargo's net, and looked towards the castle.

Between St Peter and the moat-side edge of Old Town, Doomstadt burned. Demons danced over the rooftops, hunting new prey. There were not as many as before, at least. So many had been lured by the bait of St Peter, and the fountain of horrors no longer erupted from the center of the castle. For a moment, Doom wanted to think that this meant that Helm had taken control of the Harrower, and that the worst was over.

He dismissed the idea before it became a hope. Helm's cry was a harbinger of worse disaster.

Light flashed from the laboratory tower, light redolent of flame, of molten flesh, of rotting blood. Within the flash, there was a suggestion of movement. Something huge stirred and shifted.

"Castle Security," Doom radioed. "Report."

"Your Excellency!" The voice on the line rose and fell out of waves of static. "We have lost control!"

"What is Captain Verlak doing?"

"We don't know where she is. She disappeared shortly before the demons attacked."

More ill tidings.

"Shut everything down," Doom ordered. "Kill all power."

"We're trying. It isn't working. We…"

The man's voice vanished. Static snarled, the white noise taking on mocking shapes.

There was another flash from the laboratory, a hellish searchlight stabbing a claw at the sky. Seconds later, as if in response, flights of demons rose from everywhere in Doomstadt. They began to converge on St Peter. They were coming to free their comrades. Zargo had turned the church into a lightning rod.

Doom took satisfaction in that change in the enemy's war. He could use the mistake as he tried to undo his own.

He dropped back down into the church, scything through demons once again and landing beside Zargo. Fortunov was nearby, using the last of his ammunition on the demons that still flew in the church.

"Can you hear me?" Doom asked Zargo.

"I can hear you." The priest sounded distracted. His face was taut and grey, and slicked with sweat. His hands were raised, the fingers flexing as if he were pulling on cords. He was concentrating fiercely on his demon trap. There was not much of him that could be spared to respond to Doom. There was barely enough of him to make sure his lungs kept drawing air. His breathing rasped and gasped with the fish-gulp rhythm of a dying man.

"All the demons in the city are coming for you. Hold them. Hold all of them. I must leave you."

"They will kill me," Zargo said tonelessly.

"Do not let them," Doom ordered.

"I understand." His wide, unblinking gaze was focused on the space beyond the church.

"Hold them here. Your power is stronger than your faith ever was. Hold them, and do not let them near you. You have trapped many of them already. Now contain them all in a sphere."

"A sphere," Zargo repeated.

"The ley lines will guide you. You will mirror the shape of the Earth. The power will seek this form. Let it, and defeat the enemy."

"I will," said Zargo.

It was like speaking with an automaton. But Doom had given his commands. The priest would obey.

"I'll protect him," said Fortunov.

"No," said Doom. "I have other uses for you. I may need you as a distraction." He seized Fortunov and jetted up through the stained glass window, flying through the tortured night.

In the distance, the laboratory tower was crowned with poisoned fire. The flames burned high and piercing, a blade turning back on its master, and a beacon raised by the enemy that waited for Doom.

CHAPTER 27

Doom flew in a high arc toward the castle. The demons were below, winging toward the church. There were monsters in the streets too. Zargo would have attackers coming at him from all sides. Doom had to trust that the extraordinary natural ability he saw in Zargo would keep him alive and fighting long enough. If Zargo failed, the massacre in Doomstadt would be enormous, no matter what happened at the castle.

Fortunov seemed to read his thoughts. "You should have left me," he said, rigid in Doom's grasp, his eyes riveted on the ground far below.

"Silence, or you can fly the rest of the way yourself."

The battle in the church was the distraction. Keeping Zargo alive was still secondary to destroying the Harrower.

"Are you heading for the tower roof?" Fortunov asked.

"If you wish to begin your eternity of burning early, I'll drop you there," said Doom. The eruption of hellfire was enormous. He could not pass it, and its scale disturbed him. It was the work of huge power, and was a sign that more than

Hell's legions was breaking through the veil. If every safeguard he had created was breaking down, then the horrors of the night were a mere prologue.

The automatic wall turrets opened up as Doom began his descent toward the castle. He had come in for a straight diagonal at the laboratory door, but the web of interlocking shell and laser fire forced him into a vertical dive. He and Fortunov plummeted straight down, just inside the castle's exterior battlements. He balanced his armor's power consumption between the power of the jets and the strength of the force field. He extended the shield's radius to enclose Fortunov.

A shell slammed directly into them. Fortunov jerked convulsively in Doom's grip. The shield held against the explosion, but the impact of the blast knocked them sideways. Doom fought to regain control of their dive. They dropped through a hissing crossfire of lasers, and the field flashed red. Then they were down below the angle of the guns. Doom arrested the fall at the last second, pushing the jets to their limit and subjecting himself and Fortunov to punishing g-forces as the flight went from vertical to horizontal so violently, the turn was almost a right angle.

They streaked forward, barely ten feet above the ground. Fortunov said nothing. He was either brave or frozen in terror.

Doom stayed low until they were almost at the next wall. He shot up with another sudden jolt, climbing for the parapet that surrounded the laboratory tower courtyard. His lens displays strobed on the right, warning of a missile launch. He pushed the jets even harder, gained another precious burst of speed, and crossed the parapet just ahead of the missile.

The rocket's guidance system couldn't keep up with his movements. The missile hit the parapet. The explosion destroyed a third of the wall and heaved the pavement of the courtyard up. Doom came down in a storm of fire and smoke and flying stone. He tossed Fortunov to the ground, then shot up again. The prince landed hard and rolled to a stop a few yards from the laboratory door.

Doom flew to the midway point of the tower and waited for the other weapons he picked up heading for him in the wake of the missile.

Five Doombots arced around the back of the tower. They surrounded Doom and hit him with simultaneous concussive blasts. Doom's force field went red again as it absorbed the massive influx of energy. Doom took the sudden, dangerous surge and channeled it into the armor's electrical field. The overload was huge, and the field discharged with the force of a bomb. The huge electric pulse washed over the Doombots and shorted their circuits. They dropped, inert, and Doom landed beside Fortunov.

"How much ammunition do you have left?" Doom asked.

"Less than a single magazine." Fortunov looked at the fallen Doombots. "Is there a weapon there that I could–"

"No. The enemy has control of all power in the castle. Use what you have, and choose your moment well. Whatever we see in there, do not fire immediately. You will waste what little use you might be."

"The enemy must fear you greatly if it is trying so hard to keep you out," said Fortunov.

False hope was dangerous, and Doom crushed it. "It isn't trying to keep me out. This was a display of arrogance, that is all. At most, it sought to gain a bit more time to prepare. If it truly feared me, it would have used every defense in the castle. It would have emptied the vaults of weapons. You would certainly be dead."

"Not you, though," said Fortunov.

"No. I would not have permitted that."

Doom strode toward the laboratory door.

"What is waiting for us in there?" Fortunov asked.

"Our sins. Yours and mine."

Zargo heard everything Doom said to him. He heard himself speak, but from so far away he could put not intonation into his words. It was like trying to shout in a dream. Then Doom was gone. Zargo saw him leave, carrying Fortunov. He saw what was happening in the church. He saw the effects of the adjustments he made to the gravity net, as he had it reach down and snatch the remaining demons from the nave. What he saw was at the same great distance as the sense of his body.

Zargo wasn't sure what he was any longer. The body and the mind that did battle against demons in St Peter Church had belonged to a being called *Zargo*. They might still. Or they might just be the conduit for the power, and it was the real identity now. The power was outraged by the demons. Their materiality was an insult to the Earth. They were a taint, a distortion of reality, and the Earth sought to purge itself of their presence.

They did not want to go. They wanted to stay and feast. They wanted to spread their infection until the world rotted.

Am I real? What am I?

A part of Zargo, a very distant part, even more distant than his body, feared the answers to the questions. It worried the answer was changing the longer he made himself the tool of the power of the ley lines. It worried that, if dawn ever came and the battle was over, the answer might be *nothing*.

But that part was too far away to act. It could do nothing to fight the demons, and so it was banished.

The demons gathered. They pressed harder. Something huge growled behind Zargo. Massive feet cracked marble as they walked. Whatever it was smashed its bulk through the doorway.

Zargo flexed the ley lines. A gravitational wave burst up through the floor, the anger of an invisible volcano. It seized the monster behind him. It took everything on the floor except Zargo. The new layer of the net launched its prisoners up to the others. A massive demon, a reptilian goat almost twenty feet long, stabbed at him with its horns as it tumbled upward. Their tips slashed his cassock and broke his skin. They barely grazed him, but the skin of that distant body went cold as death. The lungs breathed more painfully. The legs trembled, on the verge of a stagger. The body stayed upright, though, and the mind inside kept doing what it must. The power held Zargo up. If he died, the power would dissipate. It could not fight the demons on its own.

Be disciplined. Doom's command gave Zargo strength and precision. He weaved the energy of the ley lines. He acted on the need of the moment. He was not even following instinct. His mind and his body did what was necessary, but with discipline, as if they were machines shaped by Doom's will, the power guiding Zargo to shield himself and to contain the demons. There were two gravity webs now, a small one protecting him, and the great one that was the trap.

The demons kept coming, more and more gathering or gathered into the trap. He wasn't sure how. He wasn't sure about anything. There was only the struggle and the need to obey Doom's commands. But the pressure of the demons was becoming too great. Hell was forcing itself down, lower and lower into the cathedral, pushing Zargo's net to the limit. They were going to punish him for his presumption. They were going to destroy him by destroying what he used against them. And they were going to destroy the building that had defined his life.

The mass of the demons pressed against the walls. The pillars cracked. One of them crumbled at the base and fell, the first tree in the stone forest to die.

The demons pushed closer. They were less than ten feet above him. A kaleidoscope of hating faces snarled at him, hungry for the taste of his flesh and his soul. Distorted human faces, almost animal faces, jaws that split vertically and tongues like tentacles. Faces that were familiar, faces out of dreams, faces that were the shape of his most intimate fears. They all came closer, and even though they raged, they also sang to him, and they promised him the suffering of the world.

The outside tower doors resisted when Doom tried them. He wrenched them from their hinges, and stalked down the short hall to the laboratory entrance. The doors here had melted. Fragments of the protective rooms shone through the slag, residual magic triggered by the intensity of the unleashed energies.

"*HAVE YOU COME, THEN?*" The voice that thundered from beyond the threshold rasped like an opening tomb. Its tones jerked up and down with the electronic glitching of a machine. It hissed with the venom of Hell. And at its core, there was a trace of the human. Doom recognized Helm's voice, buried within the monster, her throat used by a will that was not hers.

Doom's jaw tightened. He wondered how much Helm had sacrificed, how far she had fallen. She had tried to finish what he had begun, and done so in the midst of the hurricane of damnation.

Though you have lost, my debt to you is not lessened.

"I am here," Doom announced to the monster, and he entered the laboratory. "I am here, and you will fear me."

The Harrower laughed. Blood ran down the chamber walls at the sound.

The demon construct was clinging to the wall like a spider, its huge bulk halfway up the laboratory roof, where hellfire engulfed the night. It had made a torso by fusing the generators together. The servo arms had become its many insectile legs, and it used them to swing itself around the walls. The turning forks were its two massive arms, the tines snapping together like claws, sparking violet spheres of discharging energy. The lodestones were its five eyes, blank yet all-seeing. The silver pool was empty, and the nanobots had formed the Harrower's skull. It was ten feet high, a fanged distortion of the human head, the silver flowing and dripping as if it were slime over bone, but in its contours Doom saw an echo of Helm's features.

She had tried to save them all, and this was her reward.

What she had most feared had come to pass.

Doom saw the ruin of all they had hoped. He felt sorrow for Helm. He would have killed Fortunov on the spot if he had not needed him. He turned away the thought of his own folly. There was never time for regret or guilt. There was only the demand of present and future action.

The Harrower dropped to the floor of the laboratory. It towered over Doom. It reached its massive arms forward. "YOU WILL COMPLETE ME," the Harrower declared. "I WILL HAVE THE PRIME CREATOR."

Violet beams lashed out from the snapping claws. Doom saw the build-up of energy and launched himself upward at the same time. The beams, wide as searchlights, crossed where he had been standing. They struck opposite walls and ripped them open. Stone turned into skin and peeled away from naked muscle. The blood of the walls gushed across the floor. Fortunov scrambled back from the deluge and sheltered in the doorway.

Do not fire, Doom thought. *Not yet. Do not prove yourself futile.*

He flew in a tight circle around the lab. He shot his blasts of force and banishment into the generators, hoping to kill the Harrower's source of power. As the demon laughed, Doom's attacks flashed back at him, amplified. They punched him into the wall hard enough to knock him through the tower and out. The hole filled instantly with the roil of hellfire. He flew back, his force field straining, shooting through the fire and straight at the Harrower.

"You will have nothing, wretch of Hell! Not me, and not Latveria!"

The beams from its arms came for him again, curving like whips. He jerked up, narrowly missing them again, and flew in a tight circle around the Harrower. The five eyes tracked him, and the tuning fork arms struck at him again and again.

Where is Helm? The shape of the skull was important. And there was no sign of a corpse in the lab. She was in the Harrower somewhere. Doom wondered, *hoped*, that she might still be fighting. She might be the chink in the demon's armor.

Dodging the Harrower's attacks, he whispered an incantation, built a massive enchantment of scouring and hurled it at the Harrower's skull. Like a gale's winds hitting the surface of a lake, the nanobots rippled into waves, and for a fraction of a second, the shape of the skull wavered. Doom saw through to its center, and there was Helm. Her body suspended, arms outstretched, a martyr crucified. The skull re-established itself instantly. It snarled at him, and though it was surrounded by eyes, its face followed him, watchful and hungry.

I see you, Helm. We will undo our folly.

The Harrower kept lashing at him, and Doom managed to stay just ahead of the beams. There was too much power in them. He knew the strength of what he had created, and he was not confident his shield and armor would survive even one hit. The Harrower laughed again, and Doom saw the change taking over the walls. The tower's wounds were festering, spreading, and the walls were fading as they bled. The red of the hellfire was filling the laboratory. The vistas of Hell were not yet visible, but it wouldn't be long. Hell itself was coming to Latveria. Doom's country would become

Mephisto's foothold on Earth. This time, there would be no stopping it unless he killed the Harrower.

I will not allow it. Latveria is mine, *and I will hold it safe.*

Doom went high, to the edge of the hellfire at the top of the tower. He focused all his will into a single attack. He gathered all his mystical strength into one contained blast as he channeled all the power he could spare from his armor into it. Then he shouted to Fortunov.

"Now! Shoot the generators! Shoot them now!"

Fortunov obeyed. He emptied his magazine into the midsection of the Harrower. It looked down at him, amused. *"WHY ARE YOU HERE?"* it mused, toying with the prey. *"YOU CANNOT HARM ME."*

He doesn't have to. Doom streaked toward the skull. *He just has to draw your attention.* He unleashed the mystic blast, and he shredded the shape of the skull. The Harrower stumbled, its lodestone eyes spinning around the absence.

The skull reformed with a crack like the end of the world, and the trap snapped shut.

"GOT YOU."

CHAPTER 28

Doom fell to the depths of a silver ocean. Vortices and riptides caught him. They battered and spun him. Lightning shot through the ocean, bursting into synaptic explosions. Beyond the silver, loomed red, the red of Hell, of an all-enclosing fire. And below, the abyss into which he plunged turned at length to the final black.

Doom fought back with sorcery and technology. He tried to blast the silver apart again, to free himself from the interior of the Harrower's skull. He could only be a few feet away from freedom. The ocean was an illusion created by a shroud of nanobots.

His blasts created brief ripples and nothing else. This was no illusion. He could have been attacking the Atlantic with a sword.

He tried to find Helm. He called out to her. There was no answer, and he dropped deeper through forever. The silver was infinite above him. The limit was the event horizon that waited for him at the end of his plunge.

Physical resistance is futile. Do not waste energy in the wrong kind of war.

Where was he? He was not in the material space of the laboratory any more. Nor was he beyond the veil and falling to Hell.

Unless he had crossed the black frontier already. Unless the lurking red glow was Hell's reality closing in on him.

Yes. The black and the red are what I know they must be. But I have not reached one yet, and the other is not real yet.

He was in a liminal space.

It was one he knew.

Even as it hurled him through the maelstroms of its currents, the silver also tried to sink into his being. It was trying to connect, and the pulses of its efforts were familiar. They were what he experienced in the moment before he completed the link with the Harrower's controls. He was in the core of his machine, and the machine was linked to Hell, but the Harrower was also trying to link to him as before. The silver ocean was not the nanobots. It was the manifestation of the power he had shaped and that was now beyond his control.

It needed him, though. Even now, caught inside, he was evading the Harrower's grasp.

The flashes and the bursts were everywhere. He was surrounded by power, pure and unlimited. The silver immensity could shatter worlds, if it was wielded by the one who knew how.

Helm had tried to control it. She had failed, and it had consumed her.

This is the temptation. It wants me to try.

If it wants something, it is limited. If it needs me, it is not as strong as it might be.

Grasp the power. Take and use it. Turn it against itself.

The logic appealed. It seduced.

You were sure you could control the Harrower's power before. Prove yourself now. Reclaim what is yours.

Excitement grew in his chest, and because it did, he realized he was on the verge of defeat. The Harrower was clever. It knew him well. It had let him tempt himself.

He snarled in contempt. Did the Harrower think his will was that weak? If it knew him and thought that, then its knowledge was tempered by huge arrogance. His creation would be taught a lesson.

Doom steeled himself to allow the link to the Harrower. It was the only move he had left.

Tumbling through the ocean, he reached out as if he were placing his arms inside the controls. His hands and forearms disappeared, embraced by silver in the midst of silver. The Harrower grasped him, eagerly, triumphantly.

The link happened.

And the silver ocean was no longer separate from him. It was the vastness of the Harrower's power, the vastness that he had created, and it rejoined him. He fell no longer. He rose, a bolt of lightning from the depths, exploding with the power of the ocean, the power that was his to take and claim.

Verlak climbed the stairs. She had started moving again when the wave of screams had moved on, the demons leaving the tower to feast on Doomstadt. She moved slowly, feeling for each step. The tower was dark, lit only by a faint red glow.

The stairs were vague dark shapes, the spiral of their ascent endless. Every movement of her arm stabbed incandescent needles up through her shoulder and into her skull.

She climbed through an absence of time and hope. She climbed with no expectation her journey would ever end. She climbed, and the red glow brightened. It seemed to come down to meet her, flowing down the walls like the descent of a last curtain.

Verlak stopped climbing. The red dropped down past her on both sides. She looked down. The spiral curled out of sight into shadows that were too deep, too hollow. If she turned back, she did not think she would find the archives at the bottom. There would only be greater darkness.

Far below, but not far enough, a mountain growled deep in its throat and parted its fangs.

Verlak climbed again, and then stopped. The walls were pulling away from her as their red became deeper and brighter. They lost their substance. The stairs were climbing in midair. Now when Verlak looked up and down, she saw the spiral go on without end. Vertigo assailed her. She dropped to her knees and clutched the solid stone with her good hand. If she lost her balance, she would fall to nightmare.

And the nightmare was rising. The walls were gone now. Suspended in red limbo, Verlak saw the lands outside the castle. She saw the roofs of Doomstadt. She saw beyond to the plains and hills and mountains of Latveria. She saw another landscape too, one with towers that dwarfed the mountains and were twisted into the architecture of agony. She saw the ground riven by lava flows. She saw the panorama of endless screams. She heard the tolling of dark bells.

The two worlds were superimposed, the reality of one about to die, the hunger of the other about to awake.

Fortunov dropped the empty rifle. He saw Doom disappear inside the demon machine. He waited in the expectation of the battle's end. He had spent his adulthood trying to destroy Doom, but for the first time in his life all his hopes rested in seeing the return of the tyrant. The demon had to fall. Nothing else was possible. Doom's arrival at the church had been a hammer blow of awe, and Fortunov had not recovered from it. Doom was inevitable, as beyond defeat as time and death.

The seconds passed. Doom did not reappear, but the Harrower was motionless. Fortunov waited. His scattered, terrified thoughts began to chase the idea that Doom and the Harrower had destroyed each other. But no. The monster had not fallen. The silver shape of the skull still flowed. The air in the laboratory hummed with imminence. The walls of the tower had not returned to their proper substance. They were frozen on the edge of translucence.

And then the Harrower raised its clawed arms, lifted its head and roared in victory. And the walls of the lab completed their transformation. They became gossamer, then fog, then nothing. Fortunov crouched on a plain of rubble. The vision of the infernal city began to coalesce.

The Harrower roared once more, and Fortunov screamed. He screamed in horror. He screamed in repentance. He screamed at the certainty that everything was too late.

The pressure of the demons forced Zargo to his knees. They

were suddenly much stronger. The power of the ley lines became more distant. His grip on the power weakened, as if he were trying to hold tight to something in a dream. Something was pulling the Earth away from him.

The demons hurled themselves at the confines of the gravity net, and the murder of the church was complete. The pillars collapsed one after another, a domino fall of destruction. The centuries-old walls fell away, parted waves of stone. Masonry and timbers rained down, splintering pews and burying the floor in rubble. Zargo clutched onto his shield and net with failing hands.

I have done this too, he mourned. The blood of the church stained him. Grief weakened him.

With no walls, the red light of Hell surrounded him. It was rising, and he had played his part in that too. He despaired. The cold from the demon-inflicted wound sank deeper into his body. It froze his core. He had almost no strength left.

A demon with a smile that wrapped all the way around its skull reached through the cracking net. Its flesh was a scalded pink. Its warm, moist fingers wrapped around Zargo's throat.

Orloff stepped out onto the roof of the hospital. Berger had tried to stop her, but she had shaken him off. She had to see.

"You're no safer in here than I'll be up there," she told him.

On the roof, she walked to the north side and stopped at the parapet. She looked up at Castle Doom. The entire building glowed red, and it seemed to be losing its substance. Though she could not see the center from this far downhill, she could see the fountain of fire rising to the sky, and knew the source of the glow came from there, where the light was absolute crimson.

A monster roared in victory, and the fire became a colossal eruption. Fire spread out across the sky. It covered the castle, and then Old Town, and it kept spreading. Orloff watched it pass overhead, then on. She turned south, numb with the knowledge of the end, and the fire spread to the horizon. The entire sky burned. The flames licked down, and she began to feel their heat.

Beyond the horizon, trumpets blared.

Then the horizon line started to change. It showed the fangs of a great city.

The power, immense. The power, his.

All he had to do was accept the grasp, and the power would flow through him forever. There would be no machine to build. There would be no difference between his will and reality.

Doom wrenched his mind back from the fantasy of omnipotence. Hell made no gifts. The tragedy of his family was proof. He thought of his mother, of her soul trapped in Hell. He had created the Harrower to end the penalty for the same mistake the demon construct wanted him to repeat.

Doom refused the power.

The silver ocean trembled. The light seemed taut, as if it might tear.

"*TAKE IT*," the Harrower said. The voice from everywhere vibrated through the ocean of energy.

Doom smiled tightly. He hadn't injured his foe yet, but

he had frustrated it. The Harrower had given up the hope that Doom would succumb to the temptations of his own hopes.

"Now we come to it," said Doom. "You must tempt me directly. The games of Hell never change. Their repetition is tedious."

"*ARE THEY?*" the Harrower asked. "*IS TEMPTATION SO EASY TO REJECT? WILL YOU TURN AWAY FROM YOUR GOAL AT THE MOMENT OF ITS COMPLETION?*"

Doom didn't answer.

"*TAKE THE POWER, AND FREE YOUR MOTHER.*"

Doom said nothing. He could barely think.

"*TAKE THE POWER, AND HELM IS FREE TOO. TAKE IT, AND ALL IS YOURS. THE WORLD IS YOURS.*"

The currents threw him in a colossal maelstrom. It spun him faster and faster, down and down toward the darkness. The great red of Hell closed in tighter. Doom struggled, but he could not tear himself from the current. Images cascaded through his mind. He saw himself as a Lord of Hell, shattering the bonds of whom he chose. He saw his throne on the Earth, eternal and unchallenged. He saw the world held by his will.

He knew that what he saw was the truth. Hell's most powerful temptations were never lies. What he saw was what would happen.

"*BECOME ONE WITH ME, AND THE GOLDEN AGE BEGINS.*"

Doom hesitated on the brink of acceptance.

At last, everything would be accomplished.

One word. One thought. A single act of will.

Yes. That was all he had to do to seal the pact.

All he had to do was stop fighting.

No.

No.

NO.

All he had to do was see the truth for what it was. Hell showed him the truth of what would happen, but hid the deeper truth, which was the price.

The images of glory and power and dominion rushed at him, a tidal wave of promises. He clutched them. He looked closely at himself. He lived the reality of his rule. The Harrower exulted as he appeared to embrace the pact, to rehearse what was to come.

Doom saw the cost. It was Latveria. His throne would be raised on a million skulls in Hell's province on Earth. He would free his mother's soul, and hurl every one of his subjects to damnation in her place.

Hell had made its mistake. Doom had overthrown King Vladimir for more than vengeance. He had done it to save Latveria. His subjects were not the fuel to be fed into the fire of his own desires. He ruled them in order to save them, as he knew he must do one day for the world.

Doom cast the promises away. "No!" he shouted. "I will not pay that price!"

The ocean trembled again. Now it did tear. Rips appeared at the edge of his perception. The strength that held him was brittle. He could snap it. There was a way. He would find it.

"*THE PRICE?*" the Harrower's everywhere voice boomed. "*YOU WILL NOT PAY THAT PRICE? BUT THERE IS*

ALWAYS A PRICE. THERE IS A PRICE FOR REFUSAL.
YOU WILL REJECT THE HELL OF GLORY AND CHOOSE
THE HELL OF FAILURE."

The maelstrom spun faster yet. It dragged Doom down
to the bottom of the silver ocean, and it cast him into the
darkness. There, the truth was waiting for him with venom
and fire. In the dark beyond hope, the Harrower assaulted
him with the path his refusal marked for him.

Doom lived what would come. He lived every moment of
humiliation and fury the future would bring. Again and again
and again, year after year after year, he would fall before Reed
Richards, one defeat after another and another and another,
defeat snatched from the jaws of victory with metronomic
regularity. He saw his mistakes, compounded by the follies of
arrogance, bringing him low, even at the moments where the
omnipotence was truly his. He saw the litany of torment that
he would be choosing for his life.

And his mother would burn.

Doom cried out as the future harrowed him.

Except.

In the flames of ruin that waited for him, there were other
truths. He saw universes threatened. He saw the shadow of
the total annihilation of existence.

He saw the threats ended, because he was there to end
them.

And there was a gap in his lived future. Hell stopped
showing him his mother's damnation.

Maybe there was hope. Maybe, in the agony to come, she
might still be free.

He didn't know.

With a roar of pain, Doom made his choice. He chose the pain of the years to come. He would condemn his mother and Helm to Hell. Because the truth was that there was no choice. He had always vowed to do whatever was necessary to save the world. He did so now.

I accept the price.

Doom refused the Harrower. He refused it utterly.

The darkness fractured.

He had returned from the darkness before through will alone. The Harrower's will was no match for his.

The darkness broke, a mirror falling into fragments. All was silver again, trembling.

The Harrower tried to pull away from Doom. He did not let it. Its being writhed. The will that had created it now turned on it.

"*YOU WILL SUFFER,*" the Harrower promised.

"Maybe." He clutched onto the hope that he could use the knowledge of what he had seen to avoid the catastrophes of his destiny. He would change this future too. He would not make the mistakes he had seen.

He would begin by destroying what he had created.

"Raise nothing more from Hell," Doom said to the Harrower. "I cast you into the furrow we have dug."

The Harrower screamed. Its will collided with Doom's and snapped. Roaring again, stabbed by all the pains of the future, he refused all that he saw. He seized the controls, because he willed them to be there, and the Harrower could not resist, and when he felt them form in his grip, he tore the core of the Harrower apart.

All that was silver exploded.

Remember, Doom commanded himself in the heart of the Armageddon flare of light and pain. *Remember.*

Remember.

EPILOGUE

"I have not been thy dupe, nor am thy prey–
But was my own destroyer, and will be
My own hereafter."

BYRON, *MANFRED*, III.IV.138-40

Dawn.

Doomstadt after Walpurgis Night. The bonfires extinguished, nothing left but piles of logs reduced to charcoal.

Doomstadt after the demonstorm. The horrors gone, the vision of the infernal city gone, swept away by the blinding silver flash that severed the Harrower's hold on the world. Nothing left but the bodies, the trauma, and the mourning to come.

On the hospital roof, Orloff looked up into a gray sky and the soft fall of ash coming to blanket the city. It puffed about her feet as she walked slowly back to the roof's exit. Her heart wanted her to run to the castle, to find Karina and know that she was safe. Her body wanted her to curl in a ball and sleep forever. Her duty to the patients in the hospital demanded that she return to them. She obeyed her duty.

In the ruins of St Peter, Zargo drew breath through a bruised throat. Warmth returned to his body. Still on his knees, he gazed at the rubble of his life and faith and identity, and he wept. He did not think he would ever rise again. The dawn that had come to Doomstadt had not come for him. Night was eternal. And still, he could feel the thrum of the powers in the earth. They were not finished with him.

In the central tower of Castle Doom, the walls were solid again, and the stairs had an end. Verlak climbed, fighting through her exhaustion. She emerged in daylight, in what had been the hall outside the laboratory. The rest of the tower was gone. She was surrounded by silence and aftermath. Near collapse, she stumbled over the mounds of shattered pavement to the gap where the parapet had been. She had to see if anything other than the castle still stood. She swayed at the edge of the drop, and looked out over Doomstadt. The city was still there, dim and grey in the fall of ash, but solid too. It was damaged, but it was real. When she saw that the hospital was intact, she sank to the ground, her breath jerking into a sob of gratitude.

At the entrance to the lab, Fortunov shook, uncertain how he had survived the blast that had disintegrated the tower. The Harrower was a twisted mass of machinery in the center of the open space.

Is it over? Are they both destroyed? It was perverse to hope at all, much less that his great hope had been fulfilled after all, but he clutched the thought as if desperation could alter reality.

The wreckage stirred.

Fortunov knew what he would see. He knew who would emerge.

Fortunov fled, terrified of the anger that would seek him next.

Doom rose. He shrugged off the debris.

Remember.

Remember what?

No. Oh no.

Remember the future.

He had seen it. He had seen everything.

Seen what?

Even the sense that there had been knowledge faded away.

I made a choice. I know that. If I made a choice, then…

Had he made a choice? The fact of a decision became a doubt, and then it was gone too. It was all slipping from him, all the memories from the other side leaving while he struggled, as if he were trying to grasp water in a fist.

Then gone. All gone, except for dread weight of griefs present and griefs to come. Nothing left but the certainty of pain.

Doom roared. He roared, and the ash fell, slow and soft and grey as the last breath of dreams.

ACKNOWLEDGMENTS

I've told everyone until they've begged me to stop that Doctor Doom is my favorite Marvel Comics character, and has been for over forty years. Writing a novel about him has led to a rather bruised arm, a result of constantly pinching myself to make sure I wasn't dreaming. So I would like to say some thanks to the people who made this dream a reality for me.

Thank you, as ever, to Marc Gascoigne, Lottie Llewelyn-Wells, Nick Tyler, Anjuli Smith, Paul Simpson and everyone at Aconyte Books for giving me this chance, and for the guidance and support that saw me through from pitch to conclusion. Thank you to Lottie for her editorial insight and unfailing enthusiasm, and if you, dear reader, have enjoyed this book, then you should thank her too.

Thank you to Marvel Comics, for entrusting me with this most magnificent of characters, and Caitlin O'Connell at Marvel for her invaluable feedback.

Thank you to Fabio Listrani for an absolutely stupendous cover.

Finally, always and forever, my thanks to my family. To my stepchildren Kelan and Veronica, my thanks for all the ways we revel in the pleasures of stories. And to my wife and inspiration, Margaux Watt, more thanks than I can list. This novel was written in the midst of the COVID-19 pandemic, but because we weather the storms as one, there was only joy in its creation.

– Winnipeg, 2020

ABOUT THE AUTHOR

DAVID ANNANDALE is a lecturer at a Canadian university on subjects ranging from English literature to horror films and video games. He is the author of many novels in the *New York Times*-bestselling *Horus Heresy* and *Warhammer 40,000* universe, and a co-host of the Hugo Award-nominated podcast Skiffy and Fanty.

davidannandale.com
twitter.com/david_annandale

XAVIER'S INSTITUTE

Two exceptional students face their ultimate test when they answer a call for help, in the first thrilling Xavier's Institute novel, focused on the daring exploits of Marvel's mutant heroes.

MARVEL HEROINES

Superhuman powers can be both a gift and a curse. A lucky few are taught to control their abilities while others master their uniquely dangerous powers alone. Explore the stories of Marvel's iconic heroines.

Sharp-witted, luck-wrangling super mercenary Domino takes on both a dangerous cult and her own dark past, in this explosive high-octane action novel.

Rogue's frightening new mutant powers keep her at arms-length from the world, but two strangers offer a chance to change her life forever, in this exhilarating Super Hero adventure

MARVEL LEGENDS OF ASGARD

In a realm beyond Earth, mighty heroes do battle with monsters of myth and undertake quests to restore peace and honor to the legendary halls of Asgard and the Ten Realms.

The young Heimdall must undertake a mighty quest to save Odin – and all of Asgard – in the time before he became guardian of the Rainbow Bridge.

The God of War must explore a terrifying realm of eternal fire to reclaim his glory, in this epic fantasy novel of one of Odin's greatest heroes.